WAR DOGS

WAR DOGS

GREG BEAR

GOLLANCZ
LONDON

The right of Greg Bear to be identified as the author of this
work has been asserted by him in accordance with the
Copyright, Designs and Patents Act 1988.

First published in Great Britain in 2014 by Gollancz
An imprint of the Orion Publishing Group
Orion House, 5 Upper St Martin's Lane, London WC2H 9EA
An Hachette UK Company

A CIP catalogue record for this book is available
from the British Library

ISBN 978 0 575 10099 2

1 3 5 7 9 10 8 6 4 2

Printed in Great Britain by
CPI Group (UK) Ltd, Croydon, CR0 4YY

The Orion Publishing Group's policy is to use papers that
are natural, renewable and recyclable products and made from
wood grown in sustainable forests. The logging and manufacturing
processes are expected to conform to the environmental
regulations of the country of origin.

www.gregbear.com
www.orionbooks.co.uk
www.gollancz.co.uk

This book is dedicated to my favorite Mustangers:
LCDR Dale F. Bear, USN, Retired
LCDR Richmond D. Garrett, USN, Retired

And by extension to all who served with them in
WW2, Korea, and Vietnam.

I also express my appreciation to those friends who helped
make this a better book, and I am honored to pass
along their own acknowledgments:

David Clark (Vietnam): "I'd like to list my military forebears, men
who served as an example for me. My father, Ken Clark, WW2
Navy Signalman; Cecil 'Duke' Crowell, US Navy hardhat diver,
WW2; my grandfather Ernest Shultz, WWI
Navy aviation pioneer; and my great-great-uncle George
Booth, First Sergeant Company D, 155 PA Infantry, Army of
the Potomac,
American Civil War."

Donald E. McQuinn (Korea, Vietnam): "My gratitude to every
Marine of my past, and my thanks to our Marines of the present
and future in the full confidence that they'll never fail to
add luster to our Corps. *Semper Fidelis.*"

Dan O'Brien (Iraq): "To the fallen Sailors and Marines of Kilo
3/12: Doc Noble, Cpl. McRae, Cpl. Zindars, and Lcpl. Lync, and all
the others who fell on the moonscapes of Iraq and Afghanistan. No
need to mention me, it seems trivial after mentioning them."

I'm mentioning Dan anyway, because he helped, and he was there.

Heartfelt thanks to all for so much.

GREG BEAR

DOWN TO EARTH

I'm trying to go home. As the poet said, if you don't know where you are, you don't know who you are. Home is where you go to get all that sorted out.

Hoofing it outside Skybase Lewis-McChord, I'm pretty sure this is Washington State, I'm pretty sure I'm walking along Pacific Highway, and this is the twenty-first century and not some fidging movie—

But then a whining roar grinds the air and a broad shadow sweeps the road, eclipsing cafés and pawnshops and loan joints—followed seconds later by an eye-stinging haze of rocket fuel. I swivel on aching feet and look up to see a double-egg-and-hawksbill burn down from the sky, leaving a rainbow trail over McChord field...

And I have to wonder.

I just flew in on one of those after eight months in the vac, four going out, three back. Seven blissful months in timeout, stuffed in a dark tube and soaked in Cosmoline.

All for three weeks in the shit. Rough, confusing weeks.

I feel dizzy. I look down, blink out the sting, and keep walking. Cosmoline still fidges with my senses.

Here on Earth, we don't say *fuck* anymore, the Gurus don't like it, so we say fidge instead. Part of the price of freedom. Out on the Red, we say fuck as much as we like. The angels edit our words so the Gurus won't have to hear.

SNKRAZ.

Joe has a funny story about *fuck*. I'll tell you later, but right now, I'm not too happy with Joe. We came back in separate ships, he did not show up at the mob center, and my Cougar is still parked outside Skyport Virginia. I could grab a shuttle into town, but Joe told me to lie low. Besides, I badly want time alone—time to stretch my legs, put down one foot after another. There's the joy of blue sky, if I can look up without keeling over, and open air without a helm—and minus the rocket smell—is a newness in the nose and a beauty in the lungs. In a couple of klicks, though, my insteps pinch and my calves knot. Earth tugs harsh after so long away. I want to heave. I straighten and look real serious, clamp my jaws, shake my head—barely manage to keep it down.

Suddenly, I don't feel the need to walk all the way to Seattle. I have my thumb and a decently goofy smile, but after half an hour and no joy, I'm making up my mind whether to try my luck at a minimall Starbucks when a little blue electric job creeps up behind me, quiet as a bad fart. Quiet is not good.

I spin and try to stop shivering as the window rolls down. The driver is in her fifties, reddish hair rooted gray. For a queasy moment, I think she might be MHAT sent from Madigan. Joe warned me, "For Christ's sake, after all that's happened, stay away from the doctors." MHAT is short for *Military Health Advisory Team*. But the driver is not from Madigan. She asks where I'm going. I say downtown Seattle. Climb in, she says. She's a colonel's secretary at Lewis, a pretty ordinary grandma, but she has these strange gray eyes that let me see all the way back to when her scorn shaped men's lives.

I ask if she can take me to Pike Place Market. She's good with that. I climb in. After a while, she tells me she had a son just like me. He became a hero on Titan, she says—but she can't really know that, because we aren't on Titan yet, are we?

I say to her, "Sorry for your loss." I don't say, *Glad it wasn't me.*

"How's the war out there?" she asks.

"Can't tell, ma'am. Just back and still groggy."

They don't let us know all we want to know, barely tell us all we *need* to know, because we might start speculating and lose focus.

She and I don't talk much after that. Fidging *Titan.* Sounds old and cold. What kind of suits would we wear? Would everything freeze solid? Mars is bad enough. We're almost used to the Red. Stay sharp on the dust and rocks. That's where our shit is at. Leave the rest to the generals and the Gurus.

All part of the deal. A really big deal.

Titan. Jesus.

Grandma in the too-quiet electric drives me north to Spring Street, then west to Pike and First, where she drops me off with a crinkle-eyed smile and a warm, sad finger-squeeze. The instant I turn and see the market, she pips from my thoughts. Nothing has changed since vac training at SBLM, when we tired of the local bars and drove north, looking for trouble but ending up right here. We liked the market. The big neon sign. The big round clock. Tourists and merchants and more tourists, and that ageless bronze pig out in front.

A little girl in a pink frock sits astride the pig, grinning and slapping its polished flank. What we fight for.

I'm in civvies but Cosmoline gives your skin a tinge that lasts for days, until you piss it out, so most everyone can tell I've been in timeout. Civilians are not supposed to ask probing questions, but they still smile like knowing sheep. *Hey, spaceman, welcome back! Tell me true, how's the vac?*

I get it.

A nice Laotian lady and her sons and daughter sell fruit and veggies and flowers. Their booth is a cascade of big and little peppers and hot and sweet peppers and yellow and green and red peppers, Walla Walla sweets and good strong brown and fresh green onions, red and gold and blue and russet potatoes, yams and sweet potatoes, pole beans green and yellow and purple and speckled, beets baby and adult, turnips open boxed in bulk and attached to sprays of crisp green leaf. Around the corner of the booth I see every kind of mushroom but the screwy kind. All that roughage dazzles. I'm accustomed to browns and pinks, dark blue, star-powdered black.

A salient of kale and cabbage stretches before me. I seriously consider kicking off and swimming up the counter, chewing through the thick leaves, inhaling the color, spouting purple and green. Instead, I buy a bunch of celery and move out of the tourist flow. Leaning against a corrugated metal door, I shift from foot to cramping foot, until finally I just hunker against the cool ribbed steel and rabbit down the celery leaves, dirt and all, down to the dense, crisp core. Love it. Good for timeout tummy.

Now that I've had my celery, I'm better. Time to move on. A mile to go before I sleep.

I doubt I'll sleep much.

Skyrines share flophouses, safe houses—refuges—around the major spaceports. My favorite is a really nice apartment in Virginia Beach. I could be heading there now, driving my Cougar across the Chesapeake Bay Bridge, top down, sucking in the warm sea breeze, but thanks to all that's happened—and thanks to Joe—I'm not. Not this time. Maybe never again.

I rise and edge through the crowds, but my knees are still shaky, I might not make it, so I flag a cab. The cabby is white and middle-aged, from Texas. Most of the fellows who used to cab here, Lebanese and Ethiopians and Sikhs, the younger ones at least, are gone to war now. They do well in timeout, better than white Texans. Brown people rule the vac, some say. There's a lot of brown and black and beige out there: east and west Indians, immigrant Kenyans and Nigerians and Somalis, Mexicans, Filipinos and Malaysians, Jamaicans and Puerto Ricans, all varieties of Asian—flung out in space frames, sticks clumped up in fasces—and then they all fly loose, shoot out puff, and drop to the Red. Maybe less dangerous than driving a hack, and certainly pays better.

I'm not the least bit brown. I don't even tan. I'm a white boy from Moscow, Idaho, a blue-collar IT wizard who got tired of working in cubicles, tired of working around shitheads like myself. I enlisted in the Skyrines (that's pronounced SKY-reen), went through all the tests and boot and desert training, survived first orbital, survived first drop on the Red—came home alive and relatively sane—and now I make good money. Flight pay and combat pay—they call it engagement bonus—and Cosmo-line comp.

Some say the whole deal of cellular suspension we call timeout shortens your life, along with solar flares and gamma rays. Others say no. The military docs say no but scandal painted a lot of them before my last deployment. Whole bunch at Madigan got augured for neglecting our spacemen. Their docs tend to regard spacemen, especially Skyrines, as slackers and complainers. Another reason to avoid MHAT. We make more than they do and still we complain. They hate us. Give them ground pounders any day.

"How many drops?" the Texan cabby asks.

"Too many," I say. I've been at it for six years.

He looks back at me in the mirror. The cab drives itself; he's in the seat for show. "Ever wonder why?" he asks. "Ever wonder what you're giving up to *them*? They ain't even human." Some think we shouldn't be out there at all; maybe he's one of them.

"Ever wonder?" he asks.

"All the time," I say.

He looks miffed and faces forward.

The cab takes me into Belltown and lets me out on a semi-circular drive, in the shadow of the high-rise called Sky Tower One. I pay in cash. The cabby rewards me with a sour look, even though I give him a decent tip. He, too, pips from my mind as soon as I get out. Bastard.

The tower's elevator has a glass wall to show off the view before you arrive. The curved hall on my floor is lined with alcoves, quiet and deserted this time of day. I key in the number code, the door clicks open, and the apartment greets me with a cheery pluck of ascending chords. Extreme retro, traditional Seattle, none of it Guru tech; it's from before I was born.

Lie low. Don't attract attention.

Christ. No way am I used to being a spook.

The place is just as I remember it—nice and cool, walls gray, carpet and furniture gray and cloudy-day blue, stainless steel fixtures with touches of wood and white enamel. The couch and chairs and tables are mid-century modern. Last year's Christmas tree is still up, the water down to scum and the branches naked, but Roomba has sucked up all the needles. Love Roomba. Also pre-Guru, it rolls out of its stair slot and checks me out, nuzzling my toes like a happy gray trilobite.

I finish my tour—checking every room twice, ingrained caution, nobody home—then pull an Eames chair up in front of the broad floor-to-ceiling window and flop back to stare out over the Sound. The big sky still makes me dizzy, so I try to focus lower down, on the green and white ferries coming and going, and then on the nearly continuous lines of tankers and big cargo ships. Good to know Hanjin and Maersk are still packing blue and orange and brown steel containers along with Hogmaw or Haugley or what the hell. Each container is about a seventh the size of your standard space frame. No doubt filled with clever goods made using Guru secrets, juicing our economy like a snuck of meth.

And for that, too—for *them*—we fight.

BACKGROUNDER, PART 1

ATS. All True Shit. So we're told.

The Gurus, whose real name, if it is their real name, is awful hard for humans to pronounce—made their presence known on Earth thirteen years ago, from the depths of the Yemeni desert, where their first scout ship landed. They wanted to establish a beachhead, make sure humans wouldn't find them and overrun them right away.

They made first contact with a group of camel herders who thought they were djinn, genies, and then, when they judged the time was right, reached out to the rest of humanity. As the story goes, they hacked into telecoms and satlinks, raised a fair pile of money by setting up anonymous trading accounts, then published online a series of pretty amazing puzzles that attracted the attention of the most curious and intelligent. They recruited a few, gave them a preliminary cover story—something about a worldwide brain trust hoping to set up offices in major capitals—and sent them around the planet to organize sanctuaries.

In another online operation, the Gurus and their new recruits led a second select group—military, clandestine services, political—on a merry geocache chase, in quest of something that might point to a huge breach of national security. There was a breach, of course.

It was the Gurus.

Working in this fashion, it became apparent to a few of our best and brightest that they were not dealing with an eccentric rich hermit with an odd sense humor. And there were genuine rewards, rich Easter eggs waiting to be cracked. Linking the most interesting puzzles led logically to some brilliant mathematical and scientific insights. One of these, quantum interlacing, showed the potential of increasing bandwidth in any Shannon-compliant network by a millionfold.

Only then did the Gurus reveal themselves—through another specially trained group of intermediaries. They came in peace. Of course. They planned on being even more helpful, in due time—piecing out their revelations in step sequence, not to upset proprietary apple carts all at once.

World leaders were gradually made aware of the game change, with astonishing tact and political savvy. Citizen awareness followed a few months later, after carefully coached preparation. It seemed the Gurus knew as much about our psychology and sociology as they did about the rules of the universe. They wanted to take things gradual.

And so over a period of six months, the Gurus came forward, moving out in ones and twos from their Yemeni Hadramaut beachhead to world capitals, economic centers, universities, think tanks—transforming themselves into both hostages and indispensable advisors.

The Gurus explained that they are here in tiny numbers because interstellar travel is fantastically difficult and expensive, even at their level of technology. So much had been guessed by our scientists. We still don't know how many Gurus came to Earth originally, but there are now, at best estimate—according to what our own governments will tell us—about thirty of them. They don't seem to mind being separated from each other or their own kind, but they keep their human contacts to a few dozen. Some call these select emissaries the Wait Staff.

It took the Gurus a while to drop the other shoe. You can see why, looking back. It was a very big shoe, completely slathered in dog shit.

Just as we were getting used to the new world order—just as we were proving ourselves worthy—the Gurus confessed they were not the only ones out there in the dark light-years. They explained that they had been hounded by mortal enemies from sun to sun, planet to planet, and were in fact now stretched thin—left weak, nearly defenseless.

Gurus were not just being magnanimous with their gifts of tech. They needed our help, and we needed to step up and help them, because these enemies were already inside the far, icy margins of our solar system, were, in fact, trying to establish their own beachhead, but not on Earth.

On Mars.

Some pundits started to call this enemy the Antagonists—Antags. The name stuck. We were told very little about them, except that they were totally bad.

And so our first bill came due. Skyrines were volunteered to help pay. As always.

———

THE SUN SETS watery yellow in a pall of Seattle gray. Night falls and ships' lights swim and dance in my tears. I'm still exuding slimy crap. Spacemen can't use drugs the first few days because our livers are overworked cleaning out residue. It comes out of our skin and sits on our breath like cheap gin and old sweat. Civilian ladies don't like the stink until we remind them about the money, then some put up with it.

It's quiet in the apartment. Empty. Spacemen are rarely alone coming or going or in the shit. If we're not in timeout, there's always that small voice in the ear, either a fellow Skyrine or your angel. But I don't really mind being alone. Not for a few hours. Not until Joe comes back and tells me how it all turned out. What the real secret was—about Muskies and the Drifter, the silicon plague, the tower of smart diamonds.

About Teal.

And the Voors, nasty, greedy SOBs who lost almost everything and maybe deserved to lose more. But they didn't deserve *us*.

I curl up in the Eames chair and pull up the blanket. I'm so tired, but I've got a lot on my mind. Pretty soon, I relive being in the shit.

It's vivid.

I HATE PHYSICS

Physics is what kills you, but biology is what wants you dead.

We're wide awake in the pressure tank at the center of our space frame, fresh from timeout, being pumped full of enthusiasm while the Cosmoline is sponged off by rotating cloths, like going through a car wash except in zero g.

This drop, we're told there are six space frames falling into insertion orbits. The first four frames hold two fasces, each fascis a revolving cylinder with three sticks like bullets. We call them rotisseries. Each stick carries a squad of Skyrines. That makes two hundred and forty of us, this drop. The fifth and sixth frames carry transport sleds with heavy weapons and vehicles and a couple of fountains. We won't see any of that until we're down on the Red.

Once we're sponged, we pull on skintights, do a final integrity check, strap on sidearms, receive palm-sized spent matter cassettes, then slip on puff packs and climb back into our sticks. Precise, fast, no time to think. Waiting in the stick is not good. The tubes are tight and dark. Our angels play soothing music, but that only makes it worse.

I start to twitch.

What's taking so long?

Then everything—and I mean *everything*—hisses and whines and squeals. I'm squashed against my tube on one side, then another, then top, then bottom, and altogether, we sing *hallelujah*, we're off!

The fasces spin outward from the frame, cylinders retro-firing to slow and get ready to discharge our sticks. I can't see anything but a diagram projected on the inside of my faceplate. Cheery. Colorful. All is well.

We've begun our drop.

The sticks shoot out of the rotisseries in precise sequence. Bite of atmosphere seems delayed. Feels wrong. Then it starts—the animal roar of entry. Just as the noise outside my stick becomes unbearable, thirty of us shoot from our tubes, out the end of the sticks, and desperately arrange ourselves, clinging to aero shields.

The shields buck in the upper atmosphere.

Over Mars.

The sky is filled with Red.

We ride ten to a shield for a few minutes in bouncy, herky-jerk free fall, at the end of which we all roll off. Comes a brief moment of white light and stove-grill heat. One side of my skintight flaps and then settles against my skin. Nice and toasty.

My drop pack spins out millions of threads like gossamer, almost invisibly thin. We call this puff. The threads expand to a lumpy ball fifty meters wide, which wobbles and snatches at Mars's thin, thin air—and then gloms on to other balls, other Skyrines enveloped in puff.

All around our jammed puffballs, curling thread tips burn away. We're suspended inside like bugs in flaming cotton candy. It's spectacular—a lurid, artificial sunrise. I'm breathing like a racehorse at the end of its run. My faceplate fogs. I can barely see, but right away, I know for sure that there's trouble. The big ball has split early. There are only three Skyrines in my cherry glow. Others have spun off in fiery clumps, and who knows where they'll land?

The glow burns down closer and closer, brighter and brighter. With gut-check jerks we slow from four klicks per second to one klick per second to one klick per minute, until, just after the last of our puff burns out, just after our packs release and rocket away, smoking, sad, finished . . .

The three of us flex our knees and land with less-than-gentle thumps.

I pick myself up, surprised I'm still alive. Bad drops are usually fatal. Quick look around. Flat, immense.

Welcome to Mars.

The Red.

No immediate threat.

Time to freely scream *fuck!* inside my helm and figure out what the hell went wrong.

———

I'm with Tak and Kazak. I think it was DJ and maybe Vee-Def and Michelin I saw thrashing away through the last of our puff sunrise. They may be no more than a klick or two off. The fasces apparently shot our sticks at the apex of insertion rather than low orbit. We've been separated from the rest of our platoon, and I have no idea how far away our company may be. They likely came down in a north-south fan, spread across more than a hundred klicks.

We could take days to reassemble.

There are no transport sleds nearby, and therefore no vehicles—no Skells or Tonkas or deuces.

Looks like we'll be hoofing it.

And no big weapons.

What's left of our packs falls, still smoking, a few hundred

meters north. That's GPS north—no magnetic field on the Red.
Good, I say to myself; sats are still up. We can receive our last-
minute tactical and regroup in order. But then my angel loses the
signal. The gyro is still good, however, and through my helm
grid, I scope out the sun.

The Antags keep bringing down our orbital assets, nav and
recon sats and other necessities. Newly arrived space frames keep
spewing them out, along with Skyrines and transport sleds, but a
lot of the time, when we arrive, we don't know right away where
we are or what we're supposed to do. We're trained to just git along.
Staying mobile makes you a tougher target. We call it drunkard's
walk, but most of us drunkards are packed tight with prayer—that
we're in range of the rest of our company, an intact sled, maybe a
fountain, or at the very least we'll stumble over a stray tent box.

After four months transvac, the pre-drop cocktail of epi and
histamines makes me feel terrific, barring a slight case of the
wobbles. I pay no attention to how I feel, nor do Tak or Kazak.
We're all sergeants. We've been here before. Our angels coordinate with fast, high-pitched screes, not likely to be heard more
than a few tens of meters away. No joy. Nobody has the plan.
No fresh recon. NCOs rule at last.

We know all there is to know, for now. But we don't even
know where we've touched down.

We bump helms.

"What strength?" Tak asks.

"A squad, no more—in this sector," I say.

"Whatever fucking sector this is!" Kazak says.

"Northern lowlands," I guess. "Pressure's about right." I
scuff brown dust along the flat, rocky hardpan and point north.
"DJ and some others skipped over that way."

DJ is Engineering Sergeant Dan Johnson.

"Then let's find them," Tak says.

"Nothing here worth staying for," Kazak agrees. "Terrible

place for a fight—no high ground, almost no terrain. Can't dig fighting holes in this old shit. Where are we, fucking Hellas? Why drop us in the middle of nothing?"

No answer to that.

We walk, carrying less than five hours of breath and water, armed only with bolt-and-bullet pistols that resemble thick-barreled .45s. Tak Fujimori has an orange stripe on his helm. Tak is from Oakland. He went through vac training and jump school with me at SBLM and Hawthorne. He is compact and strong and very religious, though I'm not sure what religion. Maybe all of them.

Timur Nabiyev—Kazak—wears blue tape. He's from Kazakhstan, on exchange from Eurasian Defense. He trained with contingents of Chinese and Uyghurs in the cold desert of Taklamakan, specializing in dusty combat—then with Italians and French around Vesuvius and on the Canary Islands. Kazak is not religious except when he's on the Red, and then he's some sort of Baptist, or maybe Orthodox.

Out on the Red, we're all religious to one degree or another. Soviets once claimed they went into space and couldn't find God. They obviously never fell from high orbit in the middle of a burning bush.

The Red here is a wide, level orange desert shot through with purple and gray, and out there, to the northwest, one little scut of ridgeline, low and round. Otherwise, the horizon is unrelieved. Monstrously flat.

Skintights sport kinetic deflection layers around upper thighs and torso that can discourage rounds of 9mm or less, but no body armor can save us from Antag bolts and other shit, which closely matches what we deal. Not even our transports have more than rudimentary armor. Too damned heavy. Ours are made by Jeep, of course, mostly fold-out Skells with big wheels, but also Tonkas and Deuces and mobile weapons trucks called General Pullers—Chesties to those who love them. For important actions, even bigger weapons are delivered on wide-bed platforms called Trundles.

When a sled drops nearby. When we find them.

Sky still looks empty. Quiet.

No more drops for now.

We are forbidden from using radio, can't even uplink by laser until—if—our sats get replaced and can scope out the territory. Then up-to-data and maps will get lased from orbit, unless there's dust, in which case we may not get a burst for some time. Satellite microwave can penetrate all but the grainiest dust, but command prefers direct bursts of laser, and Antags could have sensors on every low ridge and rocky mound. If dust scatters our targeted beams, they're excellent at doing reverse Fourier, pinning our location to within a few meters and frying us like flies on a griddle. So we're hiking silent except for scree and touching helms.

If a fountain made it, it's going to be dormant and heavily camouflaged, waiting for our magic touch. Hard to find. But if we do find one, we'll replenish and maybe grab a nap before we're in the shit.

Or there is no shit.

Hard to know what will happen.

After all this time, we know almost nothing about the enemy except they're roughly our size, on average, with snouted helms, two long arms with hanging sleeves, three legs—or two legs and a tail—and they're not from around here. Only once have I seen their scant remains up close.

If we succeed, they're scrap and stain. If they succeed—

All physics.

———

I SCAN THE horizon over and over as we walk, nervous habit. The low line of atmosphere out there is brownish pink and clear except for a tan fuzzy patch near the distant ridge that doesn't seem to be going anywhere. Did I miss that the last time? I point it out to the others. Could be vehicular, could be a recent fountain drop; could be Antags.

We'll find DJ and the others, then head that direction. No sense rushing.

My angel, mounted above my left ear, follows my focus with little whirring sounds, then finishes laying out grids and comparing the negligible terrain to stored profiles. I look at Tak, then at Kazak. Their angels concur. We dropped over Marte Vallis in southern Elysium, within a few sols' hike of a small pedestal crater the angels label EM2543a, locally known as "Bridger," probably after some Muskie who died there.

The loess laps in low, snakelike waves across the hardpan. We cross over an X and then a Y and then a W of long, broad marks like roadways, some, we know—we've seen them from orbit and from the air—running for hundreds of klicks. These are not roads but wind-doodles, cryptic messages scrawled across the flats by millions of dust devils.

According to the angels, we are transiting a low plateau of ancient olivine. A second layer of flood basalt overlaps this one a few dozen klicks south. If we play tourist and venture that way, we will see that the edges of the upper plateau have sloughed, leaving irregular cliffs about ten meters high, with several meters of rubble at the base—quite fresh, less than fifty million years old.

My boot sensor is working for once and says the local dust is pH neutral. No signs of water outflow. Still, the basalt layers overlie deep, heavily fractured, and angled plates of ancient sandstone, probably the broken remains of a Noachian seabed. That means there could be underground water way below, shifting deep flows with no surface eruptions in our epoch. All same-same. Nary a sip for us. Mars is rarely generous.

Skintight injects more enthusiasm. Christ, I love it. I need it. We're experiencing our first sol! How exciting. A sol is one day on the Red, just a little longer than an Earth day. There won't be a pickup for at least seven or eight sols. Much longer if they can't find us, which seems likely. We're probably screwed.

But for the moment, none of us cares.

JOURNEYS END IN LOVERS MEETING

We walk north, saying little.

Skyrines rarely survive more than four drops. This is my fifth. So far, I'm as clear and frosty as a winter eve, but my skintight is already pulling back the encouragement.

I hate transitions.

As the cocktail slacks off, I start to think too much. Brain is not my friend. Leathery-winged shadows rustle in the back of my skull. I may or may not be psychic, but I can feel with knife-edge prickles that we're heading into opportunity—by which I mean trouble.

With his new eyes, Tak is the first to spot the body. He swings his arm and in turn I alert Kazak. We spread out and charge our sidearms.

In a few minutes, walking steady, no leaping, we surround the body. There's another about ten meters off, and another twenty beyond that. Three in all. The uniforms are Russian, probably with French equipment. Tak bends over the first and rolls it faceup. The skintight is still puffy. The helm plate is gruesome. Can't tell if it was male or female.

Tak pokes his finger at his own helm, then explodes his hands away. *Sploosh!* Germ needles. Poor bastard was feverish in seconds, crazy for the next four or five minutes, could have even shot his or her squad before falling over and fermenting. Tak finds where the little needle punctured the fabric and ta-da gestures at its feathery vanes. He doesn't try to pull it out. Fucking germ needles can poke up as well as prick down. They can be deployed from aerostats—large balloons—or dropped from orbit in exploding pods. Both systems spray silvery gray clouds over a couple of square kilometers. The needles, each about four centimeters long, shift their wide fletches and *find* you. Then they turn you into a balloon filled with bone chips and pus.

Real nightmare batwing shit.

Our angels scree the swollen suit, just in case the dead soldier's unit is still up for a chat. No luck. It's long since self-wiped. Since we haven't uplinked since the drop, and of course have not been briefed on recent engagements, we don't know anything about these guys or why they are here. They must have arrived many sols before us—maybe weeks. Why? There weren't supposed to be major operations before our arrival. Somebody's had second thoughts since we left Earth. Maybe these guys were shipped out on fast frames, taking only a month or two rather than four…They left before us, and now they're dead, and we don't know anything about why they are here.

It's getting tougher and tougher to stay focused.

At this point, we decide radio silence is stupid. Our only chance is to try to raise other Skyrines and hear if they've found something useful.

We split three different directions.

Only then do I see Engineering Sergeant Dan Johnson, DJ, waving his hands and descending a short slope made nasty by BB-sized pebbles. He manages to skitter down on his feet, then waves again and signs that he's found a tent box. We greet him with shoulder slaps and real joy. His angel screes ours, and now we're four instead of three.

"Anybody see sparkly?" DJ asks. "I saw sparkly coming down, above and outside."

We all agree that we saw no sparkly. Sparkly is bad—it's our term for space combat observed from a distance. Space frames and sticks being blown out of the sky.

"The puff was all fucked," Kazak says resentfully. "How could you tell?"

"Well, I saw *something*," DJ insists, but he doesn't push. We don't even want to think about it. He's found a tent box, he's leading us to it. The box is up on Bridger's pedestal. Craters on Mars often sit on rises caused by force of impact hardening the surrounding regolith, making them more resistant to erosion. Scientists call the rises pedestals, and this one is about two meters above the hardpan.

We're starting to really wear down by the time we reach the box and do a walk-around. The box is at least a month old, probably also Russian or French, and still has fresh purple striping—no interference since it was dropped, no booby traps, and no germ needles to render it useless. We make damned sure of that. Safety and sanctuary. We may be in the middle of nowhere important, off course and ultimately doomed, but at least we're good for the night, which is rolling over fast, and of course it's going to be cold and dry.

Still, we're about to sleep in a tent dropped for a dead squad. I'm not happy about that, but something similar happened on my last drop, and we all survived and took down something like sixty Antags—painted them on the sand from a couple of hundred meters. A good two weeks in the shit, and the nearest I've been to learning what an Antag looks like up close.

Bolts don't leave much to autopsy after the fighting is done: cuplike pieces of helm filled with grayish skull-bits—no teeth; shreds of light armor and suit, big, wide sleeves and leggings filled with crumbling bone and charred spines. Backbones, maybe. Our gunny ignored the tissue but scooped up some of the fabric and tech and packaged it for return. We heard no more about it. It's traditional in the Corps to keep grunts ignorant about who we fight, something about dehumanizing the enemy. Well, they ain't fucking human to begin with.

DJ and Tak break the tent box's seal. The stripes turn orange-pink and then brown—safe—and the tent inflates. It carries enough air to last the night, and because it's made for five, maybe a few hours into tomorrow. Strapped in a bag outside, we find a case of MREs with sacks of water and six vials of vodka. The MREs consist of hard sausage (Finnish, the label says—probably reindeer) and tubes containing something like borscht. A feast. We stuff the vodka in our hip packs, keeping our eyes on the black sky while the tent grows and the sun drops.

We talk without butting helms, but can barely hear each other through the thin, thin air. Not that there's much to say. The smudge on the horizon has not changed, other than turning a pretty shade of violet. It may only be a big dust devil. If so, the wind conditions out there have been stable for several hours.

I look higher, bending my neck to see the zenith. Much of the time the stars over the Red shine brighter and steadier than they ever do on Earth. Their beauty is lost on me. They judge. Worse, they send Antags. The stars are waiting for me to fuck up.

After we trigger and tune the sentinel, the tent is ready. We scoop dust in our gloves and fling it in slow plumes over the striped plexanyl to provide local color. Then we circle, pull short dusters from our thighs, and brush each other down, paying particular attention to wrinkles around our underarms and gear belts. Nobody wants to itch inside the tent all night, and nothing itches like fine Martian loess. We might not notice at first; six or eight hours after a drop, Cosmoline blocks itching and a lot of other sensations, so all seems smooth and cool and baby-powder sweet. During those hours I feel like a walking ghost or some other kind of disembodied asshole. But when sensation returns—and it always does—Mars dust can turn a miserable night on the Red into something truly special.

Assured that we are now relatively clean, one by one, we squeeze through the tent's canal into our little womb, like babies in reverse. When we're all in, and I've checked the seal and found it good, I crack my faceplate. Checker always takes first sniff. The tent air is okay, clean and cold. Like Russian steppes.

———

I'M BARELY AN hour into some crazy whimpering dream about mean kids when the tent wheeps intruder alert and we all jerk up, just as *something* slips through the entrance and plops down among us puppies. Beams flash. Kazak is loudly cursing in his eponymous patois. Then his beam illuminates a helm, a face— a human face—grinning like a bandit. Behind the faceplate, we recognize the broad nose, bushy unibrow, deep blue eyes, and somber, straight mouth.

"Shit, it's Vee-Def," Tak says. As we settle down, DJ passes Gunnery Sergeant Leonard Medvedev some water and an MRE.

Still all sergeants.

"Anybody get tactical?" Medvedev—Vee-Def—asks. As we dim our lights, the beams intersect a thin haze, and we realize there's dust in the tent. Vee-Def entered without brushing down. A severe breach.

"Fuckup," Kazak says.

"Nobody got tactical," Tak says.

"Anybody see a sled come down?" Vee-Def asks.

That's too stupid a question to answer. We're here in a Russian tent.

"How many tents?" he asks.

"How many do *you* see?" Tak asks.

More quiet.

"Sticks were all fucked," Vee-Def murmurs around a swig. His eyes are wide and scared. "I came down alone. Fucking puff was burning!"

"It's supposed to burn, man," DJ says.

"No, I mean there was sparkly and the sticks caught it. Looked like space frames, too. We may be all that's left!"

We're quiet for a few seconds.

"Bullshit," Tak says.

"I saw it, too," DJ reminds us, with a resentful glance.

Bad news takes a while to soak in when you're out on the Red, because just a little bad news means you're going to die, and this is a lot. Vee-Def feels the burn of bearing evil tidings. "I don't like Finnish sausage," he says, and offers around in pinched fingers a hard little tube of preserved reindeer.

No takers. We scratch ourselves with disdain.

Then Kazak starts giggling. "Is that your Tootsie Roll, man? Or you just glad to see us?"

It's dumb and not very funny. But for the moment we're warm, we're scratching, we're alive, and Vee-Def does what he does best, he sticks the sausage up his nose, or tries to, and then sneezes and snot comes out with the sausage and the sausage is good only for the family dog, which we were thoughtless enough to have left behind.

It's not good laughter. It's harsh and tired and angry. But it *is* laughter, and there may not be much to be had this trip. We don't say it, however. Not even Vee-Def is dumb enough to say more.

We're in the month-old tent of a dead platoon, our sticks got scattered, no transport sleds, our space frames may have caught sparkly, we have almost no tactical, comm seems to be down all over—even our angels are quiet.

We could be the Lost Patrol.

Morning will tell.

MARS WILL BE HEAVEN, SOMEDAY

I can't sleep for shit. I keep going over how fucked we are.

It's extreme on the Red. The air is just a millibar above a vacuum. It's always too damned cold. While there's quite a bit of water on Mars, overall most of it is tough to get at—locked up at the poles or cached beneath old seabeds or hidden in deep-flowing aquifers. That makes water a major strategic commodity. There's always a tiny residue of moisture in the air, enough to form high, icy clouds. There's more water in the air when the seasons melt the caps, which they do with monotonous regularity. Mars can be a cloudy world. I've even seen it snow, though the snow rarely makes it to the ground. That's called virga on Earth. Same on Mars.

On a large scale, weather on Mars is totally predictable. On a warrior's scale, not so much. There are always those scribbling dust devils, and big storms can block out the sun for months, covering the Red in dark brown murk so dense and fine you can't see your hand in front of your face. Imagine a near vacuum you can't see through. But the air does get warmer when the dust absorbs sunlight.

Making oxygen is the trick. Cracking water—hydrolysis—is comparatively easy; CO_2 and oxidized dust take more energy and time. That's why we need fountains. Fountains are big, often the size of a semi cab. We usually carry a couple with us on a drop, but they can also be delivered a few weeks before we arrive, on stealth chutes hundreds of meters wide, usually at night. They plop down on the Red and if the dust is deep enough—if they're not on impenetrable hardpan—they burrow in and almost immediately pop out solar collectors and extraction vanes and whirl the vanes to collect moisture from the air.

Fountains can stockpile enough volatiles over a few weeks to keep a company alive for two or three months. A big fountain can keep half a company in combat posture for six or eight months, refilling skintights with water and air.

Command can also decide to turn a fountain into a fuel depot, reserving its hydrogen and oxygen for propellant. We've all heard of fountains letting warriors suffocate on the Red for the greater strategic good—allowing someone else to get home again. Which do you need more? A return ticket, or enough to breathe? It's a nasty balance. Needless to say, Skyrines have a love-hate relationship with fountains.

To make matters more interesting, the longer a fountain has been on the surface, the more it becomes a prime target for Antag fire. Sometimes Antags let a fountain sit for weeks, working away, storing up volatiles, and when troops arrive and settle in, *then* they blow it up. Real sense of humor. Just as we start to party—scrap and stain on the Red.

If a fountain happens to locate a shallow aquifer or cached ice, it becomes a strategic reserve and may not announce its presence even to Skyrines, but instead shoots the news up to command and awaits instructions. Too valuable to waste on grunts.

———

OUTSIDE, THE DARK is complete and the air is clear. It's not as cold outside as on the southern highlands, but it's still plenty cold—about minus eighty Celsius. Inside the tent, curled up like puppies in a litter to conserve heat, we are truly womb brothers. Freudian, but not many Skyrines know dick about Freud, so traditionally, when we puppy up, we joke about bad porn instead. Unless we're too tired. There's a whole weird genre of porn down on the Big Blue Marble, about getting it on with Gurus or Antags. We aren't told what Gurus look like and don't know much about Antags, so they can be most anything we want. Why not prime green pussy? Some people down on the Blue Marble are just too strange to live. Interesting the Gurus don't seem to mind them.

In the dim light of a single beam, suppressed to a dull orange and hanging from the center of the tent, I study my mates. They seem to be asleep. I envy them that.

Tak is my friend, we go back a long ways, but I never feel entirely secure around him. He's quiet, movie-star handsome, lean and sharp, stronger and far more perceptive than me. Ever since Hawthorne, and in all our many battles, I've felt with a spooky prickle that someday he'll survive when I won't. Still, so far we've both survived, often because of what Tak does. He's damned good on the Red and a beast in a tussle.

Kazak is a very different sort. He's our barn door exchange student, a short, stocky guy with amazingly slanty eyes and even black fuzz on his crown that descends not so abruptly to a widow's peak. He came over from Kazakhstan a few years back and got promoted before the Skyrines found out he was a Tartar shithead and closed the barn door. Perfect teeth, long on the canines. A real *Canis lupus* with a feral smile. Not the brightest, but maybe the most steady and calm in a fight or a tough situation, he can be a quick judge of character, not always correctly, often with a Mongolian twist that's hard for the rest of us to figure. I can easily imagine him slapping raw meat under the saddle of his stocky pony and chewing on it in between Parthian shots with a compound bow. I have Polish and German blood in my family. Kazak denies fervently that his ancestors once raped and slaughtered mine. "Mongols so handsome, mother ladies just spread and bred," he says. Right. When things are loose, Kazak's sense of humor is murder. His practical jokes verge on felonies. PFCs have to stay on their toes around him.

Even for all that, most of us like him because he's *our* shithead and as shitheads go, he's kind of special. I've dropped with Kazak twice and sometimes he has this look that, when he has it, very reliably informs us that our Tartar shithead will take us *all* back home with him—a fierce wrinkle in one eye that makes me, too, want to bear his children.

Tonight, squinch-faced and snoring, he looks like a troubled baby. Still, he's snoring. I envy him that.

Being likable is a gift I do not reliably possess. I can turn it on sometimes, but I know when I'm doing it and feel guilty, people should just know I'm a good guy without the charm wave…But maybe I'm not such a good guy after all. Maybe default is truth. Nobody treats me as anything special, and I prefer it that way. Nobody but Joe and Tak and maybe Kazak. They're my best friends in this whole dust-fucked war.

An hour or more passes. I'm almost asleep, or maybe I'm dreaming I'm still awake, but I'm definitely awake when the alarm goes off again. Tak gets up on his knees by the membrane, ready to throttle whatever comes through. His face creases with handsome disappointment when a blue-stripe helm pokes in. Just another Skyrine, and this time it is Corporal Lindsay— Mitch—Michelin, his face blue with cold and hypoxia.

Tak raises his hands and flexes them. Finally, somebody we can boss around. Michelin is not the most compliant corporal, however. The entrance sucks shut as he pulls out his second boot, making our ears pop, and he falls on his back across DJ and Kazak. Then he claws his faceplate open and coughs until he's doubled. It's several minutes before he can say anything.

"No beacon!" he croaks. "Fuck. Almost died."

"You're welcome," Kazak says.

"Who's here?" Michelin asks, examining us with bloodshot eyes. He sees we're all superiors. It does not faze him. Tak hands the newcomer a tube of borscht and some reindeer sausage, then, more reluctantly, a bag of water. Now we're six, too many for the tent, if it's all we've got, but what can you do?

Michelin fixes his pink-eye gaze on Tak and grins. "Praise be, I'm in heaven. Master Sergeant Fujimori is here to service me. Who needs virgins?" His lips are still purple. He does not look good, but he's coming around. He holds up the Russian food tube. "What is this shit? Tastes like weak kimchee." And he erupts an enormous fart.

"Take that bloat outside," Tak requests, fastidious to a fault.

Michelin is too weak to apologize. After he's mumbled over our names and ranks, he falls into something like a nap, more like a brief coma, and then, twenty minutes later, flails for a moment before settling down, wide-eyed and shivering.

We're all awake now.

"Christ, our sticks must have shot their loads early," he says, rolls over, and asks if we have tactical.

"No," DJ says.

Then, with a shy smile, our lone corporal confesses he *might* have something. Turns out Michelin is the only one who got a solid burst before sparkly scrubbed the sky clean. Our angels share and we analyze his download, which includes broken uplink from previous drops.

"Still far from complete," Tak says.

"None of the fountains are putting out signal," DJ says. "Maybe they didn't make it down, maybe they got taken out—not one is talking."

We meditate on that.

"Tent can keep us going for eight more hours," DJ says. We give him the look. We do not need to hear what we already know. Tell us something new or something beautiful. DJ glances away, eyes losing focus, going dreamy. It's his safety.

Tak explores Michelin's burst beyond the negative on fountains. "Well, here's good news," he says. "Euro company before us"—the guys whose reindeer sausages and borscht lie heavy in our guts—"dropped a few tent boxes they didn't get a chance to use. No data on what went wrong...but there could still be six or seven inside ten klicks."

Our angels lock, and he shows us that the tents are widely spaced around the pedestal and the crater. We'll have to hike to avoid suffocation.

Few Skyrines keep it together when we can't breathe. No matter how tough our selection and training, we all tend to open our faceplates when oxy drops below threshold and claustrophobia takes over. True story. Skyrines typically want to die a few minutes early rather than slip into lung-searing delirium. Go figure.

"Rest up," Tak says.

After that, we're quiet for another half hour. I'm on the edge of a buzzing, insect-hive sort of sleep when the tent alarm goes off once more and Neemie squeezes in to join us—Staff Sergeant Nehemiah Benchley, from our second fire team, a strawberry blond surfer with a plump face and Asian wave tattoos that ripple like skin movies on his hands and neck. He's as ignorant as the rest of us. He reports the east is getting brighter, and he saw nobody else either during the drop or while walking. He cannot explain how he lasted this long. We don't inquire. Could be we're already dead. A hypnotically dumb idea that occurs far too often to warriors on the Red.

We drink up from what's left in the tent tubes, enjoy the luxury of a good piss in our recups, and for a few minutes, the tent smells of urine and ball-sweat. Not unpleasant, once you're used to it. Like a washroom in a Russian brothel. No disrespect. Dead Russians are saving us this night.

The tent announces in a stern, prerecorded voice—in Russian, Kazak translates—that there are far too many of us and we have depleted its resources.

The sky outside the tent is getting bright.

Time to move on.

GOD SAVES DRUNKARDS
AND BAKA DUDES

Morning is really cold.

We clap on our helms, seal up, query our angels, and one by one, through our faceplates, lift eyebrows or pook out lips, meaning all our angels are quiet. There are still no bit bursts, therefore no sats in the sky. Our angels have no good news, no news at all, and so they say nothing.

The tent is depleted. We birth out and just leave it there. No sense wasting strength trying to dig a hole and hide it, and it's useless to try to burn it under these conditions, because we'd have to supply the oxygen, and on top of all that, the tent's been out here for a month and if anybody cares they already know where it is. Likely nobody cares.

More Lost Patrol shit.

"We're at the butt end of a fight," Neemie opines into our gloom.

"Right," DJ says. "Tell us something ripping, Master Sergeant Venn."

"Ripping is as ripping does," I say. "We have no commander. We are on a hunt for gasps and sips and lunch. Not that I'm all that hungry." I look critically at Michelin and then at Vee-Def, who graces us with a dopey grin we can't really see behind his helm, but we know it's there.

We keep surveying the sky. From ground level all over Mars, you can spot space frames and other orbitals, especially before sunrise or after sunset, when the angles and contrast are best. This morning, nothing presents itself but a brilliant wall of stars. Air is very clear, and that means it's not going to get much warmer.

I look west because my left hand itches and it's on my western side. That little brown blurry patch is still there, up north a ways. Looks too far off to be of consequence, but it's the only steady attraction in our tight little theater. I touch helms with Tak. "Your ten," I say. He looks. His new eyes are better than ours. "What *is* that?"

"Dust devil," he says.

"It's been there since yesterday."

"What do *you* think it is?" DJ asks.

"A cute little twist in a Fiat…and she's got a keg," Kazak interposes.

"Could be wreckage," I say. "Could be a malfunctioning fountain. Could be anything."

"Ants," Vee-Def says, meaning Antags, Antagonists. Every word gets shorter as wars go on. Guys like Vee-Def do the shortening.

"*Could* be Antags," Kazak agrees. "But they would already be here if they cared about us, no? Why waste resources just to put us out of our misery—"

"Go see," Tak says, cutting off a bad ramble. He's a steady dude. When Tak makes a decision, others nod and agree. Neemie and Michelin move off first. The rest of us follow. I look back at the tent, our lifesaver, now useless junk. All across Mars there are thousands of tons of stuff that will get buried by dust and then dug up centuries from now and sold at auction. Our job is to make sure it's Sotheby's and not Ant-Bay. Ha-ha.

Talk of sparkly has gotten us downhearted. All we want is to find another tent. Not much hope for relief and certainly we can't hope for a pickup at this point.

We probably don't have enough reserves to reach the brown blur in the west. But maybe we're on a drop line, a regular pattern of deliveries in theater, across the plain. A mystical pilgrim's trail that will lead us to a few more days of life, and no asking God for more, that's already too much.

———

HIKING ON MARS in the morning chill is a treat I'd sell to any starry-eyed explorer for a hot shower.

Decades ago, a bunch of them came to Mars and set up parking lots full of white hamster mazes, then dug deep networks of rabbit tunnels. They claimed Mars and called it home. We call them all Muskies after a visionary entrepreneur, Elon Musk. From what little I've read, he founded an online bank, made cars and spaceships, promoted a vegan lifestyle, and fought for years with Blue Origin's Jeff Bezos, Virgin's Richard Branson, and a dozen other competitors around the world for launch facilities and orbital domination. Eventually, they pooled resources to fulfill the dream of putting people on Mars. But Musk had the name that stuck.

For almost twenty years, settlers kept crossing the vac and arriving on the Red, and then, abruptly, the migrations stopped—mostly because the best settlements maxed out and the others were starving or worse, like Jamestown in Virginia. But a few hundred stalwarts survived, and for a time Muskies were highly regarded, successful pioneers...Until people tired of spending money on the colonies, none of which ever made a return on investment.

So the investment stopped.

After the Gurus arrived and told us that Mars had maggots and we had to go out there and exterminate them before they grew into wasps, the Muskies became a liability. The brass decided we couldn't defend them, or save them if they got in trouble, once the Battle of Mars began in earnest. I've never seen a Muskie, even at a distance. There may be a couple of thousand left alive, but Earth hasn't done squat for them in years. As far as anyone knows, Antags don't bother with them, either.

The original settlers paid between $10 million and $100 million each for their *Mayflower* moment. Our strategy prof at SBLM likened them to the guy who lit out in the 1930s for the Pacific Islands to get away from the hurly-burly and ended up on Guadalcanal.

EVERY SKYRINE IS SOMEBODY'S BASTARD

We march. Radio silence isn't all that big a deal now, but we keep our talk to a minimum. The sky is still empty. Looks as if what's going to be here is already here.

Walking on lowland hardpan with only a softening of dust, or low ripples cut through by devil tracks, is easy enough, not like sand or deep dust, and we weigh about one-quarter what we would on Earth, so we could conceivably jump along like John Carter or a moon astronaut, but that's not recommended and not even all that much fun after the first few leaps, because you never know when your boot will come down on a stone big enough to turn your ankle. There are fucking rocks all over.

There's a lot of confusion still about how Mars came to be what it is today. Parts of Mars are pure nightmare, from a geologist's standpoint—so much evidence of big gushes and rivers and lakes and even oceans of past water, present water not so evident, but there all the same—so much difference between the southern highlands and the northern lowlands—plus the biggest visible impact basin in the solar system, Hellas Planitia, surrounded

by peculiar terrain both older and younger than the impact...
Smart people spend lifetimes trying to riddle it.

Mostly, I leave it to them. But I have my theories. I'm willing
to believe all these little rocks fell out of some giant kid's
pockets. He walked around in dirty sneakers for hundreds of
thousands of years, picking up rocks and stuffing them in his
dungarees. Whenever his balls chafed and tugged his pants leg,
he dribbled a stony trail. Johnny Rocker. That explains all these
ankle-turners.

We could legitimately pray for a thin cloud of fine silt to blow
over, but the sky is not cooperating. Martian dust is a major heat-
grabber. Temperatures rise, batteries last longer. Insolation—
solar energy—drops quite a bit, but we aren't laying out solar
panels and our skintights have little in the way of photovoltaic
capacity.

DJ says he's in sight of the next Russian tent. He's quite an ace
at finding tents. We knew roughly where it was, but he climbed
the pedestal and located the tent box in an old gully. And then he
reports it's got warning colors.

"Germ needles," he says.

The box is filled with shit that kills humans.

That leaves us with maybe two hours of breath.

———

By DATE OF rank, I rule in this fragmented squad, but I don't give
orders because nobody cares until we get our recon and tactical
becomes important. Besides, if I go all commando voice—*Now,
men! Listen up*—they're likely to ignore me and turn to Tak.

Which is fine by me.

I'd sure like to hear from Gamecock, our company
commander—Lieutenant Colonel Harry Roost. I don't much like
Roost—he can be a by-the-book hardass—but I respect him. He

would be strong and direct out here, if not reassuring. We don't need a hand-holder. We need a lifesaver with a sense of purpose.

———

THINGS DO NOT get better. Before we reach the next tent box, Tak spots debris a few hundred meters off and we divert. As we get closer, all I see is a skipping series of strike marks, scorch and scatter—a few craters where chunks hit, while the rest went on and plowed long, shallow graves in the hardpan.

We gather around the edge of the strike zone and eyeball the extent. This was once an entire space frame, and it did not fall empty. It came down full of sticks and fasces. There are dead Skyrines everywhere. And a transport sled, split into pieces. Skell-Jeeps spill out of the shattered capsules like the bones of half-born babes. All useless. Even dangerous. Kazak warns us to stay clear of anything that looks like a reactor.

We gingerly poke around, looking for oxygen generators, tanks, packs of skintights, anything that could keep us going for a few more hours. Nobody talks. We don't examine the bodies. They came down hard and they're mostly just scattered rips of fabric, squashed helms...freeze-dried stain. They had probably just emerged from Cosmoline, woozy and sluggish, and were getting cleaned off, suiting up, attaching puff packs, prepping for the drop. The space frame must have just then been hit by ground-to-sky bolts or lasers, or sky-to-sky, no way of telling. When seen from a few dozen klicks, or from the ground: sparkly. Just as Michelin and Vee-Def said. Major sparkly to take down the company's frames and all our sats and, since we have yet to find a fountain, maybe all those as well.

The trunk of the frame might contain extra cargo. We give it a quick search. Nothing here, either. Pure Skyrine waste, nothing to see. Move along.

We have about half an hour. We'll be dead long before we reach the brown blur. Just keep marching toward the rough position of the next tent box. Kazak suggests we fan out, not to offer a compact target. We break into three groups.

"What's that tower of haze out there, really, do you think?" Tak asks. He's about ten meters away, skirting the pedestal's rim.

"Something stupid," DJ says, about thirty meters away. "Making itself obvious."

"Or something strong that doesn't give a fuck about being spotted," Vee-Def suggests.

That's possible, but I don't want to hear it. If it's strong and boastful, it doesn't belong to us. Antags are winning today.

"Maybe it's a secret sect of Muskies," Neemie says, moving closer.

"Shut up," I say. "And keep the spread."

We go wide again. Fifteen minutes of oxygen, give or take. Soon our angels will warn us we're down to last gasp and that will seal the deal. Maybe that's why we call them angels. They could be the last thing you hear.

Hey, Skyrine—it's a good day to die. They don't actually say that, but it might be cool if they did.

———

TIME TO DESCRIBE a skintight. It's a remarkable piece of equipment, even when it's failing, even when you know you're going to die. Your standard Mars-grade skintight is a flexible and seamless suit woven from a continuous monomolecular strand of carbon coilflex, set into a bilayer gel mostly comfy to the skin. Moisture is recycled or broken down into oxygen, depending on the need. In the field, the skintight absorbs skin waste and conveys it through tiny tubes to storage packs around the butt, which gives Skyrines a big-bootie profile. Every few days you remove the extract from the butt packs and throw it away—a useless lump of oil and dead skin and salt and other gunk.

The helm and the angel process video and tactical memory. Skintight fabric contains circuitry for battlefield diagnostic, which sends our health status to the angel for uplink, so that birds on high can tell our commanders how we're doing down on the Red.

Skintights do nearly everything except walk and fight and they do it quietly and without complaining. Some say they are like the still-suits in *Dune*, and they do bear a resemblance, but ours do a hell of a lot more than conserve and filter water.

Every Skyrine has a love-hate relationship with his skintight. Can't wait to get home and get it off, but then he misses the convenience of never having to worry about pee or crap or sweat, and feels, when naked, that one is minus a real friend, perhaps the best friend ever. Some old hands have to relearn bladder control when they're back in civvies. All the designers need do is make skintights sexually accommodating and Skyrines might never have to come home again.

Yeah.

That said, a skintight whose batteries are running down, whose oxygen is running out, whose water is turning sour, feels less like a friend and more like a jar full of pickle juice.

We are sinking deep in the jar.

THE WAY IT SPOZED TO BE

Immediately after drop, or on the way down, you're supposed to receive updated tactical and maps with known objectives and concentrations of Antag forces clearly laid out, appropriate to your squad's assigned chores.

Ideally, you'll drop within a short hike of a fountain or, barring that, a cluster of tent boxes, and somewhere in the vicinity your transport sled will also come down on stealth chutes, spiraling in within a couple of klicks of the company's drop zone, though they are pretty targets and often don't make it intact.

Skyrines are trained to make do with what they got. But when you got next to nothing…

Every Skyrine drops with at least one basic weapon, his sidearm. As I said, they look like fat .45s. Someone named them Yllas, don't know why. They don't shoot bees. They fire bullets and bolts. Bolts are deadly to anything they hit within five hundred meters. They home on whatever you're looking at with about ninety-nine percent accuracy. The pistols carry a small spent matter cassette and that has to be switched on to charge the plasma about thirty seconds before combat. A single spent matter cassette can charge and launch about sixty bolts. Gun captain—a rotating duty—collects all used cassettes. Spent matter waste is bad shit and we're supposed to be sensitive about ecological issues. In truth, however, there are a lot of cached bags of it out on the Red; no time in combat to search and recover if, for example, our gun captain gets zeroed. Vee-Def is supposed to be gun captain for this drop.

Kinetic rounds work in vac, of course—gunpowder supplies its own oxygen. But cold can reduce range, and target practice on Earth doesn't train you for Mars, where windage is usually very light, the thin air very cold, and the gravity drop much slower. Our other weapons, lasers and even weak-field disruptors, can be affected by heavy dust.

Skyrines have been trained to fight in nearly all conditions. Training is so you might not get killed before you gain experience. Newbies start on the Red with nothing but simulations and a month of Earth-based live fire—not nearly enough, in my opinion. You only really improve by doing.

———

AND HERE'S WHAT we think we know about the Antags, or at least, what we're told: They probably don't come from our solar system or anywhere near. That means they arrived on a big ship, tech unknown but capable of crossing interstellar distances. It's tough to visualize how huge interstellar space is. Vast, vast, long-long-long distance—repeat a trillion times until you feel really small and silly. Mostly empty light-years and deep cold.

But we haven't found that big ship, have no idea where it might be hiding, and can only vaguely guess how they get from there to Mars. Or anywhere else they take a fancy to. So far, just Mars, we're told.

But then the grandma said...

Titan! Jesus.

HEAVY HAND

Maybe I'm seeing things.

A couple of lights are floating up in the sky, competing with Phobos for my attention, bright enough to be space frames, but they could just as easily be Antag. Their *Grasshopper*-class boats are about that bright in orbit—clusters of pressurized tubes filled with transports and weapons and combatants.

Tak raises his hand. Michelin raises his and shouts there are sats still up—and then I see a thin blue line drop down quick, hit the dust, miss Vee-Def—then try again. This time the line touches him, then shifts over to Tak.

"Bit burst!" Tak shouts, loud enough to hear from five meters. We've been found.

I get my blue line next, and my angel is suddenly happy to show me where we are, where there might be supplies and weapons—the immediate logistical picture. Only three of us receive the laser lines, so our angels exchange for the next few seconds while we're chattering like schoolkids waiting for the bus.

"Something's coming," Tak says, having finished a quick

skim, tagging data he finds immediately important. To my surprise, it's not survival data—nothing to do with tents or sleds.

It's a warning.

"Big stuff coming down," Tak summarizes, concentrating so hard his eyes cross.

Michelin cranes his neck and looks up at the sky, squinting. He covers his helm with gray-gloved hands. Then he crouches. Instinct. We watch him, bemused.

"What is it?" Vee-Def asks. "Landing parties? Big Mojo?"

Big Mojo is rumored to have been seen once, four years ago: a kind of massive Antag orbital capable of shaving off huge, battalion-strength landers and dropping them to the Red. The lights we see aren't that bright. But they're also not what we're being warned about. Whatever's out there, whatever's on its way in, the mass is enormous, and there are nine to twelve of them, maybe more, separate objects tracked by our few remaining sats, which have finally and most kindly supplied us with what they know—just before we suffocate.

"Biggest may be a hundred million tons," DJ says, winnowing the numbers down to basics. "Others, smaller—five or six million."

"Jesus," Neemie says, his voice husky. His air is going fast. So is mine.

"Why tell us this shit now?" Michelin asks, lifting his head from his crouch.

"We're within five hundred klicks of point of impact," I say. "Approaching at more than forty klicks per second, which means they're moving in…I think fast…from outside Mars's orbit? Solar orbit? Extrasolar, from the Oort?"

Does that make sense? Wouldn't the Antags want to slow them down, whatever they are, or do they just plan on skimming atmo and making another go-around?

"What can we fucking do?" Michelin cries.

"How soon?" Neemie asks.

"Doesn't say."

Some lights now roll into view low in the west, very bright objects indeed, very big, one actually a crescent—and moving fast. Right for our collective noses, so it looks, so it feels.

Then, just as we are about to fall on our knees and wait for the big bright things to fly by or hit us square, Vee-Def finds practical info in the bit burst and shouts, "Three more Russian tents! A whole pallet! A hundred meters that way—" He points.

We run. No questions, no disagreement. We got maybe ten minutes of air.

I look over my shoulder and nearly take a header. But you can stumble quite a ways on Mars and still recover, if you're fast with your footwork. What I see, as I keep my footing and keep running, is that the objects in the sky are *tumbling*; the motion is obvious—bright, dark, crescent wobbling. Quick count: one scary big one, visually wider than Phobos but, I hope, I fear, much closer, and nine or ten smaller, but by now you can see all of them rolling around way up there like happy seals in an ocean swell.

Tak and Kazak find the pallet of three tent boxes and we cluster around as Vee-Def and DJ and Michelin slice the containment straps and separate the boxes, check the stripes—safe—then pop the seals. Two tents spring out, nearly hitting me and Michelin, and then roll and lie there, all innocent and beautiful. The third won't disengage from the box. Its air reserve is empty. It's not quite useless, however—Vee-Def harvests its water packs.

We got maybe four minutes to get one or both of the remaining tents to inflate before we climb inside, but even if we do that—

The first object hits the atmosphere. It draws a superfast ghostly white flame across the sky. The flame lingers and turns pale purple. The object strikes beyond the northwestern horizon.

It is *gone*. Not so bad. Then a brilliant flash seems to roll out of the west, quickly fades to a gloriously supernal mauve, while a pinkish dome shot through with coiling white clouds blooms at the center of the strike. The dome rises into perfect mushroom cap, supported by—nothing! No central pillar of smoke or cloud at first, but finally it seems to fill in, condense, and we see the mottled grayish stalk, tossing out curving streamers of purple and white.

We stand in awe. I'm gasping—Cheynes-Stokes breathing, not good.

The first tent has nearly inflated.

Then the ground shakes—*heaves* violently, tossing us like bowling pins. We end on our butts, clutching at the hardpan, while all around, dust leaps and pebbles and rocks do a crazy, jiggling dance.

A few dozen meters away, the hardpan *cracks open*, taking in the pallet and the bum tent—swallowing them whole. Almost gets DJ as well, but he scrambles toward us like a desert beetle. The crack stops a few arm-lengths from my faceplate. The sound is awful, a hard-packed, rhythmic pounding that shakes our skulls, our bones, makes the fabric of our skintights ripple, like standing too close to a Japanese drummer in full frenzy. My head pulses with each wave, and then—the waves seem to bounce off something and come back from the other side, from the east. What the fuck is that about?

We look west again.

A translucent wall of air passes over, buffets us, and suddenly we are surrounded by a muffled, pressing, scary quiet.

"Cone of silence!" Tak calls out, lying flat beside me.

"What?"

"We're in the cone! The shock wave's bounced against the upper air and arced over!" he says.

I have no idea what he means.

"More coming!" Michelin shouts. We all manage to look up. The sky, the horizon, is a soundless, eerie sort of awful, shot through with gray streaks spreading from that too-perfect mushroom cap, then obscuring it. That might have been the big one. If it wasn't, we won't survive, because it isn't over. A half dozen others *skip* this way and that across the sky and through the clouds like stones on a pond, finally plunging...

The shock is amazing. I'm tossed maybe five meters up and flip over and land on my back, hard enough to knock me silly. I try to breathe. Everything hurts. Broken ribs? If my skin-tight tears, I'm cold meat, but that may not matter, because the stars have fled—there's only a low gray ceiling, seemingly solid, impenetrable. But white specks fall *through* the ceiling.

I'm just a big ball of pain but then, old memories, I reacquire an agonized pair of childlike eyes and say, It's Christmas, look! Snow. Snow is falling all around. Flakes and chunks, some like grapple, some big as my fist. Falling all over, bouncing off me, off the hardpan. I don't bother to get up. Maybe I can't and I don't want to know that.

Pretty soon I'm buried in it.

Damn, we were almost in the tent.

Then come the rocks.

NOT YET A HERO, HUH?

I wake up and see Tak leaning over me, looking into my face. Fingers do the ICU, UCME?

Yes. Yes.

It's heavy outside.

The air is like nothing I've ever felt on Mars, warm and dense. My angel has been sounding a continuous wheep-wheep of alarm. I get up on one elbow. There's a blanket of ice and snow all around, punctuated by black rocks big as my fist, big as my head—new rocks, flung from hundreds of klicks away. Some are still smoking.

Impact heat.

Scattered between the snow and ice and the rocks are pools of fizzing liquid water, bubbling like hot springs. Terrific. We've made it to Yellowstone.

We're on Planet Perrier.

I try to say that over comm. I want to show Tak I'm still clever, still able to make jokes, but I've bitten my tongue and my mouth is full of blood and it splatters on my faceplate when I try to talk.

Tak shakes his head. Holds up two fingers. I get up to help him find the others. DJ is buried in a drift. We shove aside rocks and ice. He's limp when we pull him out, but recovers enough to join our search. Kazak we find next. He's alert and looks as if he might have just had a refreshing nap. Leaps up out of the rubble, brushing snow and dust from his plate and shoulders.

Michelin is also still alive, but his helm took a rock or something and the plate is cracked, not yet through the seal. Still pressurized. All our skintights are okay, miracle of miracles. No rips.

We immediately try to relocate the other tents. Maybe the one has finished inflating. If it hasn't, or if both got swallowed by another crack or pierced by rocks, we're down to nothing, don't know how we lasted this long, must have been mere minutes yadayada all the shit that fills one's head as the body does, like a robot, like a trained dog, what it's supposed to do to keep your pretty soul wrapped in flesh.

We find the tent. It inflated, but then—ruptured, big holes where rocks went through. But the canisters still have air and we take turns charging our skintights. Just a few minutes' worth.

Where's Vee-Def? Neemie?

We find the second tent box. Shadows close in around my eyes like groping fingers. My lungs are awful balloons filled with fire.

Tak inflates the tent. The noise all around has returned. It's unrelenting. Mars is cosmically bitching: whistling, hissing, sighing—then, letting out with a shrill, high scream as something much too grand shoots overhead. More big stuff coming down? No way to know. The gray canopy of clouds still looks solid. The local pools still bubble and spit mud, local air still feels thick, but everything is cooling rapidly, and now the water is turning into steaming, crusty, carbonated ice—sinking into the dust or soaking into hardpan.

Fog suddenly condenses all around. It's like a big Walt Disney brush painting us over. We can't see much of anything. Wiping my faceplate, fingers streak away dust and water. The water vanishes from my fingertips and leaves just the dust. Never even had time to become mud.

I pick my way around and kick at the last of the snow, vanishing before it can liquefy. This stuff is not water! Like dry ice or something else. Weird.

Something in me remembers where Michelin was, and I turn just enough to walk back and find him. He's trying to get up. Tak bumps into me. We both check Michelin over. His eyes are wide, concerned. He swipes at the fog.

Tak holds up five fingers.

My cheeks hurt I'm grimacing so hard.

Kazak joins us. The fog begins to clear, swirling up and away in ghostly eddies. The sky shows patches of grainy black. Funny I haven't noticed the sound for a while, but it's down to a constant brumble-grumble with odd pops that make my ears hurt.

Then it gets real quiet. That's not much better, in my opinion. We all stand hands on shoulders, supporting each other, supporting Michelin, who's regaining his balance, some of his strength, touching his faceplate, no doubt wondering how he made it through.

Vee-Def and Neemie come stumbling out of the last unwinding mist. They spot us. Shamble our way. Tak holds up seven fingers. Praise Jesus. We gather around the one intact tent, brush ourselves off as best we can, and crawl one by one through the tent's tight canal. No immediate appointments. No place else to go. We are tired, lost, beat-up little puppies. Too many for the tent, regulation, but nobody cares. We've got air, water.

The ground is still vibrating as I manage to find some sleep. Then, maybe five minutes later, Michelin wakes us by flashing a beam around, and says, sitting up straight, hair on end, full of revelation, "That ice—some of it was dry ice, methane, ammonia—really *old* shit!"

"So?" Kazak asks, ticked off.

"The Antags dropped a fucking *comet*!" Michelin concludes, and stares around at us, one by one, jaw agape, impressed by his own intelligence.

We stare back. Fuck yeah. No disagreement.

"Heavy hand, man," Vee-Def says, shaking his head in admiration. "Taking charge."

NOT DEAD YET

Caught in a weird, ethereal glow as we wake, we untangle, sit up, and one by one, peer through the clear tent panels. Tak's face when he looks shines like hot bronze.

The sunrise is amazing. I've never seen such colors on Mars, like a Pacific island postcard, great streaky plumes of dust catching first light of morning, all red and orange and gold. Our resources are not encouraging. Plus, we're hungry. We don't complain, but now we think on it.

We suit up and emerge. The world outside doesn't seem to have changed substantially, after all the hurly-burly. The brown blur is back, just about where it was. The sky is a little lighter—more dust kicked up—but the snow is gone and the puddles have all fizzed away. It's once again a dry, desolate hardpan.

Dust settles quickly on Mars, once the wind stops.

We stand out in the cold like anyone would, wrapped in crossed arms, whapping our shoulders, waiting for salvation or at least something different. Skyrines do not stay impressed for long. About the only thing that would impress me now is a portal opening directly ahead and taking me straight to a Jack's

Popper Palace. Beer. Burgers and fries. I'm hungry enough that that would impress the hell out of me.

Kazak hears something. "Sounds like a mosquito."

"Skell coming," Vee-Def says. He has the best ears of our small bunch. Tak has the best eyes of anyone in the company; new eyes, brilliant blue. Even so, I spot the Skell-Jeep first, a little bug whining over the horizon. It flies a big chartreuse flag, the color most obvious out here—green and yellow severely lacking on Mars.

The Skell veers to avoid fresh pits and then it's upon us. Glory yet again—we have our division deputy commander! Lieutenant Colonel Hal Roost, Gamecock to his troops, is driving the Skell while a United Korean *sojang*, a major general, two small stars attached combat-style to a blaze strap on his chest, rides shotgun. The general cradles a Facilitator—a wide-mouthed rocket launcher. The general also has two Tchikoi flechette pistols strapped to his belt, wrapped in transparent Baggies with finger holes, dusty-desert fashion.

This pair is grim, abrupt, no congratulations, no small talk. Gamecock signals radio silence is still on. Our bad. We are, however, under the circumstances allowed to communicate by scree or laser, angels targeting each other, or by shouting in our helms, and that gives us a chance to clearly hear Gamecock announce that our forces are in temporary disarray.

"We took major sparkly on delivery. The drop was severely fidged. Some orbital jock must have spooked at the first G2O." Ground-to-orbit. That could explain our high stick release.

"Well, they're all dead now," Gamecock says. "Good to see you made it." Gamecock gestures over his shoulder. "We need to reevaluate our leisure activity. See that blur? That——is a game changer. Probably some sort of Antag factory. We don't know whether it came down with the dirty ice or was lying there waiting for supplies."

"Master Sergeant Venn saw it before the strike," Tak says.

Gamecock nods, good info. "Whatever, now it's got everything it needs to crank out adverse goodies."

And to think we were moving toward it. Like jacklighted deer, I guess.

We look at the Korean general, wondering if he'll contribute anything. His face, behind a dirty faceplate, is haggard. His skin-tight is exceptionally dirty. He's been out in the open for some time.

"Pardon," Gamecock says. "This is General Woo Jin Kwak. He dropped with an eastern platoon the week before we arrived. Lost most of his men. The survivors are south of here. Good news, they've found an old Chinese fountain and may have the codes to activate. So that's where we're going to regroup. Then, we're going to attempt to establish two-way with whatever sats are still working and conduct some recon. Learn what's going on. What's expected of us. For now, that Chinese fountain is our destination. And it is over *there.*" He points south. "We'll know nothing more about the Antags until we have orders and command tells us go see," he says. "And to do that, we need to stay alive and accumulate resources."

"Leave now," Kwak says, and swings up his arm. Command structure among the signatories in our fight is not supertight, despite the fact we're supposed to be buddies and cooperate fully. Korean general and all, we don't move unless Lieutenant Colonel Roost tells us to.

"Climb up, travelers," Gamecock says.

The Skell-Jeep is big enough to carry us all, if three hang from the waist bars. Tak and Vee-Def and I hang. Gamecock drives us south. Judging by the bent frame and a skewed wheel that thumps us about, the Skell has taken a couple of tumbles and a roll or two since it popped out of its capsule. It's a real beach buggy ride.

Pretty soon, recent craters become more obvious. The comet chunks split before striking atmosphere. A lot of loose ice skipped around way up there, creating a total impact zone of maybe ten or twenty thousand square klicks. Just guessing. Pin-point aim considering where comets usually dwell.

I'm asking myself—we're all amateur astronomers up here—how the Antags can maneuver fucking comets without our knowing, since trans-Martian space is scanned from Earth and the Moon every few hours. Maybe the Antags covered it in soot before moving it downsun. No matter. That level of theory is way above my pay grade, but I stuff it aside in a mental cubby to ponder later, perhaps before returning to timeout.

I like having things to ponder as the Cosmoline sinks in, the bigger and weirder the better. One of my favorite ponders is the Galouye question—is all this, the entire perceived universe, a gigantic computer simulation? There's a philosopher named Thaddeus Cronkle way down in London who claims he has proven that it is, and that we can run what some boffin or other called a Taylor algorithm to figure out which operating system is running the show. We're all Neos. Cool shit, that, real calming. Better than contemplating heaven, because all Skyrines go to heaven, not an exclusive club, and if it lets *us* in, I doubt it's much like what we've been told. Paradise, like Mars, is never what it's spozed to be.

The Skell takes us through even rougher scenery. There was fighting south of us before we dropped. Remnants of bivouacs lie all around, scattered as if by massive S2G—sky-to-ground—laser or bolts or torpedoes. We watch in respectful silence. There are bodies. Lots of bodies, and they may have taken orders from the Korean general.

He doesn't look left or right.

––––––

A BIVOUAC ON Earth means a temporary encampment where troops have not had time to pitch tents or set up any structure. On Mars, of course, there is rarely any sort of bivouac without tents or other cover. We steal words from the past and abuse them.

Gamecock does not enlighten as to our tactical. He's as lack-wit as the rest of us. And the general still doesn't do anything but sit there, his gloved hands grabbing the seat bars so tight they look like they might split. He's seen rough shit. The way he's not looking at the pits and debris, maybe he saw it here.

Tak, hanging on beside me, studies the field of recent battle with screw-lipped concentration, like he's constipated. Neemie is motion sick but holding it in. Only Vee-Def keeps a steely squint toward some far destination, wherever it may be. Heroic. Stoic. So unlike him.

The overloaded Skell climbs a slope and tops a barchan—a big sinuousity of blown sand about fifteen meters high—and rolls for a time along the crest, then turns with a sickening, tire-scurry lurch and descends, sideways, sliding, threatening to roll—but Gamecock corrects just before we hit the hardpan.

Without warning, just beyond the dust-deviled edge of sand, the lieutenant colonel takes us straight over rutted, ancient mud, nearly knocking me loose, and with another lurch, down into a deep furrow. He brakes the Skell to a trembling halt within five paces of a rough lean-to. The lean-to is made of capsule and tube parts and covers a big tent, a command tent.

Beyond the lean-to, the furrow splits, carving a Y in the flatness. Gamecock jumps from the Skell. We're quickly the center of attention as heavy rank emerges from the lean-to. This Y-shaped depression is our recon point. It is full of Asian and Russian brass—two Chinese generals and three Russian colonels. Boy are they happy to see us! Now there are sergeants and a corporal to boss around, along with Gamecock.

Kwak dismounts slowly, passes his weapons to a Russian colonel, and turns toward us. Face pale, resigned, he gathers strength to summon us into the command tent. Where is this honcho's staff? Each one of these officers should have security and staff and a whole lean-to or command tent apiece. Clearly, they have fallen on hard times.

I glance at Gamecock and then at Tak, whose constipation has relaxed into focused wonder, and share a silent fear that here, buckaroos, there are far too many cowboys and not nearly enough Indians.

Tak touches helms with me. "Why so many generals?" he asks.

"Somebody fucked up major ops," I guess.

THE STRAIGHT SKINNY—OR NOT

The lean-to is jury-rigged and works more as concealment than protection or support. The command tent beneath resembles an old hot air balloon, sagging and rippling under the curved and cracked aluminum and plastic. A one-person airlock replaces the birth canal entrance, but operates much the same way: you enter, wrap yourself in membrane, air is squeezed back into the tent, then you unzip an inner panel, unwind, and step inside. We make sure DJ and Vee-Def brush down thoroughly, not to disgrace us.

Tak and I silently assess the situation once we're in. This is not a place of safety or refuge. They've probably been using the tent mostly as a place to talk. First, the pressure is no better than it would be most of the way up Everest. Even so, the thin air smells of death—foul-sweet, clogging. None of the officers looks fit. Most have sustained crush or strike injuries. Wounds tend to get nasty in low pressure. Flesh needs oxygen at decent pressure to purify and heal, otherwise anaerobes move in. I long to seal up my skintight and leave. We all do.

Gamecock introduces us around the ragged circle. Despite wanting to gag, I'm in awe. Here we are, grunts from a fragmented squad, sharing the air—however foul—with commanding officers from three partner regions and five nations. These guys hang out with world leaders. Certainly a group worth rescuing, and that may improve our chances…

Major General Kwak proves adept at English and is in slightly better health than the others. He tells us, in a tight, pain-racked voice, that they have a little water, another day's worth of air, and—at the northern branch of the furrow—something that would be invaluable if it weren't broken: a Chinese fountain, covered with sand and dust, not by design, but by the local weather. It's at least two years old, from a previous drop.

"Can you fix?" he asks with a hopeful rise of one brow.

Gamecock and DJ confer in whispers. I can't hear what they're saying. I know that DJ had tech training on fountains but was never certified.

As a Russian named Efremov pushes out a sag in the tent, Kwak slowly steps over to a fold-out table supporting a small projector. "You must be asking, why are so many generals? Because commanders must study ground before committing troops to battle." He gives a wry shake of his head. "We arrived with many space frames, an orbital command station, many satellites. Seventy-five transport sleds, hundreds of vehicles. And now they are destroyed or scattered. We made emergency drop, and are now here."

These impressive combined ops did not include us. They must have arrived separately from our squadron, weeks before.

"We have not been able to establish comm with our other forces. We do not know where they may be, or how many survive. We were unfortunate…" Major General Kwak pauses, chest heaving as he works to suppress Cheynes-Stokes. With so many in the tent, long speeches are clearly not in order, but that's never stopped generals.

Kwak continues. "Our ships encountered Antagonist defenses in orbit with at least forty of their...snake-trains, upon their own insertion and entry." He looks less sure of his words and refers to a Russian colonel, who translates for us, "Snake-trains...The general refers to Antagonist resupply caravans. Carrying weapons, troops, great amounts of volatiles."

"Comets?" Gamecock asks.

"We think so, yes," Efremov says, and drops down on his knees. These few words and he's almost out for the count.

"Clearly, something large," Kwak resumes. Determined to finish this grim briefing, the general refocuses with shuddering effort. "There is only one of our satellites still in orbit, though that may be down now as well. No more frames will arrive for at least a week. Until we understand how our present forces are dispersed, and what strength remains, we are merely observers. Are we agreed on this intelligence, gentlemen?"

Everybody's agreed, if not happy.

A Colonel Orlov pushes up and struggles to do his bit. "Chinese fountain...inoperable. We lost engineers in the drop. But it may still be reworked—repaired."

"We have an engineer," Gamecock says. DJ looks apprehensive. "Do you have proper tools?"

"Possibly," Kwak says. "But not many spare parts."

The officers confer in Chinese and Russian. Then another officer enters the tent and looks around: an Indian with a swollen face, chapped and cracked lips and cheeks, his right arm badly broken and hanging in a crude cable sling. Lots of starboard breaks here. A command sled could have landed hard and injured everybody inside, all at once.

"We are in regard to repair and refit," Kwak tells him.

"Most excellent." The newcomer reaches out his left hand to

Roost, thinks better of that gesture—no good for Muslims, and who knows?—withdraws the hand, looks around with sunken eyes. "I am Brigadier Jawahar Lal Bhagati. Who here is capable of our salvation, and making do for all?"

The old fountain seems to be our last hope.

Gamecock puts a hand on DJ's shoulder. "Sir, this man is the best we have."

God help us.

"Most excellent!" says Bhagati. "We have scrounged tools, and may have the right codes to activate. Let us begin."

BRIEF HOPE

The next few hours, I'm designated quartermaster and scurry back and forth carrying tools and a few of the dwindling water packs. Still no food to speak of, but we can do without that for days longer.

DJ seems to be making progress with the fountain, but it's getting dark and very cold, minus one hundred Celsius, and we're not going to be able to stay outside much longer. Keeping warm drains batteries fast. During cold snaps or night, Skyrines are supposed to squeeze into a tent or at the very least huddle in a ditch and cover with dust. Last man pushes dust over the group and then burrows in as best he can. Back on Rainier, we trained extensively on how to huddle and cover. Like puppies, as I've said; puppies seem to know how to assume the most efficient piles.

Tak had corpsman training back at SBLM, and despite his own contusions and a couple of cracked ribs, he tends to the beat-up officers in the half-inflated tent with a steady, blue-eyed gaze that is equally good at calming horses.

Our squad, by the way, is code-named Trick and is made up, in full complement, of two fire teams. Tak and I are part of fire team one—weak-field disruptor, rapid-delivery bolt rifles, and multitrack launchers. If we arrive with all our weapons, of course. I don't know why we still use code names. We don't even know if Antags understand human languages. But we sure as hell don't know *their* languages. No one, as far as we've been informed, has ever intercepted comm between Antag units or their ships or equipment. Nothing to help us make a Rosetta. Maybe they just don't *talk*.

Which is one reason I don't like calling our enemy *Ants*. Ants communicate all sorts of ways. Ant colonies are a single organism, a single mind, mostly, with the individual insects we call "ants" acting both as muscle and neurons. Each ant serves as scout, worker, and a little bit of the colony brain. The colony as a whole gathers intel around its field of action and then solves problems like a distributed network. They communicate by touching feelers and sensing chemicals they leave behind, trails of clues that also serve as a kind of GPS. I'd hate to fight ants, especially big ones. Gamecock, like Vee-Def—like Joe—persists in calling our enemies Ants. Sometime I'll tell you about my nightmare of getting stung all over.

Christ, it's getting cold. I'm starting to feel comfortable, ready to settle in and go to sleep, so to keep awake, I walk back and forth in the ditch between the half-inflated command tent, where the generals and colonels are hanging out—with the exception of Gamecock—and back up to the northern branch of the Y to the broken Chinese fountain. My ankles are knotting, so my gait is more of a controlled stumble. Worse, there's a sickening smell in my helm. I hope it's not my own gangrene. At the very least, our skintights are well beyond pickle juice; the scrub filters are failing and the residue must be turning rancid, which is absorbing oxygen…Everything needs recharging, replacing. Including me.

Finally, I post myself by the fountain, too tired to move. Sleep is a soft and lovely thought. Lovely easeful death. Through a darkening tunnel, I watch DJ's feet. He's shoveled out an angle of dust at the base of the fountain and unscrewed a hatch, into which he's now shoved the upper half of his body. His feet twitch and every now and then he bends his knees. That's how I know he's still alive, still working.

Fountains are impressive pieces of equipment. They used to arrive by balloon bounce, but since they've gotten larger, more expensive, and more delicate, they're more often delivered by stealth chutes or even chemical fuel descent. This Chinese model is smaller than some and may have bounced down hard when it arrived. Maybe it wasn't packed right. At any rate, Colonel Orlov explains, on one of his own slow, painful passes up the trench, that some of its collection tanks have been crunched and its self-diagnostic unit has refused to activate, under the stubborn belief that it won't do any good. Fountains can get neurotic.

DJ's boots twitch, his knees flex, but other than that, he's a cipher.

The fountain suddenly decides to pop its top and push out a collection vane. Orlov and I give out a weak cheer. Kazak, Michelin, and Efremov join us, hopeful. But the vane doesn't unfold or spin, and it's no good if it doesn't spin.

DJ finally shoves out of the bay and shakes his helm. "All busted up inside," he calls out. We can barely hear him. Kazak and Michelin and I touch helms with him like footballers in a huddle. "The parts that work are unhappy, and if I reroute the bus, the parts that don't work will suck all the power. Drain it down to nothing. Don't know what more I can do. If anybody finds a parts kit, let me know, okay?"

We amble in slow lurches for the command tent, loopy from the smell in our suits. None of us wants to spend a night puppied with a bunch of senior officers, but we don't have any choice. Die outside or steal air and heat from the brass.

BLONDE ON A BUGGY

We're in serious trouble, no doubt about it. We barely make it through the night. I lie in our pile, moving only when Kazak kicks in his sleep. He kicks like a mule.

General Bhagati is doing poorly. Blood poisoning, best guess. His own once-friendly germs have decided he's a dead man. That happens a lot to warriors in battle. Germs seem to think we're all walking corpses.

First light, we seal our helms and leave the tent to stand under the pink dawn. The sunrise is abrupt and not at all spectacular— not that we care. Point comes when beauty is lost on a fellow. My head swims. Helm stinks like a refrigerator whose power has been out for a couple of days, skin itches all over, and I assume the others, like me, will soon consider just popping a faceplate and getting it over with. A miserable end for Trick Squad.

Where did it go wrong? I'll get into that later, I decide, when the freezing cold really sets in. You get warm, comfortable, and last thoughts come easier. At least the itching will go away. Maybe.

I sit on the edge of our ditch and catch occasional dim speech sounds from around the tent, but it doesn't mean much, mostly in Korean or Mandarin. I took some Mandarin in high school and junior college, but not much sticks with me. I wanted to take an internship in Shanghai but got turned down because of an ultraslight criminal record—boosting an uncle's truck when I was thirteen. Skyrines don't mind criminals. They beat that juvenile crap out of you, then raise you from petty crook to stone killer. Skyrines start out as Marines, but then we get shipped to the desert and mountain centers for a lot of additional training. There's also the entire Right Stuff gantlet, including a madhouse LSD psych evaluation that demands a Nuremberg trial. I remember that vividly, more than the routines of piss-poor torture, also known as VPP&T—Vacuum Physical Prep and Training. Hawthorne Depot, Rainier, Baker, Adams—Mauna Kea. Military medicine has been pushed to the ethical limits, and way beyond. Blood doping and juicing aren't allowed until you're a finalist, but then the docs really go to town. I added fifteen pounds of solid muscle, then was starved fifteen to make up for it. My body fat ratio…

Shit, I don't care. I'm sitting on the edge of the ditch, thinking vaguely about women—but not yet thinking about good old Mom. According to hallowed combat tradition, the last thing a mortally wounded grunt asks for is Mom, but in the vac and on the Red, nobody can hear that final whimper.

Michelin sits beside me. We bump helms and he says, very hoarse, "They're all down there yelling at DJ in Mandarin. I hate officers. He doesn't know Mandarin. I do, and they are talking shit. Blaming him for killing us all."

"How's he taking it?"

"DJ may know machines, but he is the densest piece of wood in the forest. He's mostly ignoring them."

My head is really spinning. My eyes take snapshots at the end of a long, dark pipe.

But I'm not yet blind.

"See that?" I ask, pointing north.

"What?"

"That." This could go on for a while, but Michelin manages to focus. He grabs my arm.

"*That*...is a vehicle!" he says.

"Not a Skell," I observe.

"Definitely not one of ours."

"Still, it's pretty big. Antag?"

"No idea. Not a Millie." Millies are millipede-like Antag transports, with dozens of segments mounted on big tires.

"We should let the others know," Michelin says.

We don't move. We're fascinated by the progress of the approaching vehicle. It's maybe ten meters long, a cylindrical carriage with big, curved, punch-blade tires. It's not one of ours, but it certainly isn't Antag.

We slowly remember that we've seen its like in old vids.

"It's a Muskie bus...isn't it?" Michelin says with boyish wonder.

A squad's spooky antennae can spread news quick and without words. The rest of our Skyrines, except for DJ and Gamecock, suddenly appear in the trench, climb to the edge, and squat next to us.

"What's so funny?" Kazak asks. Nobody's laughing, but he's hearing laughter, I guess.

"It's a Muskie colony transport," Michelin says. "A bus."

Gamecock joins us last. We let him shove into the center of our lineup. "Fidge this," he says. "DJ reports no possible joy with the fountain. I'm getting ready to hitch a ride with the Horseman." By which he means Death. But then he leans forward, squints, and sits up straight, squaring his shoulders. "Do you see *that*?" he asks.

"We all see it," I say.

"Then maybe it's real. Have you ID'd it?"

"It's a Muskie bus," Michelin says.

"Everyone sure it's not Ant faking a Muskie?" Gamecock asks. He sounds beyond tired. We're all near the end. My angel has been telling me every five minutes or so that the skintight filters have maxed out. I'm thinking about shutting it down, just to let myself fade in peace.

But there is that bus. If Gamecock sees it, too, and Michelin says it's a bus, it had better be a bus.

Meanwhile, as the shared hallucination is being scrupulously eyeballed by us ragged group of perch-crows, nobody seems willing to initiate and engage, not even Gamecock. Kazak and Tak do rock-paper-scissors. They come up evenly matched, rock against rock, three times. Spreading fingers is just too damned hard.

"Fate calls on us both," Kazak says. "Sir, Tak and I would like to go beg a cup of sugar."

Gamecock nods, but he's not agreeing, exactly; his carbon dioxide has shot way up and he's about to fall asleep, then die.

Tak punches his arm. "Sir!"

The lieutenant colonel pulls back. He looks around, behind, down into the ditch, across the broken fountain and the sagging command tent. "Am I in charge here?" he asks dreamily.

"Yes, sir," Michelin says. "You're all we got. The Russians are dead. The Indian is dying. Chinese and Koreans are huddled in the tent, and the tent is out of air."

While we're considering our lack of options, the cylinder out on the flats rolls forward again. Toward us, it seems. We've been surveilled and someone has decided to investigate. Bless them. Bless all Muskies. Survivors. Self-sufficient, quiet…mobile.

Gamecock finds a last grain of resolve and taps Kazak's helm. "Stand down, both of you. Let them come to us," he says. "DJ, go knock up the generals and tell them we have visitors and not to shoot."

DJ hustles, as much as he can move at all, down the slope into the ditch, where he pauses, gets his bearings, despite the fact there's really only one direction he can move—along the ditch— and then lurches forward again.

I turn my attention back to the flat. I don't trust superb coincidence. What in hell would a Muskie be doing out here? The nearest settlement is at least six hundred klicks northwest. Somewhere near the center of the comet impacts.

The bus is now about fifty meters off.

Gamecock raises one arm. Waves it slowly. The vehicle slows and stops again. My vision is almost gone. Through the fuzzy end of a dark gray barrel, I make out a few more details. There are patches all over the fuselage. The curved blades on all six tires are scratched and dented and look to be from different batches, varying in color from titanium gray-orange to rusty steel. Bus has been around for a while. A prospector? I've not heard of such out here, but even Muskies must have hard-core purists who can't stand to be around *anybody*. Pity if the bus is carrying just one gnarly old miner with a chaw-stained beard and the phys of King Tut.

DJ returns, it seems right away—but that could mean I've nodded off without knowing it. Tak is shaking me by my arm, and Kazak is trying to rouse Michelin, who's not responding.

"What's with the generals?" Gamecock asks DJ.

"Asleep or dead," he says. "That fountain was our last hope. Sorry, fellows."

"Not your fault," I manage to say. I can hear them okay, but I'm not sure they hear me. Sound is funny on Mars. Everything is funny, or soon will be. I'm hypoxic. I don't even notice that someone is approaching us on foot, not until a tall, slender figure in a lime-green skintight is almost upon us. Very tall. Maybe two meters.

Carrying slung tanks and a pressure hose.

The figure's helm lases ours. A female voice inquires, "Give refill? Or you walk a me back my buggy?"

We all try to walk, but it's a bust. We tumble over on the ridge and slide past her, if it *is* a her; I hope it's a her. Mother or female angel, *really* an angel. I'm good with either. Michelin directs her to Gamecock. She attaches her hose and pumps oxygen for a few seconds, and when his eyes flutter, she disconnects and makes rounds, giving us each a few minutes. My concentration returns, but my head hurts like hell. The tunnel is wider but I'm seeing double and can't stop blinking.

Then the female does her rotation again, charging our suits with at least an hour's worth of gasps. When she's finished with the second rotation, she steps up over the ridge and into the furrow. We all sit on the other side of the ridge and enjoy just breathing, waiting for our wits to reassemble. It's going to be a long wait.

Our savior comes back leading the Korean general. Tak follows. Our eyes meet. He shakes his head as he walks up the ridge.

"Sorry," the female says. She sounds young. "Coudna get t'em in time. We should get a my buggy and te hell out. Ot'ers sure come soon."

Her voice is high and a little hard on consonants and *s*'s. I had read about thinspeak... pronunciation adapted for high altitude or thinner air. Now I'm hearing it. Plus a true Muskie accent. She's the real thing. Through her faceplate I see a wisp of white-blond hair and large, blue-green eyes. She's very tall. Have I said that already?

"Are we the last?" Gamecock asks. "I mean, our company..."

"Havena seen else a-one. Sommat set off transponder an hour ago. I tracked a way off course and found you."

DJ must have activated the fountain's beacon. He may have inadvertently saved our lives. But likely he also announced our presence to anything that gives a damn within a hundred klicks.

We march to the buggy's airlock, helping each other along. DJ and Michelin tend to Major General Kwak.

"Second gen?" DJ asks the ranch wife as she returns to assist. We're all on radio comm now.

"Don't be rude," Tak says.

"Born a Mars," she confirms. "All guys? No fem?"

"No women," Gamecock says.

"Damn. Be good, now." She gives us each, one by one, a foot up into the lock. "Carry us all, buggy's got just juice enow make te eastern Drifter."

Great. Whatever that is.

Her eyes meet mine as she hands me up, right after the general. She's strong, despite being slender. "Welcome on't, *Master Sergeant Venn*." She sounds out my name precisely. It's on my chest strap.

I smile. "Thank you."

"Get te hell in," she says.

I am the last. She climbs up and seals the door. In the cramped lock, she hands out brushes unlike any we've seen—labeled "Dyson." Like magic, we're clean in a few minutes, with nary a speck kicked loose. She dumps the brushes down a little chute. "Gecko tech," she announces with that amazing smile as the lock finishes its cycle and she pushes open the inner hatch.

We tumble into the relatively spacious cabin, about two meters wide and four long. Forward, through the wedge-shaped windshield, I can see the ridge, the unmoving vane of the useless Chinese fountain…

The distant horizon.

The young woman—she can't be more than twenty-three, twenty-four Earth years, half that Martian—sits in the forward seat and takes the pilot's two-grip wheel. The bus responds with a whine, a deep groan, and a whir of electric motors, and we back away from the ridge, turn north, roll a short distance, then turn southeast.

We take seats on cushions or slings spaced along the bus's interior. Unmarked bins and plastic crates fill most of the cabin, leaving us with little space to call our own. We do not complain.

"Rough go soon," she says. "Strap in if you can, otherwise hang a tie-downs."

Vee-Def assumes a husky feminine voice. The husky part comes easy. "Buckle your seat belts, gentlemen, it's going to be a bumpy ride," he says. He's quoting someone, I don't know who, probably a movie star, but that's okay. Everything's okay.

Tak and Michelin and I try to treat the general's wounds, which have purple edges, not good; we don't know if he'll last more than a few hours. He slips in and out of consciousness, murmuring in Korean.

The young woman focuses on the drive. The bus does not appear to be equipped with other than the most rudimentary guidance. I can make out a kind of sighting telescope in the roof just behind the driver's seat, probably for taking star fixes. Grid lines on the lower half of the windshield. No side windows, no way for us in the back to look out at the passing spectacle that is Mars.

A bottle of tasteless water is passed around. Even the general takes a long drink.

I feel almost human.

"Remove t'ose skintights," our driver says.

"Yes, ma'am!" DJ says, grinning like a bandit.

"Scrub t'em out while t'ey charge a buggy taps," she continues. On Mars, among the Muskies, there are now several kinds of accents and dialects and even some newly birthing languages, we were briefly informed in basic. But we weren't instructed in any of them.

"Pull your pouches and toss t'em a recycle chute. I t'ink we have filters a fit, back a rear bulkhead, top right drawer. T'en, scrubbed and clean, climb in your suits again. We're going outside onced we get t'ere."

Those of us who can, follow her directions. We don't mind being bossed by a tall blond ranch wife. That's what our DI at Hawthorne called Muskie women, when he mentioned them at all. *"Don't think you're going to save all those ranch wives... They are off-limits. They do not fidging care. To you, they matter less than Suzy Rottencrotch."* That sort of shit. I am deliriously grateful. I feel the way a pound mutt must feel, rescued just before they seal the hatch on the death chamber.

We're all War Dogs, adopted by a very tall, strong ranch wife.

———

WE'VE STRIPPED TO Under Armour when the first big jolt hits. She wasn't kidding. We're off the plateau, off the hardpan, onto real washboard. And heading toward the eastern Drifter. Whatever that is.

"As Raisuli said, *It is good to know where one is going*," I quote. Skyrines headed for the Red dote on desert war movies, even flatties. Oddly, Vee-Def does not get the reference, which makes him sullen.

Tak and Kazak finish their chores first, scrubbing and repacking filters, despite the lurching and jolting, and suit up again, then move to the front. Michelin is next. I'm slower, luxuriating in the simplicity of being alive.

Glancing at the ranch wife, I feel the vague pressure of crotch interest. I'm reviving enough to ask what life is like for her, up here, and how I may be of assistance, that sort of hormonal shit. Feels good. But of course, Michelin has moved in first. Michelin imagines himself our Tango Foxtrot Romeo. Not even the obvious competition of Tak sidelines his self-assurance.

He's trying to strike up a conversation.

The ranch wife shakes her head, twice.

Michelin doesn't get that she's fully focused on the job at hand until she shoots out her long right arm and claps a spidery hand over his mouth. "Shut*T*up, please," she says. "You want a roll t'is t'ing?"

The long arm's reverse elbow swivel impresses us all. We goggle in admiration.

"No, ma'am," Michelin says. He grins like a sap back at us, then squats down behind the control cab—and promptly goes to sleep.

Major General Kwak is in severe pain. He doesn't complain, but we can't pull off his skintight, not around that splinted arm. I rummage in the rear bulkhead and find the medical kit in a drawer just below the filters, marked with a red cross, and with Tak's help administer some morphine. Nothing more modern in the way of painkillers, apparently, but this will do for now. The general regards us with tight eyes, nods his gratitude. Muzzes out. I start looking for a transfer bag or rolls of tape to repair his suit. Either we patch the skintight's arm, which is showing too much fray, or we bag him entire, or he's going to have to stay in the bus. Will the ranch wife mind us using her safety gear, depleting her reserves, air and water?

That leads me to ask myself, what is she doing out here all alone—and how do we possibly fit into those plans? She could just as easily dump us in a hole. We've never been of much use to Muskies. Maybe their neutrality has taken a more practical turn and they've gone over to the Antags. It's all about survival. I might do the same. How is it bad thoughts return so quick when you know you're not going to die, not right away?

More sharp lurches and nearly vertical ascents. The suspension squeaks and groans and the tire blades whang like steel drums, bending until they crimp, then snapping out on the uproll with an energy that makes the whole cabin shudder.

I can't sleep.

But then I wake up and the young woman has stopped the bus, climbed out of her seat, and is stepping gingerly back through our sprawled group. She sees my eyes are open, faces me, and says, "I have a make report and count for what I've used."

"Right," I say. "Can I help?"

"Doub*T* it." She gently nudges the general, who does not react. "Chinese?" she asks.

"Korean," I say. I'm on my feet, working out the tingles from being jammed up with the others. I bump my head on the cabin roof. How she manages to hand-over and stoop so gracefully is beyond me. She's beautiful. She's the most beautiful creature in the entire universe. Gosh.

She cocks me a hard side glance. "I'm a dust widow," she says. "Know what t'at means?"

I shake my head.

"I've gone t'rough t'ree husbands sin*T*s I war nine. Your atten*T*on mean as much to me as a sheet mite's. Understood, Sold*T*er?"

"Marine, ma'am. Skyrine."

Nine would be something like eighteen, in Earth years. And that no more than a few years ago, best guess.

"You know my name," I say. "What's yours?"

Another hard look. She grimly faces forward. "Teal Macken-zie Green," she says. "Nick for Tealullah."

"Nice name," I say.

Kazak is awake now, listening. Vee-Def and Tak confer in the farthest corner, under the bulkhead drawers. Our commander, Gamecock, is curled up like a pill bug. Kazak and I nudge him. He's cramped something fierce—that happens when skintights go sour. Lactic acid burn is a misery I wish on no one. He stretches as best he can, grimacing.

"Tell us about this Drifter," he says to Teal, the ranch wife, the dust widow, whose beauty is undiminished and maybe even enhanced now that she's scowled at me.

"Not till we get a shelter." She finishes the seal on her bright green suit, a bulky older model, likely custom-mod to fit. It has different-colored patches on limbs and torso. First owner was apparently shorter. "A wheel is jammed and we're about fifty meters a whar we need to be. Anybody fit a get out and push?"

We all volunteer. Gamecock picks the strongest, includes me and himself; we're jammed in the lock again and then outside, and none of us is sure the skintights will hold suck, after all they've been through.

PARADISE LAID UP

U.S. kids are taught that the first settlers on the Red were the superrich and a few of their friends. They made mistakes. A lot of them died. The survivors recruited others, paid for them to fly up—which got harder as news returned about how so many camps were consolidating, failing—disappearing. Mars is a hell of a long ways from Earth when there's trouble. Jamestown and Croatoan all over again.

But the tough got tougher. They learned and stuck it out and, gradually, the settlements began to expand. Began to really and truly succeed. The survivors became heroes.

Then arrived the third wave, including hard-core folks who found Earth too civilized, too restrictive—too stupid. Rugged individualists, political fanatics, IQ theorists seeking to isolate and improve the human gene pool. Diehard bigots and supremacists, happy to turn Mars into a spaghetti western. My high school history teacher, Mr. Wagner, fairly liberal, left his students with the impression that Mars was pretty much a lost cause. Still, it sounded exciting—romantic. Frontier towns with attitude. A boy could still dream.

Our strategy prof in basic at SBLM added a few more details: "Before the arrival of the Gurus, private sector colonies on Mars denied Earth's taxing authority, and even tried to declare their terrestrial and orbital assets exempt from government interference. After our war began, when the government took over all launch centers, the colonies protested, refused to pay their cable bills—stopped recognizing Earthly specie. Their access to interplanet broadband was cut. Blackout followed. Silence.

"We know where the settlements are, mostly, but we are not authorized to contact them, to intervene in their defense, or to commandeer their assets unless absolutely necessary—and only then with prior authorization from ISC."

Back then, International Space Command was in charge of our war effort, until Germany, Canada, and all of South America withdrew and the United States fragmented politically into war and pax states—those that accepted the story told to us by the Gurus, and those that did not. Forty U.S. states supported, those most likely to get richer from Guru tech and science. Ten did not, mostly in the South and Midwest. Cuba abstained and declared itself neutral, despite having achieved statehood just a few years before.

International Space Command regrouped and was renamed International Sky Defense, or just plain Sky Defense. Some of our equipment still carries the old logo. Most of the Northern Hemisphere countries joined in and contributed to the effort, India and China massively—big industrial needs, lots of Guru bennies. Two-thirds of our forces are now Asian. You learn quickly how tiny a slice Western civ cuts from Earth's pie.

The Sky War entered its thirteenth year and at the age of twenty-six I became a sergeant. Timeout does not add to seniority, only active duty on the Red. There are a lot of inequities in the Corps, but bitching gets you nowhere because, as always, brass is polished brighter than me and thee.

THE LAST OF my squad—so far as any of us know—has been rescued by a ranch wife who is taking us with her to a mysterious site she calls the eastern Drifter. As I've said, I'm not completely ignorant of Mars geology, but I have no idea what a Drifter might be or what it might look like. Yet now, apparently, we are there.

The bus shudders to a halt on a rugged slope of dust-pocked lava. Teal has pushed her vehicle as far as she can, two hundred meters up this slope, beyond which rises an odd, knobby hill about fifty meters high at its peak and, from what we can see, about two hundred meters wide. Teal locks the wheel and joins us in the rear.

Our skintights are now charged with sufficient air and water to last us at least a few hours. The landscape we see as we exit the bus's airlock is fascinating but tough to riddle. Thirty meters to our left—north—is a mound of deep brown and black stone, not lava, weathered almost smooth. To me the mound resembles a half-sunken head. I make out a beetling overhang like a rumpled brow. To the right of this head, south and west, lies an angled ridge like a muscular black arm, its "hand" clenched into a fist, protecting a kind of rocky harbor. A giant seems to have risen out of the planet, head, neck, and one shoulder, then laid an arm across the lava field, trying to shove itself up, but somehow got stuck—freezing solid before it could climb out and walk away.

Sunken giant. Shit. For the first time in many hours, curiosity takes strong hold. We need to know what our ranch wife is doing out in the middle of nowhere, on the edge of our tactical theater, not too far from our ODZ—Orbital Drop Zone. All alone—except for us.

Teal completes her circuit, then butts helms with Gamecock and makes her needs known. She'll go back to the wheel and steer, but she wants us to roll the bus the last few dozen meters into the curved embrace of the giant's arm. I hope there's something waiting there other than a metaphorical armpit.

I take position near the bus's right rear wheel, careful not to let the edges of the blades touch suit or gloves. No wonder our ride was rough. The wheels are worn almost razor-blade thin. Everything about the Muskies seems threadbare, last-ditch, desperate. And yet, the dust widow saved *us*.

Gamecock comes up beside me, along with Tak, and we decided how best to move the bus to where the lady wants it to go. Our effort is mighty, the progress slow, but we manage in about fifteen minutes to close the distance. Then Teal locks the brakes, steps out again through the airlock, holds up her hand, and marches off into the shadow of that massive, crooked arm with a wonderful, long-legged stride that combines hop and jog. A true princess of Mars.

The sun is just over the upper forearm and shines in our eyes, so we can't see her in the shadows. A minute or two later, she returns, shaping out of the darkness like a green ghost, and tells us to push some more.

We push.

Hard-packed sand and dust form a decent floor inside the arm. In the shadow of the wall, my eyes finally adjust and I see, set into the giant's upper chest (I can almost count the ribs), a solid metal gate about ten meters wide and nine meters high. Beside it is a smaller gate, more of a door. The big gate has been opened, I presume by Teal, exposing a black cavern. The gate's outer surface has rusted to a close match for natural Martian brown. Hardly visible at all, except up close. The stony wall surrounding the rusted gate is coated with a thick layer of lava, alternating rough and glassy, as if a melted flow slurped up the giant's arm. In the armpit and crook of the elbow lean two dramatic intrusions of massive, six-sided columnar basalt.

Vee-Def leans in to say, "Muskies are vegan, right?"

He probably saw a movie about cannibals on Mars.

"They certainly won't eat *your* stringy ass," Kazak assures him.

I am only half listening. The giant has faced wind, water, and lava for a long, long time—why not just wear away, sink down, give up? "It's still trying to swim," I tell myself.

Michelin emerges and lends a hand as we push the bus across the threshold, into a cramped, dark airlock barely wide enough to accommodate the wheels and skinny dudes sneaking around each side. He tells us the general is doing poorly, might not last more than a few hours unless we decant him into full medical. "He's got something he wants to say to Gamecock. His English is better than my Korean, but he's going in and out."

As our ranch wife comes through the narrow gap to the left, shining a bright single beam, I see glints and realize the roof is low, low indeed. How the bus fits at all puzzles me until I notice that it has hunkered down on its suspension and the bottom of the fuselage is now just a few centimeters above the lava floor. Teal's light reveals unnatural-looking grooves crisscrossing the walls and roof. I'm no expert, but the cavern, the lock, seems to have been dug, blasted, or melted out of a large mass of metal-bearing rock, leaving basalt columns as structural support.

Teal opens and climbs through a smaller hatch in the inner wall, and we stand around for a few minutes until the gate closes behind us. Then she returns and inspects the outer seal.

"Airtight," she says. "After I open te inner, we'll push and park beyond."

"Have you been here before?" Tak asks.

"No," she says. "But I know of it."

"Is this the eastern Drifter?" I ask.

She looks past me. "Get everyone out when we're t'rough."

"Our Korean general is going to need some help," I say.

"Stretcher in te boot." She taps the bus's stern, showing us the outlines of a flush equipment bay. In short order, with her help, I pull out a rolled and folded stretcher and prepare it. "From here is slope," she says. "Should make pushing easy."

With that, the tall young lady returns to the bus's midsection, lifts herself up, squeezes flat, and climbs in.

The inner lock door now pulls aside, back into the rock. Very neat engineering, I think. An echoing blat of the horn tells us to resume pushing. A few minutes later, we're inside a chamber about three meters below the floor of the outside entrance. DJ and I close the second gate behind the bus. This one has a thick polymer seal that grabs hold of the circular metal frame. Encouraging, but still no pressure.

The inner chamber is high, dark, possibly natural—a relatively smooth half ovoid about twenty meters across. What would leave a big egg-shaped hollow in the dense, metal-bearing stone? Hot gas? Steam? The floor is dust and sand, compacted from material that could have drifted in before the airlock was finished. In the gloom, we see nine other vehicles in a tight half circle pushed close to the northern wall. They look old and worn-out.

Teal clambers down from the bus, all arms and legs, with an unfamiliar, almost alien grace. She looks back at us, at me, gestures for us to follow—and is once more definitely human, definitely female.

Command would surely frown upon fraternization with Muskies, if they thought it likely or even possible. But the fact is, we've received no instruction about them one way or another.

We do know how to treat our sisters in the Corps. They're fellow Skyrines, no more, no less, *ever*, as long as we're in service. It's a hard code and both sides are held responsible. Tak and Kazak once served rough justice on a flagrant violator of the sister code, a corporal named Grover Sudbury. Sudbury had raped and beaten a female PFC in his crummy apartment outside the depot at Hawthorne. Tak excluded me because I had a list of sketchy fitness reports and might have been DD'd if caught.

But I saw the bastard after they had finished with him, crawling bloody and mewling across the deck of a second-floor walkway. They had finished by shoving him through a door that was closed at the time. Corporal Sudbury did not appear capable of standing, much less fit for duty. Months later, the Corps booted him in disgrace.

And then, Sudbury just vanished. Nobody ever heard from him again. Remember his name: Grover Sudbury. There have been a lot like him in the last couple of years, far more among civvies than Skyrines.

So I know when to stop thinking about sex. But I'm tired, pretty sure we're doomed, and the dust widow is exotic, not like women back on Earth—not like any female in the Corps. Great fun to watch.

We ferry the general out of the buggy on the stretcher. He's mostly out of it, awake but delirious. Vee-Def keeps him from plucking at his faceplate. I glance at my glove and wrist joins, usually the first to reveal increasing pressure. We're still in Mars normal.

Michelin stays close to the ranch wife. "Where exactly are we...?" He runs a glove along the dark stone walls.

"Te Drifter, I told you," she answers softly, reluctantly. Does she regret bringing us here? "Te eastern Drifter."

"But what *is* that?" Michelin asks, glancing around for assistance. We know as little as he does.

"Te garage will pressure, if t'ere pressure on t'other side. T'at's the inner lock. If a pressure, you strip, go naked—except for te general. Brush down now. Doan a want you bring in bat*T*le sand."

I'm not sure what she means, *battle sand*, with that brittle *T* of thinspeak—spent matter waste? What do the Muskies know about that? That's all she'll tell us until we open yet another smaller hatch, less rusty, quite thick, serious about keeping stuff in and out. An inner sanctum must lie beyond.

Gamecock has said little throughout our trek. Now he bumps helms with Tak and they seem to reach some agreement. I hope it doesn't mean we're about to commandeer this place or otherwise take charge.

As we open the thick hatch, enter the inner lock, and crowd in around the stretcher, I feel a deeper, almost creepy sense of awe. This formation is so very different from anything I know about Mars. The stone is remarkably dark and looks exceptionally dense and hard. Every few meters, ceiling and walls are shot through with glints of large metal crystals—wider than my hand. Nickel-iron, I guess. Beyond the polished crystals, there are more runs of grooves and other signs of excavation. Must have been a bitch to carve and finish. If the Muskies did all this, years ago, then they're a lot more accomplished than we were ever taught at SBLM.

Vee-Def comes close to me, grinning at whatever he is about to blurt. He bumps helms. "Vast!" he intones. "Fremen warriors! Vast!" At my recoil and grimace, he shouts, "Duncan Idaho, right?"

Neemie and Michelin ignore him. I doubt Vee-Def reads much, he's probably quoting one of the many movie versions. Never a drop of rain on Mars. Snow, yes, but never rain.

The fabric around my wrist finally dimples. The airlock is pressurizing. Our ears feel it next. Teal opens the opposite hatch. A tiny, dim light flicks on out there somewhere. It looks far away.

"Batteries on. Might still be good. If I don't pass out, join me?" She pops her faceplate. She doesn't pass out.

The dimple around my wrist gets deeper—we're surrounded by maybe two-thirds of a bar. Then she cracks open the hatch we just passed through and air rushes by, filling the garage.

"Go ahead," she says, once the wind subsides, and peels out of her own suit. In a few minutes, we're all naked. The relief is amazing. I do not want to ever put on a skintight again. Slumped and rumpled on the deck, our suits stink, but the air seems good, even fresh—not a bit stale.

Not that I'm paying much attention to the air. The ranch wife wears only squared-off panties. I cannot help myself. My God, she is amazing. I never knew a woman could be that tall, that slender, that spidery, and still be so beautiful. Even the general ogles her with a pained grin and asks us to remove his helm.

She doesn't seem to notice; possibly doesn't care. We're not part of her tribe. We're not Muskies.

Why bring us here? What use could we be?

And what the fuck *is* this place?

WHAT THE LOCALS RECOMMEND

We have ready access to the garage, and as little star lights flick on in the high ceiling we start to inventory supplies on the bus—Teal's buggy—and on the older vehicles, which it turns out are already pretty stripped down.

Then Teal wanders off, leaving us in the dim glow. She returns a few minutes later wearing dark green overalls—ill-fitting, made for a shorter individual, worn through at knees and elbows, but more decorous than near nudity. Draped over her forearm is a stack of similar clothing. She tosses it to the floor. As I pick one out of the pile and give it a shake, my fingers rub away green dust. I bend over and swipe the compacted floor with my palm, bringing away the same dust, along with a few grains of grit.

"Algae?" I ask nobody in particular. DJ and Vee-Def are scratching and trying to make their overalls fit.

Teal kneels beside the general and gives him more water. "Can you talk?" she asks him gently.

For the moment, his delirium has passed and his English

has returned. "Must tell them soon," he murmurs. "Looking for this. Looking for just this." The general settles back, closes his eyes. Teal scowls in concern. She glances my way, aware I've caught her lapse. Her face goes bland.

Tak and Kazak squat behind the general, taking it all in. Gamecock is probably waiting for the right moment to suggest to our hostess that careful, thorough recon might be a fine idea. He does not like the shadows. Nor do any of us.

The ranch wife seems to be deciding who our leader might be. She focuses on Tak—of course. I'm used to that. He and I have been on liberty together from Tacoma to Tenerife. Women always look his way first.

Tak, with a dignified nod, directs her to Gamecock.

"My name is Teal," she says to the colonel. "Nick for Tealullah Mackenzie Green."

Gamecock introduces himself as Lieutenant Colonel Harold Roost. After him, we all divulge our proper names and ranks—all but the general, who has drifted off again. Tak gives him another dose of morphine. Teal warns him, that's it, no more. Although I'm wondering if she prefers that the general would simply fade away…

"T'ere a much trouble here," Teal says as we rearrange, like kids around a campfire. She becomes the center of our attention, but we might be a pack of dogs, she might be talking to us just to relieve boredom, for all the emotion we seem to arouse. "We stay away a trouble, but now it comes a-doorstep, right a T'ird Town, my Green Camp."

"There's more than one town nearby?" Gamecock asks.

She doesn't answer this, but keeps talking, eyes over our heads, searching the darkness and stone. "I come here until te bad time passes."

"Bad time," the general says. Perversely, the morphine seems to perk him up. Maybe he drifts off to escape the pain.

"ST'ere a battle coming?" Teal asks Gamecock.

"We're stragglers from a bad drop," he says. "Waiting to regroup."

"So t'ere wor more..." She nods slowly. "Many?"

Gamecock lifts his lips, adds nothing.

"I figured," Teal says. "From te buggy, while heading sout'east...Kep rolling by broken ships, buggies, abodes—tents—bodies across te flat. Hundreds."

"Human?" Gamecock asks.

"Hard a know." She throws out her hands. "Couldna stop. I had a make speed a get here."

The general struggles to sit up. His eyes are bright, feverish. "Knew about this. Looking! Long time past," he says, "big strike. Big as a moon. Ice and stone metal core. Heat of impact tremendous, but shove ice deep, superheat steam, blow out... Biggest basin! Chunks not mix."

Teal watches him with a veiled glare, as if he is a snake trying to bite. She gently pushes him back down, then changes the subject. "Tell what you can, what a-happening a t'ere," she says to Gamecock.

"Major effort," Gamecock says. "Troops and supplies, survey parties."

"Robots?" she asks.

He shakes his head.

"Why na robots? Why people? Far Ot'ers supposed a be smart, from anot'er star, right?"

We've asked ourselves that same question. Same reason, I suppose, that robot football never caught on. Real bones, real snaps.

"Robots can't replace a Skyrine," Gamecock says.

Teal sniffs disdain. "Figure t'at out, save yourselves."

"Where's the fun?" Michelin says. "Life is being there."

"Deat' *S*'a never going home," Teal responds. *Death's never going home*. Right. She crouches again by the general, checks his neck pulse; her knees show through holes in the jumpsuit. Fascinating knees. "We stay ou*T* way. We'd like a know how long 'twill last."

The general's eyes flutter. "Hard battle coming."

Gamecock's face is stony, but I suspect he's still trying to figure out what he can say in front of this noncombatant, whether we need to commandeer her supplies, her vehicle… everything in these caverns.

It's Tak who speaks next, maybe out of turn, but what the hell. We owe our lives to her. "We dropped without tactical," he says. Gamecock swivels on his ankles to face him, brow wrinkled. "No complete update. We're pretty ignorant."

"*I* know," the general says, voice weak. "I tell more. But *she* must not listen," he says, staring at Teal.

Without a word, Teal rises and walks toward the darkness where she retrieved the jumpsuits. "Let me know when you're done," she calls.

We sit for a moment in silence, out of uniform, worn to nubs. The air in the hollow is cool, strangely sweet… Active environmental. All of it just adds to our enormous puzzle.

Gamecock looks down at the general's face, then up at the rest of us. "Get ready to listen," he says. Closer to the general's ear, he says, enunciating each word, "Sir, we're secure. You need to tell us what you know."

The general swings his head right and left, scanning us, the side of the bus—then looks straight up at the stone roof. "This is retreat, reservoir," he murmurs. "Place to hide." A wave of pain racks him.

"Maybe it is," Gamecock says.

"Much more," the general says, eyes searching for relief.

Gamecock gestures for Tak to give the general more morphine—
a half dose. Tak complies.

"What's the plan, sir?"

"Old plan, year old," the general says, eyes moist. "Land and
reinforce, lay forts and tunnels, claim low flats, establish networks of resources, fountains, depots. Big drops, rocket descent
pods. *Big* effort from Earth, funded by Russia, China. Lots of
my soldiers. Informed not much enemy orbital. All wrong. We
arrive, Russians first. All wrong. Lots of enemy orbital, recently
inserted, take us down, Antags have *big* ground presence, dominance. We fight. Lose big. We know so little!" He looks away,
ashamed. Nothing to be ashamed of.

"We were in transit when all that went down," Gamecock
says to the rest of us. "We were meant to be a backup or modest
supplemental to the big push."

"They could at least have told us," Kazak complains.

"Antag G2O mopped us from the sky. All but one of our
satellites were down." He pauses, then adds, "That's what must
have happened."

"No resources, no weapons, can't do much down here," the
general says. That seems to be it, then. We're all we've got, and
we're relying on the hospitality of a ranch wife and her peculiar
cave just to stay alive.

Michelin and Tak and I go back to the others. Gamecock
stays with the general, in case he has more to say.

"Muskies!" DJ says. "Bless 'em. Sure talk strange."

"Not that strange, after so many decades," I say, thinking on
Teal, idly considering what it might be like to go AWOL and
join the Muskies—not that we have another choice, right now.
Hardly any command. Hardly any AWOL involved.

"What the hell is this place?" Kazak asks.

"Surprised there's still air and water and power." Tak shakes
his head. "Don't know how long it's been empty."

"If it *is* empty," Vee-Def says, eyes searching. "Like the Mines of Moria. Orcs everywhere, man." He spreads his hands, makes crawly motions.

"Fuck that," DJ says.

Tak stretches his neck, then does a few yoga moves. I follow his lead. "She's not telling us much," he says, assuming downward dog.

"Why should she?" DJ asks. "What I'd like to know is, why is she out here all alone?" He puts on a squint-eyed frown that could be either suspicion or skepticism.

Gamecock and Michelin join us. "The general is out. We peeled back his skintight. Gangrene. He needs surgery."

"Good luck with that," Kazak says.

"He said something odd before he passed out. Mumbling in Korean and English, back and forth, about broken moons, uneven settling…" He shrugs. "I'm not sure this place is any kind of surprise to command."

"They've been looking for it?" I ask, again feeling that spooky prickle.

"We don't know what orders the first wave might have had. The general's not exactly making sense."

"Teal didn't look happy when he was talking," I say.

Gamecock glances between me and Tak, settles on me. "You've been studying her."

"Sorry," I say.

"Not at all. She's receptive."

"BS, sir," I say. "She glammed Tak."

"I'm a good judge," Gamecock says. "Go after her. Find out what this place has to offer, how long we can stay, how long we *should* stay. Whether we're alone. If this is a big ore concentration, then it's dead cert the Antags will have scoped it out."

"And we haven't?" Tak asks.

"No need asking our angels," Gamecock says. "They won't

carry strategic data we don't absolutely need, and that includes planet-wide gravimetry. Still, that kind of info has got to be pretty old...Why wouldn't the Antags know?" He shoves all this aside with a push of his palm. "Go," he tells me.

The others smile as I stand. I shove my hands into the overall pockets, feel something cold, then, surprised, pull out a metal disk about the size of a quarter. I hold it out, catch the light, see that it's featureless on one side like a slug, but made of what could be silver. Very white silver. And on the other side, there's a long, coiling string of tiny numbers and letters.

"Holy crap!" Neemie says, and grasps at the air. I pass him the slug. Neemie's father runs a rare coin shop in Detroit. He looks at it up close, turns it over, rubs it in his fingers, sniffs it. "It's platinum," he says. He passes it around and when everyone is done marveling, as much as any of us have the energy to marvel, Kazak hands it back to me.

"A sample of the local ore?" Gamecock asks.

No idea. I replace the purloined platinum in the pocket where I found it and move off after Teal.

———

THE DARKNESS BEYOND the antechamber to the buggy barn is broken only by occasional star lights, low-power jobs about the size of a grain of wheat. They look as if they might have been glowing for years.

I can see Teal's footprints in the damp green dust that lightly coats the tunnel floor and almost everything else. A few minutes and I arrive at a juncture connecting other tunnels, right, left, straight ahead, up...and down.

Way down. I pull back and lean against a wall, heart pounding against my ribs.

Almost fell into a shaft.

Maybe she wants us *all* dead. That would make sense, given the situation. Maybe she thinks, or was told, that there are troops out here looking into the family secrets. She could pick us up off the Red, fake concern, take us to the very place someone's looking for, but it's a mine where she can just dump us down a deep, deep hole...

I nearly died in a mine at Hawthorne. Joe pulled me back at the very last instant. Rocks rolled from under my boots into a pit, splashing into stagnant water dozens of meters down.

This hole is about four meters wide. With considerable care, I walk around it and try to pick up Teal's footprints on the other side, but the floor beyond is suddenly bare—no dust, no prints. However, I hear distant padding sounds...echoes of someone breathing. I hope it's Teal.

The walls are marked again by regular grooves, scoring the stony surface in a fashion that makes me think machines might have done the excavation, leaving grooves so that other machines could use them for stability or guidance. Maybe the machines are still down here. I imagine a mobile printer/depositor, serviced by a truck carrying buckets of slurry for different builds...going from place to place and building stuff for the miners.

Another thirty meters and I hear a voice off to one side, coming from a cubby. Teal emerges, rises to her full height, and looks down on me in the dim light.

"Are t'ey coming?" she asks.

"No," I say.

"Just you?"

"Just me." I take out the coin and hold it up in the palm of my hand. "Found this in a pocket. Any idea what it's for?"

She glances, sees the coiling string of numbers, gives a little shudder. "Caretaker," she says. "Must be his jumper."

"They left caretakers behind?"

"Maybe. Hang onna't." She moves on. I follow. She's slowed down a bit, as if she can't find what she's looking for.

"Do you mind my asking, again, maybe—have you been here before?"

"No," she says.

"How do you know where to go, what to do?"

She answers, "My fat'er told me."

"Was *he* ever here?"

"Na more questions."

"We're grateful, of course."

"W'afor t'ey send *you*?" she asks as we walk. She points behind us to the rest of my squad.

"They're concerned."

"T'ey t'ink I like you?"

No words for another ten or twelve paces. Then, Teal says, with a short intake of breath, "Your soldiers han't riven or forced. T'ey leave us be. I could guess it so. Flammarion lies on sa many t'ings."

There's a crater on Mars called Flammarion, also one on the Moon. They used to name craters after dead scientists. Flammarion was an astronomer some time ago, but what his or her namesake is doing here, or has done to Teal, or has told Teal about us, I can't even guess.

On we move another couple of dozen paces.

"T'was tip time I left Green Camp," Teal says. "Sa bad came a me. Ally Pecqua stole my widow's due, and Idol Gargarel…He chose me a make t'ird gen with te Voors."

"Third gen? Force you to have kids?" I don't know anything about Voors. Another settlement, I guess. Trading females. Doesn't sound appealing.

Teal looks sidewise, face cold in the faint blue light of the star bulbs—lost and cold and sad. I want to punch Ally what's-the-name and Idle Gargle in their throats for making her sad.

Teal continues, "I stole te buggy and just drove away. Stealing transport is killing crime in te basin. You're not te only ones in trouble on Mars.

"I'm not here a rescue you. You need a rescue *me*."

NOT YOUR FATHER'S FUTURE

Sitting in the Eames chair, looking out at the early morning gray, I tap fingers on my knees. Reach into my pocket. Fumble with the platinum coin. Then I get up to pee. Wander into the kitchen. Open the refrigerator. Nothing looks good. Most of it has spoiled. No fresh veggies. Should have picked some up in the market. Not thinking. Not planning ahead.

Walking ghost, out of my box.

I drink a glass of water from the tap. *Soon time a break and out*, Teal would say.

Walk some more and sync my terrestrial compass. Take advantage of my liberty, with or without company. But I don't want to. I don't know what to do with what I know. Could be dangerous to tell anybody. Joe told me to stay away from MHAT. Maybe I shouldn't even be *here*.

I can wallow in confusion and self-pity in the blue and steel apartment only so long before ape-shit darkness closes in and worse memories gibber and poke.

On top of the amazing, the good, and the awful that came after I acquired the coin, I have echoing in my head the jagged haunt of Teal's own story, of high frontier injustice and a young woman's flight, and how none of us could save her from the value of that primordial, metal-rich *Drifter*, nor from her betrayal of a hard ethic pushed way beyond the intent of the original Muskies.

Humans can be such shits.

A Skyrine shouldn't tangle in matters that have nothing to do with why we fight. Shouldn't invest in an outcome neither his own nor the war's. Stay in the box. But last night's fitful sleep, second night back—after a day spent in seclusion, squeezed into the leather chair, wrapped in soaking towels, seeping out through sweaty skin the last of the Cosmoline—staring out the window at the passing ships and ferries and pleasure boats, the pulse of Guru-motivated wealth and commerce, the whole, big, wide fidging world—

I heard echoes of Teal's voice, her accent, her choice of words. What Teal said before she betrayed her people's trust and led a wayward bunch of Skyrines to the Martian crown jewels:

You need a rescue me.

Despite everything, despite the Battle of Mars and our very real chances of losing the entire war, I can still hear her voice and believe, *insist*, that Teal is alive, can still be found, though I have no more power to return to Mars right now than one of those wheeling gulls.

Not unless I take another tour. Something I have vowed not to do. Something Joe would definitely discourage.

But there's one thing I did vow. I promised Teal that I will deliver the platinum token.

I just don't know to whom.

HOBOS AND DRIFTERS

The answer to where all the air comes from is a few hundred meters ahead, down a tunnel with many branches, most of them dark—no star lights. We don't go there.

Teal breaks into a lope. I have difficulty keeping up. She knows how to push and kick away from both floor and ceiling in the lesser gravity, not so Mars-bound as to have lost her terrestrial strength. I have no idea how Muskies raise their daughters; maybe there's universal Spartan discipline. The Green Camp big shots might insist their children train to become accomplished gymnasts. She sure moves like one.

Is her story, barely begun, a tale of patriarchal tragedy, rigorous discipline—or hypocrisy and cant, all *Scarlet Letter* and shit? I am truly both sympathetic and intrigued—but then I come up abruptly to where she stands on the edge of another shaft, actually a very large pit. I nearly bump into her. She blocks me with her outstretched arm, glaring at me yet again. Am I really that clumsy?

Beyond the rocky edge, a wide, echoing gloom fills with rising plumes of hot mist, fresh and moist and somehow electric.

Slurps and the wet claps of bursting bubbles echo through the steam. Nothing like it in my experience on Mars. For the first time, I feel that I am actually smelling a living planet, not just the dusty shell around a fossil egg.

Teal backs us away a couple of steps. "Onced t'ey called t'is Devil's Hole," she says. "I didna know t'was so close."

"Hot pools," I say. "Not sulfurous. Clean, sweet."

"T'ey *wor* sulfurous. Fat'er said you could not breat' here a-t'out a special mask. And still, t'ere's niter." She leans and points to a patina of white crystals flecking the black stone arch. "First team here suffocated. Bad air seeped inna t'eir suits. Second team took better suits and dosed te deep pools wit' oxyphores. Buggied in borax and potash from te farm flats, dropped oxidized dust and mine tailings inna pools. Oxyphores converted all into life, food—air."

Oxyphores—the green dust?

"T'ird team dug more garages, brought depositors and printers, made machines, explosives—carved and blasted deep. Too deep, as 'Turn out. Cut a stony barrier right inna hobo. Flow fast, alive. Deep flood. You know a hobo, what t'at is, Master Sergeant Venn?"

"Not in your sense, I suspect."

"Hesperian history. You learn geology in school?"

No need to tell all. "Fighting means knowing your ground."

"*Hobo* should be spelled with double aitch, *H2-obo*. Means an*T*ient underground lake or river flowing, sloshing, around volcanic chimneys and hard, rocky roots, seek an old familiar bed a run free, flood or carve more, t'en, as always, up t'ere, freeze, dry up—blow away. But keep a flow deep down, down here. No matter how t'ey dam and block, hobo kept breaking t'rough, flood entire. No need for sa much water, we already had enough from te soft lands. Te miners struggled a pump and get back a work. T'ey failed.

"My fat'er was a tail end of fift' team. When t'ey pulled out, he set te sensors a let towns know when te hobo played down, sloshed ot'er way. T'ey planned a come back and resume mining. Ore a big lodes of iron, nickel, platinum, iridium, aluminum. Of course too much water, even for Martians. All could a let us build more towns. Many more. If we wor making more babies or bringing in more settlers. Neit'er which we do, now."

"Because of the fighting."

"Afore t'en. Te first troubles started afore I wor born."

"Troubles?"

"Come wit' me."

She takes me through a narrower tunnel. Here, the star lights seem brighter—the walls reflect their feeble glow. Beneath the green dust, my fingers feel the neutral warmth of pure metal in large patterns, irregular and beautiful crystalline shapes.

Then it hits me. During daylight, Mars dirt is warmer than the thin air for the first couple of centimeters, but gets colder the deeper you dig. Down here, something is keeping the Drifter's thick walls pleasant to the touch. The Drifter may be sitting above an old magma chamber, one of the last signs of Mars's youth.

This place is *fabulous*. I doubt it would be possible to over-rate its strategic importance. How could it have been kept secret from Earth? Or from the Antags, for that matter?

But if Gamecock heard the general right, maybe it isn't secret—not to Command. Someone could have spilled the beans and told Earth, and Earth could have finally decided to look up satellite gravimetry from decades past.

Confirm an anomaly.

Maybe command decided this is something worth finding and fighting for. Enough water and materials to support a couple of divisions, thousands of drops and ascents, for decades to come. No need for fountains.

Yet the Antags are still dropping comets.

And nobody told *us*.

My head reels trying to figure the ins and outs.

Teal comes to a ladder, metal rungs hammered into one side of a square, vertical shaft about three meters wide, rising into darkness. I can just make out a platform ten or fifteen meters above.

"Climb wit' me?" she asks. "I doan wan*T* go it alone."

"What's up there?"

"My father said a watchtower, dug inna rock near te top, face west."

"There's air?"

She gives me a tart look and takes to the rungs. There is indeed a platform about halfway up the shaft. I'm not at all good at orienting underground, not sure which way I'm pointed, but guess we're well up in the hill that rises over and beyond the sunken entrance—the "head" of the Drifter. The pure metal gives way to dark reddish stone streaked with black. The platform is rusty, coated in greenish powder, and creaks under our weight. Rust-colored water streaks and shimmers down the stone.

How long since the flood subsided? Days? Weeks? And who would be alerted that the Drifter was again open to mining and manufacture? How long until they all decide to return, in force, and find us?

Niter. Sulfur. Depositors and printers. They could easily make weapons, explosives.

Another ladder climb and we pass through a metal hatchway into a cubicle, bare rock on three sides, metal shutters on the fourth—and cold. Deep cold. Electric heaters have been mounted low in the stone walls, but not turned on. The chill sucks the heat from our bodies. We obviously won't be staying long.

"'Tis as I heard," Teal says, shivering, stooping—too tall for the cubicle. "T'is was built a guard over ot'er camps shoving in."

Where there are people, there will be competition. Conflict. It's what humans do best.

"Maybe we shoulda worn skintights," Teal mutters as she twists the plastic knurl. "Doan know if…"

With a ratcheting creak, the shutters pull up and aside. There's thick, dusty plex beyond, lightly fogged by decades of blowing sand—despite another set of shutters on the opposite side. Teal keeps turning the knurl and the outer shutters lift as well. The wide port provides a view of the sloping entrance to the northern garage and the rocky plain beyond. That damned brown blur still rises in the northwest. Odd. The comets should have wiped away any weather pattern.

I point it out to Teal. "That's been there since we arrived. Any idea what it might be?"

She shakes her head.

Because the plex sits under a meter of rock overhang, there's no view of the sky much above the horizon. And we can't look straight east or south.

Teal reaches up and unscrews a cover in the cubicle's roof. My fingers are numb. I can barely feel my face.

"T'ree-sixty," she says, swinging aside the cover and pulling down a shining steel periscope. She plucks at its metal bars, not to freeze her fingers. "As told."

"Who told?" I ask.

"Fat'er. Look quick," she says. "Canna stay long unless we find te control booth and gin te power."

I keep my eyes a couple of centimeters from the nearly solid rubber eyecups, but manage a circling, fish-eye view of the land around the promontory and the cubicle. Like a submarine under the sand!

Nothing…nothing…

Around once more, and then, to the southeast, I see a dusty

plume, much closer, and beneath that, approaching the Drifter: three vehicles, neither Antag nor Skyrine.

More buggies.

"Muskies coming," I say.

She gives me attitude about that name, but takes the view. She rotates the periscope several times, always pausing in the direction of the buggies' approach.

"From te Voor camp," she announces.

"Voor? Who are they?"

"Voors, Voortrekkers," she says. "You know not'ing of us!" She stows the scope, closes the shutters, and returns to the ladder, muttering, "Got a way gin main power."

Right. She descends from the lookout and I follow, fingers so numb I can barely hold on to the rungs. If we find a control room and power switches and equipment, maybe we'll also find the miners' stock of reserves: medical supplies, skintight repair kits, food. Enough to give us time to wait for reinforcements. Which have *got* to be on their way. This was supposed to be a big shove, right?

Maybe we've found what command was looking for all along.

PATRIOTS AND PIONEERS ALL

Teal is in the tunnel, running east. I reach the bottom of the shaft barely in time to see her disappear into darkness. Training tells me to get back to my squad—Voortrekker sounds suspiciously old-school—but I'm conflicted. I don't know what sort of trouble we could face, what exactly to tell Gamecock or Tak or the general, if he's still with us. Would the buggies carry miners returning to their digs—happy to see us, happy to have our help? Somehow, I don't think so. But can I trust Teal to tell the whole truth?

I doubt our angels will answer any of these local questions. They're rarely conversant on matters not immediately important to our operations, and settlers have never been an issue.

And why not?

How stupid is that?

The star lights here still glow, but dimmer, doubtless on fading battery power. I cross through many gaps filled with shadows. I'm feeling my way and my pace is slower than Teal's. The tunnel weaves for fifty or sixty meters through raw metal and then basalt and outcrops of what looks like pyrites—fool's gold, crystals of iron sulfide. Lots going on in the eastern Drifter.

The tunnel opens into what could be another buggy barn—but empty. The green dust here is thick and pools of moisture stain the floor's compacted sand. Teal stands on the far side, beside another lock hatch, feeling the seals with her long fingers, then pushes her face close to detect loss of air.

The temperature is cooler but not frigid.

"Western gate still tight," she says, glancing back at me. "And welded shut. My fat'er told me t'ere now only two gates, two ways in, sout'ern and nort'ern. When te Voors took te Drifter, t'ey wanted exclusive, made*T* defensible wit' small force."

"Do the Voors know we're here?"

"T'ey know *I'm* a-here," she says.

"How?"

She shakes her head and walks to our right, toward a glassed-in booth mounted high in the empty chamber, where a dispatcher or controller might sit, looking down upon the garage floor. She climbs the ladder and pushes on a door in the booth's side.

I stand below and look up. "Tell me what happens if they get in," I say.

"If t'ey find me, t'ey take me back. If t'ey find *you*, t'ey kill all."

"They can fucking try," I say.

"T'ey have guns," she announces, working to pry open the booth door. No go. It looks welded shut as well. She descends, eyes darting like a deer seeking a canebrake.

"We need to know the truth," I say. "Why did you come here? What if those buggies are just bringing back miners?"

"T'ey wouldna come back just now," she says.

"Why not? The hobo's down—"

"Because t'ey're *afraid*!" she cries. "You think t'is just a mine? You donna know a t'ing!"

"Afraid of what? Us?"

"Na!"

"What the fuck is going on?" I ask, voice a little too high. I try to stay in front of her and intercept one of her looks, but as she sets foot on the floor, and I push in, she grimaces, reaches out with a long, agile arm—and slaps me. I don't know a single Skyrine who reacts well to being slapped by anyone bigger than a child. My hand is up and about to return the favor when the look on her face collapses into anguish, and she lets out a piercing scream.

That stops us both cold. We face off in the middle of the chamber, breathing heavily. She twists about, hands out and clenched, stretched to the limit.

"We *have a* find it!" she cries. Her voice echoes—broken, lost, hollow. Then she falls to one knee, as if about to pray, and hangs her head. "It warna just the hobo drove out fift' team. My fat'er wouldna say all. Even so, he told me come here when if t'ere is na ot'er place a go. Drifter safer t'an Green Camp, if I wor put a te dust. But he said I must go alone."

This floors me. "Even so, you rescued us," I say, trying to reestablish common ground, common sympathies. "Maybe you thought, like you said, we might be able to help. You don't think anyone else can or will help...right?"

She shakes her head. "I doan know why I pick you. You're na our people. You're na even friends."

"We're *human*, goddammit!" I say. "We're fighting for everyone."

"Na for *us*," she says softly. "We doan want you here. Likely t'ey doan want you here."

"The Voors?"

Teal forces her calm, fixed face, stands, and wipes her cheeks with the back of her hand. Then, looking down and blinking, she reaches a decision. "Sorry. Na call for sa much at once*T*."

"Yeah," I say.

"If t'ere be power, we switch *T*'on afore Voors reach te sout'ern gate. T'en we lock and stop t'em outside."

Her lingo is getting too thick for me. One sound, inflected, passes for a page in a dictionary. "We haven't checked the eastern gate."

"Na time. T'ey're close."

"We're fighters," I say. "We should check and if necessary post watches at all the gates—"

"Voor buggies haul twen*T*'each. T'at wor sixty. You?—" She holds up one spread hand and three fingers. A stern look.

"Okay. But they're just settlers. What kind of weapons would they carry?"

Her withering glance away tells me I've asked exactly the wrong question. "T'ey find lost guns on te dust—maybe yours?"

"Nothing they're trained for. Nothing they have codes or charges for. They're not Skyrines."

Teal has this expression, avoiding looking at me, like she wants to tell all—but it's hard. Long years of indoctrination and resentment. No love for the Earth that cut them off and joined an interplanetary war. Then, her stiffness slides away. She's come this far. There's no turning back. She focuses, makes a face—she has to speak to me in a way I'll understand, and so she reaches back, speaks more slowly. "T'ey're *Voors*. Dutch, Germans, Africans, some Americans—whites only. Independent, old history. Smart, cruel—fat'er-rule. They came first a join Green Camp, t'en cause trouble, break wit' all, took a *trek—t'eir* trek—fifteen hundred kilometers. Claimed and routed a French camp—Algerians, Moroccans, some Europeans—cleaned t'em out, sent most a die on te dust. Rebuilt. Regimented. T'ey used French printers a make weapons, said a fight off solders from Eart' coming a destroy t'em. Na a body at Green Camp or

Robinson or Amazonia or McClain said naught a t'em. We'd all been cut from Eart' already, na more supplies, na more uplink—pushed on our own, we couldna afford te bigger fight." She takes a deep breath, shakes her head.

"Who found the Drifter first?"

"French camp. T'ey did sommat little mining, t'en pulled out. After, te Voors worked a hard five years until t'ey breached te lava dike and hobo surged. T'ey're the fourth and fift' teams. T'en...t'ey withdrew, but keep claim."

"What did they leave behind?"

"Buggies back at te north gate, clot'ing—some supplies. I doan know how else much."

"Your father was a Voor?"

"French. Voors let him live a-cor he war white. But t'ey sent his first wife out te dust. She wor African, a Muslim. Fat'er left Algerian camp just after Voors close te Drifter. Went te Green Camp..." She gets that distant look, too much history, too many nasty tales even before she was born. "Married my mot'er, and t'ere wor me."

The Drifter was closed due to the hobo for more than twenty years? Nine or ten Martian years? And we happen back just in time for the reopening! This isn't making even a skeletal sort of sense.

"The Voors, do they partner with Antags?" I ask.

She makes a face, I *would* think that—then shakes her head vigorously. "We call t'ose Far Ot'ers. We wor told Amazonia sent folks out te dust a meet t'em. Nobody's heard a t'ose since."

"If the Voors left good stuff here, what could we expect to find? Mining machinery? Food?"

"Fat'er say t'ere wor a printer-depositor, barrels of slurry, maybe safed food, surely spare parts, enow te gear up quick—all in upper chambers so na get swashed. T'ey keep all locked, wrapped, and sealed—stake and reclaim onced hobo sinks.

But…" She reaches into her pocket and takes out another platinum coin. Shows me a string of numbers and letters inscribed on both sides. Similar to the coin I found. Different numbers, however. "Codes te get in."

"That's how you got us in?"

She nods.

"And the power?"

"Hydro deep, far below. Where te hobo still flows." Saying all this, Teal looks sick with doubt and uncertainty. She has no idea what we're capable of.

"Where do we look for their cache?" I ask.

She walks off a few steps. "Fat'er show a chart, but t'wor old."

We work our way around the chamber, searching the deep shadows for exits, side tunnels—and find a dark hole hiding behind a basalt outcrop. No star lights, but wide enough to allow a buggy. The big tunnel cuts through metal and black rock. No grooves. Why?

"T'is was made near te end, I t'ink," Teal says. "Afore t'ey left."

If the Voors are indeed hard-core bigots, renegades, killers—patriots intent on making their own nation because they fit nowhere else…Are they also the most rational of pioneers? Would they attract and keep the best engineers, enough to plan and carry out a long-term drainage operation? Or did they just keep blasting pits and tunnels way down below until they tapped into the hobo? Ruining or drastically delaying their schemes of conquest, forcing them to abandon the Drifter…

Waiting, fuming—angrier and angrier.

"Your father was their chief mining engineer?"

"Geologist," Teal says.

"Did he go to Green Camp to offer them his expertise? After the Voors…"

"He told enow a keep t'em interested, so t'ey'd allow him

a stay. But he never told all. He kept saying te hobo would be down soon, because wit'na the Drifter and its promise, we have na value. Ally Pecqua and Idol Gargarel finally got tired, arrested him. T'en t'ey stole my widow's due, and he knew 'twas over for bot' us. When he wouldna tell more, t'ey sent him out te dust. I wor next. Sa I left."

"Was it always that bad?" I ask.

"Rationals love a correct and trouble. Cut off from Eart', t'ey only got harder and meaner."

Makes my neck hairs bristle. Still, though we owe Teal our lives, I have no way to verify her story, no way to know how a meeting with the Voors might turn out. Maybe they're just tough. Maybe they're fighters. Maybe we are better off with bigoted fighters than corrupt Muskies. I've certainly known enough bigoted good ol' boy Skyrines. Nasty boys in town, terrific in a fight.

SNKRAZ.

At the end of this wide tunnel lies a wider, square chamber, and within the chamber, a great big knobby shadow surrounded by even darker boxes and drums. The walls are equipped with shelves—some cut out of the rock. Right and left are smaller antechambers. Teal pokes in and out of them in sequence, silent.

Then she emerges from the last.

"Is that a printer?" I ask.

She nods. "Never seen one t'at old. 'Tis big."

"And the drums...slurry?"

"Plastic, metal, alumiclay, a t'ere—" She points. "Sinter chamber. Make almost any machine part. May gin up te buggy, te other buggies. If I can switch and ramp power."

"Where would we do that?" I'm acutely aware our time is running out. The Voor buggies were less than ten klicks away when last we looked.

"Track a star lights," she says. "T'ey'll get brighter. Te genera-
tor and t'ermal source should be near te emergency reserves."

"Your father said that?"

Another nod.

We walk together back up the slot, find a dark offshoot we
missed, venture along for a dozen meters.

"T'ere's a big battle out t'ere," Teal says. "You, te Far Ot'ers."

"Yes, ma'am." I walk a couple of steps behind her. She's liable
to fling her arms back as she feels around in the dark, and she's
strong. Don't need to lose teeth.

"You have any idea what Eart' did, cutting us off, cutting us loose? How many you have killed a loneliness and
Eart'-grief?"

"I'm not sure I understand."

"We're morna half crazed. Cost me my first husband. He had
Eart' family too."

"Oh?"

Her accent gets deeper. She's going home in memory. "He
worna used a narrow places. Came star-eyed, filled a freedom-
talk. Romanced my family and won me young, t'en spent most
a his time far-minding it, away in his t'oughts—back a Eart'.
Cut off, he lapsed, sorrowed, didna see us, didna see me. Vasted
up here." She pronounces this "vaysted," a portmanteau word,
a cruel bundle of her first husband's life. "Gone stir," she adds
softly. "After t'at, never saw me clear. Saw only his Eart' wife.
Tore t'ings, violent, til te camp passed judgment and sent him
out te dust. He just wanted a go home."

Not just the Voors are hard, apparently.

I'm not about to point out what we were told, about Muskies
not paying their cable bills. Not paying taxes. Or any of the rest
of it. Our lives may depend on this young woman's tolerance, if
not her favor.

Quiet minutes as we push along, until we see a single star

light hanging on its almost invisible wire—but brighter than the others. Another fifty meters, in darkness and complete silence except for our breath and padding boots, and here the star lights are brightest of all—five bunched together, as if marking a location. Should have brought Tak, I think, with his new eyes. But mine have caught a black hatchway she missed.

"Here," I say to Teal, who has gone on, perhaps distracted by her memories.

Doubling back, standing beside me, she pulls out her platinum, feels around the hatch—finds a small panel, slides it open, revealing a display and keypad. She lays the coin against the panel and punches in the string of numbers. The hatch clicks and together we pull it wide. Beyond brightly glow a lot more star lights, hundreds suspended from the ceiling, outlining the walls of another larger chamber, also square and about twenty meters on a side. The illumination is bright enough to dazzle for a few seconds, but we can clearly make out a medium-sized electrical panel, and beside this, the steel cap to a thermal source. Hot water from below ground? Nuclear? Likely not spent matter. That's never been shared off Earth. Just as well…

Teal seems to be following memorized instructions. In a few minutes, moving from station to station, she's got the station humming, buzzing, snapping inside its ranks of transformers, storage cells, fuel cells. The star lights brighten and the room lightens to clarity surrounded by stony gloom, except where a vein of that crystal-patterned nickel-iron reflects cloudy brilliance.

"Hydro still strong inna deep works," she says.

"Can we lock the southern gate?" I ask.

"Maybe," Teal says.

"Do you know how?" I ask.

"Control room," she says.

"This isn't it?"

"SubstaTon for te nort'ern upper works. T'ere should be a substaTon for sout' and east, also big deeps and central digs—a main board for te whole installaTon."

In the new brightness, I see that Teal's face is still slick with tears. This was her father's domain. He worked here…For the Voors. Told her what he knew.

But all that he knew?

"You know where that is?"

Her large gray-green eyes flick, searching, looking beyond me. "Maybe," she says, and returns to the wide tunnel. At the junction, she points left. "T'is way."

She moves ahead. My squad's survival likely depends on what we find. I'm already remiss in not telling them what I know about the Voors. I judge we have about ten minutes to prepare for the new buggies' arrival. If this chancy operation succeeds, and nobody gets in our way, we might be able to rejoin the battle—the war. To live is to fight.

But I'm thinking on this woman, no doubt about it. Some points down the trail I'm going to find out all I can about the Muskies, about Teal's people at Green Camp, if she still thinks they're her people—whatever they call themselves. Little Green Men and Women. Maybe they're all just Martians now. Very romantic, that. More history. More culture and language.

More about what made her what she is.

The brighter lights reveal all we missed before: a sunken door, a fallen sign, a set of steps carved into the rock, leading up about fifteen meters through a smooth-cut corridor to another chamber. This one is lined and sealed by black, shrink-down plastic sheeting. Teal sets to removing the plastic, not an easy task, and I help. In a few minutes, we unveil a much wider shuttered viewport facing southeast—and beneath that, a dusty and decades-old control panel, sporting a holographic display panel—tiny projectors mounted on a strip above the panel—

The works. A southern watchtower to complement the northern—but also a command center.

I stand behind her as she takes a seat on a hard plastic chair. Most of the equipment here was likely made by the old, bulky printer-depositor; that is how Mars was furnished, replacing old-style manufacture and factories—but demanding slurries to feed the printers: solvents, polymers, powdered metals and ceramics...All the necessary materials that could be shot through a printer head onto a laser-hardened or heat-set or fusible object of manufacture. Including weapons.

All of which had to be shipped from Earth, or mined and purified on Mars.

Seven minutes. I'm trying to imagine the motions of the Voor buggies, the men inside—or men and women. How long will it take to get back to my squad? What can I deliver in the way of knowledge, strength, advantage, if I leave this command center before it's even up and running?

Teal looks at me, takes a deep breath, then flips open the cover to a number pad. Carefully, she lays the coin on the pad, then keys in the string.

We both jump as the panel powers up. Lights pick out projectors, which begin to whir and whine after so many decades of disuse. The panel sensors recognize our faces, find our eyes, the projectors align, and color patterns and even crude, unfocused images flicker before us. The first views are external and seem to fill the volume over the panel in exaggerated 3-D.

Teal waves her hand over a flat square in the center of the panel and brings one image forward, spreading it wide with her fingers. We now have a live view—I assume—of much of the southeastern slope of the Drifter, the rear shoulders and back of the swimming giant. She calls up other cameras, all external, and then, with a side glance, the first internals—thumbnails of dozens of chambers within the Drifter's bulk. At Teal's command, the thumbnails expand into brighter, more detailed images, rising between us and the dark walls. One shows a sloping surface made of crystals, surrounded by darkness but outlined by star lights. That view suddenly goes black: camera failure, security— or did Teal just delete it with a flick of her finger?

What she's summoned from this watchtower control panel is a tally of tunnels, shafts, digs, forming a map that turns slowly before us, expanding in jerks as more are added, as more old cameras return to life. The Drifter was a big operation, and it appears the flooding has not permanently damaged most of it.

Coins, codes, cameras everywhere…Multiple points of security. The miners had seriously worried about claim-jumpers, interlopers—maybe Skyrines or Antags, though it seems this place was left to the hobo before our war began.

Soon, the grand map finishes filling out. I recognize the upper works—the gates and tunnels we've passed through, along with where we are. There are many, many more tunnels and chambers, not yet explored, all in green. But there are also extensive and deeper excavations, some very deep, judging by the comparatively small profile of the upper works—and many of these are marked in blue and red.

Teal pokes her fingers through the blue and red traces. "My God," she breathes. "T'ere's na'one here, and 'tis still changing!" She shoots me another look, sees I have no idea what she's on about, then blanks the map and expands the southern garage and its "harbor," another encircling wall of lava.

The three Voor buggies are pulling up outside a wider, taller version of the northern gate through which Teal brought us earlier. She flicks through several vantages around the rocky harbor and sandy floor. "A t'ird of te eyes are down," she mutters. "Might come back onced t'ey warm. Can you see enow?"

The buggies have halted, having arranged themselves in a defensive triangle, tails together, noses pointed outward.

Nobody disembarks immediately. No way to know how many
Voors we might face, what arms they carry, if any...

Then a hatch opens in the middle buggy and a stocky figure
in patchwork skintight emerges, hesitates on the step, reluctantly
descends.

"Voor?" I ask Teal.

"Looks like."

"Recognize him?"

The projectors whine and complain as she turns to frown at
me. "I doan know any Voors."

"Is he a leader, a scout?"

She shakes her head.

Another figure climbs down, in similar skintight—taller than
the first by a foot, broad across the shoulders, brawny. Not at all
like Teal, but still homegrown, I guess, since there hasn't been a
colonist transport for years...

And then a third, much smaller—skinny, even puny, and a
fourth, about mid-sized. All look male to me. They stand out on
the rock and sand before the southern gate, not moving after they've
arranged themselves in a curve beside the middle buggy. I assume
they're all Voors. There's a stiffness, a tension in their grouping—
but nobody has emerged from the other buggies, not yet.

"Any comm?" I ask.

She shakes her head. "Not'ing like," she says. "Doan know
about radio."

"They might not know we're here."

"T'ey know *summat* is here," she says.

"How?"

Silence.

"Would Green Camp sic Voors after you?" I ask.

"T'ey might."

"That bad?"

Another nod.

"To arrest you?"

"Common interest," Teal says with a lost downbeat. "Two years back, Green Camp and the Voors drew up a share claim, for when te hobo draws out. My fat'er helped make te deal, to stay important and keep us alive. Green Camp t'inks Voors might haply force t'at claim if others jump. T'ey might t'ink I'm jumping. If t'ey see *you*..."

Christ, I'm beginning to feel like I've stumbled into a Jack London novel. And fuck you if you think a Skyrine doesn't read old books.

The Voors haven't moved. By posture alone, they look apprehensive. Then they turn as the point buggy's lock hatch opens. Three more Voors descend, another varied group—also male.

From the last buggy, three more step down—making nine. Still nowhere near capacity for the buggies.

But then three figures in different skintights emerge from the lock of the middle buggy. All Skyrines, and all female, prominently displaying their sidearms.

Latecomers? Stragglers? Male and female needs transvac are sufficiently different that we often ride different sticks and join into combat-ready units in theater, on the Red.

Teal zooms in without my asking, and I manage to scan their blazes: U.S. Seventh Marines on one, ISD Second Interplanetary on the other two. I make out three flags: U.S., of course, and—among our favorite allies on the Red—Malaysian and Filipino.

From the other buggies, six more Skyrines descend, also female and heavily armed. Between them, I count four flechette guns, two armor-punching lasers, and a microwave disruptor, effective against Antag equipment in past engagements, but according to recent tech skinny, maybe no more. The last to step down from the point buggy is a Filipino gunnery sergeant, and she hefts a strong-field suppressor, about as big and impressive a weapon as any one of us can carry.

Teal sweeps over to a captain's parallel bars, and a stenciled name well known to me: Daniella Coyle. Captain Danny Coyle. I barely suppress a whoop. "Holy shit," I say. "Sisterhood is powerful!"

Teal is puzzled by my triumph. "T'ey're yours?" she asks.

"I am *theirs*," I say. "Outlaw ladies held up the Dodge stage. Time to make them welcome!"

BACKGROUNDER, PART 2

Now is not the time to get into all the branches and divisions and shit, but while we're watching more internationals and ladies arrive on our scene, light 'splainin' is in order.

International Sky Defense (ISD) is our overarching authority. Its symbol is a flaming shield protecting a speckled blue marble, Earth, kind of like SHAEF but spacey. At its highest level, ISD Joint Command is staffed by politicians and retired military commanders from all signatory nations. Joint Command, everyone assumes—but no one I've met actually knows—reports to the Wait Staff, representatives of the Gurus.

Below Joint Command, each signatory nation assigns warriors and resources and helps pay for ISD's orbital assets, transfer craft—space frames, sleds, and such—and weapons, including R&D.

The United States "loans" Navy, Marine, Air Force, and Army warriors to ISD. Other countries assign, we loan; same difference. Skyrines sometimes combine not just with international units, but with other U.S. services, mostly Army or Air Force—and since we're already under NAVSEC, the secretary of the Navy, and he's mostly obedient to Joint Command, that means we can run into warriors from just about any branch of service, and any signatory nation, recognize them more or less as partners, try hard to respect their command hierarchy, and work together efficiently, mostly without invoking esprit de corps, which can make Marines pugnacious.

Historically, that's how we see ourselves—Skyrines are nothing more nor less than Marines who ride rockets. Some say we're a touch more civilized than ground pounders, but frankly, I don't see or feel that, and once all the battles are won and the Antags have fled back across the sea of stars, we will happily revert to the well-trained, tightly disciplined, rudely judgmental bastards we have always been.

Even with all that, when we're off the field of battle and engaging in additional training or just plain R&R, we manage to get into some lovely threaps—that is, swedges, stoushes, dustups, squash-downs, knucklers, blennies, bruisers, fwappers, scratchers, jawbusts, jointers, joists, jaunts, jousts, teethers, chirps, flips, funsies, fisticuffs, ball-tug, dentals, gouges, or, in more common parlance, disagreements, tête-à-têtes, contretemps—fights.

Eskimos = twenty words for snow. Skyrines = twenty-plus phrases for getting scrappy, in that friendly sort of way where we rarely kill each other.

If you don't understand where fights will begin, and who is going to be on your side, and who is just *not*, you can get into trouble fast. Among the ISD signatories, U.S. Marines buddy up well with Filipinos, Koreans, Japanese, the few Guamanians we run into, Fijians (Pacific Islanders in general), New Zealanders (especially Maoris), and Australians. We get along okay with Brits and the French. The Italians have wine and MREs to die for and the most beautiful women I've ever seen in space, except for all the rest. We love the Indians and Pakistanis and Sri Lankans and Tibetans, and of course, there's Kazak and the 'stans, good people all.

Skyrines mostly get along with the Chinese, but we can have issues with Russians, though both are terrific at the beginning of a drunk and downright fierce on the Red.

Canada, Germany, Austria, Spain, most of Eastern Europe, all of South America, and Africa—but for Somalia, Ethiopia, and Yemen—are not signatory.

————

WHILE TRAINING AT Hawthorne, we used our one day of R&R to visit Lindy's 1881, a rough local bar in the small, square desert town. There, by severe happenstance, we met up with a stack of eleven Russian exchange officers. They had been invited to Hawthorne to lecture and critique U.S. training practices. What numbnuts depot clerk let them out all at once to do the town has never been revealed.

The encounter started off jovial. The Russians tried to explain, over beer and cold peppered vodka, how training at Socotra—off the tip of Yemen—and in Siberia was so much harsher and more realistic than anything we went through here at Hawthorne. Kazak disagreed and gave them the stink-eye. His people and theirs have history. It was obvious words would soon lead to deeds. After a few minutes of verbal give-and-take, Tak, Kazak, Michelin, myself, and four female Skyrines conferred how best to deploy a Fist Marine Division.

One of those sisters was then–First Lieutenant Coyle, chaperoning her brood and standing aloof from us grunts, but nodding to the music and enjoying the ambience—until she saw she could not get her chicks out fast enough to avoid the coming scuffle.

The sisters walked between their brothers and formed a loose line between them and the Russians. This encouraged the Russians to smirk and question our masculine courage. They gave each other encouraging looks and foresaw easy mayhem followed by another round of cold vodka.

The locals, a crusty, paunchy crew, well past their middle years, cleared chairs and tables and sat by with big grins.

Meanwhile, Michelin casually took post by the bar's rear exit.

The Russians led with three burly toughs. At a barely perceptible nod from Coyle, the sisters withered and allowed their line to dimple, then to break up. Brothers and sisters re-formed into flanks on both sides of the long bar, opening up space at the side of the establishment for our rear echelons to maneuver.

And so we did.

The Russians, no strangers to bar fights, observed these tactics through a vodka haze and finally recognized the seriousness of their plight. Smirks turned to frowns.

Kazak, with a wink at Tak and me, said something *very* offensive.

Game on.

Our Russian allies whipped out a steel grove of navy-issue Iglas—wickedly practical blades—and, from puffy pant legs, slowly pulled knotted climbing ropes and lengths of tow chain. Brows furrowed, knuckles white, balancing from foot to foot, they swayed one way, then another with choreographed precision, like flags in a wind, toward our flanks—admirable to see in men so full of Russian spirits.

And then—they chose their opponents and leaped.

Kazak gleefully ran Tartar interference through the melee, snatching at knotted ropes, taunting, dancing away with wiggling fingers from the slashing Iglas—sowing wholesale confusion. Tak and I worked around Kazak's quantum indeterminacy and doubled in at the conclusion of his feints, disarming four of the biggest Russians and dislocating their shoulders with precise sweeps-and-bows.

First Lieutenant Coyle and our sisters dealt summarily with the younger, less experienced, and thus meaner chain-wielders. After their wrists were snapped and they were disarmed, Coyle, with a lovely flourish, sent Russian officers reeling one by one down the length of the scarred wooden bar to the rear exit, where Michelin booted them through a banging, shivering screen door. Bruised and battered Russians piled up in the rear parking lot.

Just before our brave allies pushed off the oil-stained gravel to return for another round, earning our respect and doubtless forcing us to trade lives for Skyrine honor—U.S. Marine Brigadier General Romulus Potocki slammed through the front door, bellowed like a bull, and, before anyone could react, underhanded a stun grenade between the tables.

When the smoke cleared—everyone in the bar reeling and most of us bleeding from the ears—Potocki called us all to attention. Those who could still hear alerted to his presence, and the rest, observing them, followed suit. Even the Russians, slumping through the screen door and past Michelin, stood up straight, if they could.

All but one beardless stripling who had hidden behind an overturned table, and now rose with a howl to whip his chain around Tak's head.

At that, Coyle herself stomped the poor kid into a tight, dusty corner. And Potocki watched her do it.

A few minutes later, the MPs showed up.

Kazak and the ladies came through this deafer than posts but otherwise unscathed. I acquired a couple of Iglas and a slice across my bicep that took three days under Guru paste to heal. Med center restored everyone's ears.

Tak lost both eyes, but in short order—the next day—the Corps issued him a fresh pair, bright blue. Within hours he was better than ever. His raccoon-mask chain-whip welt took longer to fade—the rest of our time at Hawthorne. We became local heroes. Skyrines bowed theatrically in the mess. Attitude and spirit.

Most fun we had had in weeks. And we all had inappropriate dreams about First Lieutenant Coyle.

Five months later, on the Red, with nary a bitter word, some of us teamed up with those same Russians and seven hours after our drop engaged a dense Antag redoubt in the center of Chryse, near Shirley Patera. We reduced the enemy to smoke and chaff. Some of the Russians received decorations.

The kid who had chain-whipped Tak was not there. He had been demoted, by request of the Gurus in Moscow, and sent back to Novosibirsk to hump a desk.

I'm happy to see our sisters, delighted to see Coyle, and I hope she remembers me. We work well together.

HOPE IS THE THING THAT FLOATS

Teal and I descend from the watchtower, make our way as quickly as we can down the tunnels, and within ten minutes Teal has climbed into the southern garage booth and opened the outer gate. The three Voor buggies—plus the nine Voors and nine Skyrines—are soon inside an even bigger hollow, a hangar carved out of basalt, with rows of steel support beams shoring up the roof.

After the buggies park, three more Skyrines escort the drivers down from each. There are nowhere near sixty Voors, as Teal feared; there are only twelve. I'm curious why they would take three buggies.

The Voors, all pale males in their twenties or thirties, line up beside their vehicles. One is a skinny old dude, likely first gen. Their skintights are as cadged together as Teal's, but reddish brown, with black helms and leggings and white-tipped boots.

I finger in magnification and look more closely at the new blazes. The Skyrines are from First Battalion, which in the past has been assigned early recon and ground prep—sneaking around the Red in the dark before a battle, surveilling Antag positions, correcting and refining maps, choosing drop sites.

How these new arrivals have made their way into my lofty presence does not encourage confidence. Still, they have a strong-field suppressor. And they know how to handle the locals.

Before Teal and I descend, I give out a sharp, four-tone whistle, and Captain Coyle greets us at the bottom of the booth ladder, sharp-eyed, pistol drawn and charged. She's in her late thirties, whippet-wiry inside the skintight, red hair, plump cheeks, and black eyes visible through her helm. I am out of uniform, but I've strapped my blaze to my arm, and I pull up my sleeve to show the bump where I've been chipped and dattooed. Captain Coyle runs her glove over the dattoo, then consults her angel on name and rank and current disposition, while the other Skyrines listen in, all ears, some grinning—expecting their situation is about to improve. Maybe, maybe not.

Coyle is not yet reassured. With a side glance at Teal, standing a few meters back, she faces me. "Master Sergeant Michael Venn," she says, echoing the display in her helm. "Sixth Marines, out of Skyport Virginia last deployment. Have we met, Venn?"

"Affirmative, Captain."

"Can't recall just where. Can't read your chip, but the dattoo tells the tale. Are there more of us around here?"

I tell her about our broken squad, the Korean general, how we survived on Russian tents and could not save an assortment of top officers. The captain listens, stern-faced. "We came down about two days after you," she says, "maybe three hundred klicks south. Similar situation, looks like. Then we ran into these boys. Real charmers. SNKRAZ."

Sho 'Nuff KrayZ. Recent update from SNAFU, *Situation Normal, All Fucked Up*, which our alien sponsors do not like to hear.

Captain Coyle takes the suppressor from Gunnery Sergeant Maria Christina de Guzman—mid-twenties, oval-faced, small and supple and very fit looking, with strange, cold eyes—and tells her to prep the Voors. Here, in decent pressure and only a mild chill, Gunny de Guzman orders the Voors to strip to their Dutch undies. I don't know what "Dutch undies" means, but Sergeant Anita Magsaysay snickers and the others look pleased.

For their part, the Voors are tense and pasty-faced as they pull off their skintights.

I know that in Coyle's opinion, though she's being polite, I'm still under suspicion. No angel to lase, no read on my chip, dattoo purely surface, no bona fides other than a whistle that could have been compromised and a detached blaze that could belong to anybody; I could *be* anybody. I try to look relaxed and friendly.

Teal simply looks frightened. She obviously believes the Voors were sent to kill her. But under firm prodding, the Voors do as they are told, silent, resentful, eight of them young and skinny and scared, three in their thirties and not much fatter, one emaciated elder with burning eyes.

Sergeant Mazura b. Mustafa—of middle height, narrow face, big black eyes, and luxurious lips—binds the Voors' wrists with tough plastic straps. Several of the almost naked men study Teal as if trying to remember the sketchy portrait on a wanted poster. They could believe we're going to restore their liberty, allow them to continue their settler ways—do what they came here to do. After all, Earth policy is hands-off, live and let live, right?

Only now are we joined by Gamecock and Tak and DJ, who goggle at this turn of events. Gamecock approaches the captain, who opens her plate and shoots out a gloved hand. The ones in control, for now, begin to relax a little. DJ and Tak exchange friendly greetings with some of our sisters. They are polite but edgy, worn down from whatever they went through before they encountered the Voors—and from having to deal with these gentlemen on apparently less than cordial terms.

And those cold eyes. Something's different about some of our warriors in this gathering…

But I dismiss all doubts.

"Anyone speak Afrikaans?" Captain Coyle asks. She removes her helm and shakes out a short mop of sweaty black hair.

"I do, a little," Teal says. Four of our sisters, alerted to her presence, take this opportunity to gather around her, scoping her out, admiring her fashion sense, I suppose. Teal puts up with their curiosity, but after a few minutes, Coyle reins it in.

"Ah, Captain, first ranch wife we've seen!" Magsaysay complains.

"She's tall," says Lance Corporal Katy Suleiman.

"Taller than you, Shrimp," Mustafa says.

"Everyone's taller than Suleiman," Magsaysay observes.

"She's pretty, though," says Corporal Juana Maria Ceniza. She experimentally pinches the fabric on Teal's arm, eyes wary as a fox's.

"Cut that shit, Ash!" Coyle warns.

Ceniza lifts one brow, but pulls her hand away and backs off.

"Go on," the captain encourages.

"Radio talk mostly," Teal says, shivering at our ladies' interest. "*Taal*, t'ey call it."

"Their English is piss-poor," Coyle says.

"T'ey speak English well enow when t'ey want," Teal says. The Voors squint hard at her. One makes a rude gesture, which is knocked down by Corporal Firuzah Dawood, a short, stocky gal with a shaved scalp and a dancer's way of moving around the captives. Nothing escapes her, and she's not afraid to be brusque.

"You hitched a ride?" Gamecock asks Coyle.

"Not hardly, sir," Coyle says. "We saw them heading our way, took residence behind some rocks, and offered up a pigeon. No way of guessing their intentions. To our delight, they stopped."

"For little ol' me," Ceniza says. She grins, thrusts out a leg, mocks pulling up a skirt. Objectively, I assess that she might be the shapeliest of our sisters.

"As soon as they saw Ash—Corporal Ceniza—they screeched to a halt and came out mad as hornets, weapons drawn," Coyle says. "A bunch of gallant males surrounded her, and the boss man blessed her out—I think. Accused her of violating Muskie neutrality."

"Some sort of dispute with the condo association," Ceniza says. "Assholes were going to strip me on the Red." Her mates seem prepared to get angry all over again. They close in on the Voors, palming sidearms—but Captain Coyle raises a hand. The Voors bead sweat and glare.

"We popped out from hiding, desert fashion," Coyle continues. "They wisely decided not to go up against Sergeant de Guzman." Coyle returns to the gunny the strong-field suppressor, also known as a lawnmower. De Guzman, had she been so ordered, could have cut the Voor buggies into sausage slices with a few sweeps.

The eldest Voor, the one Coyle calls the boss man, raises his bound wrists. He's a small, skeletal guy with a high pale forehead, a fringe of wayward gray hair, a small, sharp nose, and a thin-lipped, white-stubbled face. "Talk, we talk, Colonel," he says to Gamecock, fellow male, trying to appear conciliatory if not actively friendly. His black eyes shine like aggies. "We need to *talk* what is happening."

"I'll listen in a moment," Gamecock says. "For now," and he looks hard at me, "I need to catch up on every little thing that's happened in the last hour." He turns to Captain Coyle. "And the last few days."

"Yes, sir," Coyle says. "The Voors appear to have something to add to that conversation."

"That we do, and damned essential!" the old Voor says.

Teal does not look happy, but there's little she can do. She's now effectively reduced to the same status as the Voors, until we find time to sit and share and get things straightened out.

Until we understand what the hell this Drifter station is, and what's going on around it, and what it implies both for the settlers and for our little war.

IN HEAVEN AS IT IS ON EARTH

In the early years of Mars colonies, idealism and pioneer spirit drew "investors" with promises of a new and better life under the hurtling moons of Mars, never closer than tens of millions of miles from Earth, often much farther. That appealed to an intriguing subset of humanity that held, even within that narrow purpose, many different opinions about life.

The first pioneers on Mars were packed into small, chemical fuel spaceships, up to twenty at a time, without benefit of Cosmoline sleep, to suffer in high-tech discomfort the months-long journey.

When they arrived—if they arrived, for as many as half died during those first voyages—they found supply and construction vessels at their landing sites, ready to be arranged into those famous white hamster mazes, while primitive versions of our fountains swept the air and soil of Mars for the ingredients essential to life.

High adventure.

Bravery and creativity and passion were essential to the success of those early settlements. Remarkably, nine out of ten of the new settlers survived the first few years, thanks to the genius and foresight of a small slate of terrestrial entrepreneurs, most of whom never made it to Mars.

They were too old. Age was the single greatest factor in casualty rates during transit. Men and women over forty were ten times more likely to sicken and die. Some said it was physical frailty; as I look back on those voyages through the lens of my own experience, I am more inclined to believe it was a fatal pining for Earth's basic luxuries—wide-open spaces, blue skies and clouds and rain, clumped dirt, clean, fresh air, the mineral tang of good water—that drove older travelers into decline.

So many pioneers had been convinced that a heaven of simulated reality would make up for all that was lacking on Mars. It did not. They should have studied the examples of pioneer families on the Great Plains, hunkering in the murky shadows of sod huts, the ladies—away from home and friends and society—driven to spooning laudanum while the men hunted or plowed hard, rocky fields, turning grim and leather-faced as weather and natives challenged, their children seemed to run wild as animals, and the last reserves of sanity dwindled.

Some dreamers believed that Mars could be terraformed—remade in Earth's image. Barring that long possibility, they imagined great domed frontier towns with outlaws and sheriffs and saloons, or their high-tech equivalents. One such dome was erected, inflatable, a thousand meters wide. It lasted six months before being destroyed by a double calamity of meteor strike and high wind. No others were built, but the concept will likely return if Mars ever finds peace.

But what I'm really working up to is an explanation for what the hell Voortrekkers and their ilk were doing on Mars.

People who build utopias need places to put their nowheres. The groups that followed the first waves of settlers to Mars were filled to overflowing with grumble. Not a few felt constrained by Earthly trends that discouraged bigotry and patriarchal dominance and denied power to those who espoused biblical or economic purities. People seeking to build personal empires hid behind these idealists, then rose up to take advantage of their lapses, their unmet necessities...by imposing order and discipline, which utopias typically lack and desperately need, especially when conditions get harsh and death looms.

Once these pragmatists were in power, all over the Earth hard-core malcontents took subscriptions for specialized settlements and shipped dozens or even hundreds of chosen ones—prepackaged and compatible seedling societies—to Mars.

And so we now face Voortrekkers, not the actual Forward Explorers of South African and Rhodesian history, but a group of dedicated reenactors that espoused many of those ancient hard-core attitudes.

No blacks, no wogs—hard ways for hard living.

Latter-day patriarchs running roughshod over history.

———

KAZAK AND MICHELIN have joined us in the southern garage. DJ is tending to the general.

Being outnumbered has done nothing to subdue the old Voor, who is already stepping up his rhetoric. His name is Paul de Groot. He's been on Mars for thirty-two years. "Listen up!" he shouts. We fall silent as his shrill voice rings across the hangar.

"Bit of a stinker, sir," Captain Coyle mutters to Gamecock.

"We are Trekboers! You've commanded my wagons, you'll know our names and where we stand!" De Groot makes a point of walking around his men, tapping their heads—a reach for some, as he is the shortest—and naming them. "This is Jan, this is Hendrik, this is Johannes, that is Shaun," and on down the list. The broad-shouldered brute I saw from the overlook is named Rafe. He has a quiet stealth that concerns me. Pent-up, strong, like a coiled snake. I wonder if he and the stinker are father and son. For all I know, they might *all* be his sons.

The Voors settle to parade rest. Teal looks even more miserable.

"Understood, sir," Gamecock says, breaking in just as Captain Coyle is about to lay down her share. The captain is not impressed by any of the Voors. "We're willing to come to an accommodation, providing it's mutually beneficial. We need information—"

"You're here a-learn what this pipe does!" de Groot cries out, though everyone else is quiet. He clamps his teeth with a click, levels his shoulders, and thrusts out his jaw. "Trekboers protect what's ours." His dialect is different from Teal's, but then, he's trying to speak English. To my ear, he's easier to understand.

Gamecock approaches him. "You were willing to murder us," he says. "That could explain our general lack of courtesy, don't you think?"

"No such!" de Groot says, but in a lower voice. "We have little to share and no kindness on principle."

"Leave that be," Gamecock says. "Captain Coyle tells me you have information that could go a long way to patching up our differences. If we can establish mutual trust...for now."

De Groot sniffs. "This is *our* pipe," he says. "Our station. We keep it under hold, patch and drain it, waiting, a-hope of return and mining. And living! But you can understand, we do not want its quality a-shouted any who listen. Strange ears, out on the dust!"

"We can agree on that," Gamecock says.

The old Voor turns to Teal. His face sharpens and his lips purse as if he is about to spit. "You are the *hoer*," he says. "Do you know this one?" he shouts to all of us, advancing until he sees the sisters and Gamecock have palmed their sidearms. Then he nods like a dip bird and backs off a step. "She betrayed her camp, and now she betrays all *us*. None should be here! *This* is our salvation, our hope. We follow *her*, a-stop her betrayal." He flings his arms at the heavy dark space. But then his bluster fades, he seems to deflate a little, and he nods at Rafe, the big fellow, who steps forward.

"We come from bad news," the broad-shouldered young Voor says softly. "Piet Retief Kraal and the Swellendam Pipe have been destroyed. The Far Comers have not bothered with us until now, but our *legerplaatze* are silent. And this woman's camp—silent a-well. It may be all were murdered by ice, rocks."

"The comet took out a *settlement*?" Gamecock asks.

"All we had, gone," Rafe confirms, sensing, hoping for a turn of sympathies. Shaun and Andres, both young and light-haired, lean against each other. Andres is shaking.

"We *think*," de Groot says, watching this emotion with gimlet eyes. "Same compass. No radio after. Shock nearly scrubbed our wagons. Our brothers wanted a-look, but I am hard man, *we* go on. If the *leger* is there, it is there. If it is gone…But the others, they disagree. They take a wagon and leave."

"The ranch wife saved you," Coyle says in a wondering undertone.

"*Hoer* has luck a-get out in just time," de Groot counters. His voice rises for effect, and he thrusts out his bound hands. "She *knew*. She's glove with the Far Comers!"

Our tall rescuer has frozen in place, face screwed up and drained of color. "T'at's a *lie*," she says very softly.

Rafe continues, "As *vader* says, what's done is out. We have a-decide new all soon, friend or foe, or we're over. We are finished, *dood*."

By which he means, I assume, we are dead.

"Now all listen," de Groot resumes, building up again, able to inflate and deflate apparently at will. He folds his twisty-tied hands in front of his crotch, lowers his head, gazes up at us under his brows. "This pipe is hope, but only if we fix and restore. And here the *hoer* could help, if she tells what she knows—and trims time so doing."

Gamecock has been listening without comment until now, but he quickly arranges us to block the Voors just as they move forward, despite their plastic shackles, to begin these labors.

"You are not in command here, sir," he reminds de Groot in a confidential voice.

"It's *our* pipe, damn!" the Voor named Shaun cries, and the others bristle, but de Groot shushes them, waves them down with his hands like a conductor with an orchestra. I swear that Rafe is just waiting for a chance to make a stupid move. Tak and I instinctively take a couple of steps left and right to flank him. He's big. They would all die, but maybe that's good enough for their pride under the circumstances—who can say? Humans are invariably wild animals. We learn that early in boot. I doubt it's any different on Mars.

"Do you know our history, this place?" de Groot asks. "Where we are, where we stand, where we suffered and suffer now?"

"We've left you alone," Gamecock says. "That's what you want, isn't it?"

"We stand in fear of soldiers taking all, and now—*she* brings you!" De Groot tries to jab a knobby finger at Teal, who narrows her eyes. The Voors are bound—she is not. I suppose that's a telling point.

"Where in hell are we, Venn?" Gamecock asks me, aside. "What is this place?"

"We could tell," de Groot says.

Gamecock looks between us, concentrates on me. "What have you learned?"

"Far from all I'd like to know, sir. This woman's father told her this mine, Drifter, pipe—whatever—was a place where she could retreat if things got bad at her camp. Apparently, they did."

"How?" Gamecock asks Teal.

"Long story," she says, swallowing hard, eyes still tracking the Voors.

Gamecock looks back at me. "Venn, what the hell is all this about?"

"The settlements, towns, laagers, whatever they call them— have had it rough, Colonel. They've managed to explore and build camps, but I think their population hasn't grown much."

"Hard times!" de Groot says. "Hardest for Voors!"

"You fight for what isna yours!" Teal cries, her brittle restraint snapping. "You raid and kill and *t'ieve*!" Gamecock is losing control of the discourse, but at least there's information emerging, of a kind. He looks at me to indicate he will interrupt if passions overflow, or if the talk is not useful.

I stand aside.

"We were told by her station, this *hoer* has left, she is angry, she is going a-our pipe," de Groot says.

Teal looks down. "Na such," she murmurs.

"Her *vader*, he was an engineer," Rafe says. "He left the Trek-boers long past. Went a-Green Camp."

"Lost the Trekboer way," de Groot adds firmly.

"You killed his wife!" Teal says, eyes up, accusing.

"At Green he lost his wife again!" de Groot says. "Man is good at losing wives."

"How many camps know about this place?" Gamecock breaks in.

"Just Voors and Green Camp," Teal says defiantly. "Te Voors killed most te Algerians."

"Not such," de Groot says. He's about to add something, but, looking around at all the brown faces, his Adam's apple bobs and he clamps his jaw.

"My fat'er told na else but me, and t'en Ally Pecqua took my intended and made him her own." An old story. Teal is intent on saying more, letting out her frustration. "Among te Rationals, wit'out a husband, I am a burden."

De Groot snorts. "Among Voors, women are *value*."

"White women," Teal says.

Our sisters study the Voors closely, eyes narrowed to slits. Rafe notices and nudges his father, who looks around, less smug but no less defiant.

"They were fools, but we partner," de Groot concludes with a deep sniff up his long nose.

Gamecock listens with a serious and sympathetic expression. To Teal, he says, "Your father told you how to get around this place, where to find food and resources."

Teal nods. Her eyes are dry, weeping done.

"You did not intend to bring others with you, including us."

"No. But t'ey woulda died out t'ere," she says, eyes like head-lamps in the shadow.

Gamecock turns first to Captain Coyle, whose expression is neutral with a touch of grim, then to de Groot, and observes his reaction. I watch Rafe, who cringes in anticipation. He knows de Groot just can't keep still and shut up.

"We *live*!" de Groot shouts. "We feed our people! We trek and settle and build, flee battles, *soldate*, but even so, lose families and land! And now, because of *your* war, the *laager* is *gone*!" He stares around as if his look could pierce us all. "We have waited years. When the water is down, the pipe is no longer flooded, we mine and build and make crops. Here there is much metal—but down below, vents, *vluchtige*—pockets of methane, ammonia—*stikstof*—nitrogen!"

"And sulfide," I explain under my breath to the colonel. "They seeded oxyphores in the pits."

Gamecock frowns. Biology is not his strength. Skipping over

that, I add the important point: "Enough water still flows to power the old generators. And they have a printer. Quite a few barrels of slurry—metal, ceramic, medical, and nutrient."

"How many?" Gamecock asks.

"Hard to know, sir. Lots. They finished most of the installation before the hobo—before the water rose and they left."

"Drifter. Pipe. Hobo," Gamecock says, trying to absorb the words.

"Why not just pump out the water and sell it?" Tak asks.

"Water iss *everywhere*," Rafe says. "We got water."

"That gives *suurstof*, oxygen, hydrogen," de Groot says. "But very little *stikstof*, not so much *metaal*, not like this, just ready to dig and melt. This pipe means *huise*, *kos*, food—life! But what is that now? *Nutteloos!* No use!"

His agony is honest. His eyes fill with tears. Everyone is still, quiet. The other Voors seem embarrassed. Rafe flexes his arms, tugging at his twisty-ties. Hard times indeed.

"I never wanted *t'at*," Teal says.

"You led them straight here!" Rafe says, not shouting, but with deep resentment.

"So did you," Captain Coyle reminds him.

"Not our choosing," Rafe says.

The tension is rising. Gamecock feels it. We all feel it. Teal can feel it most acutely. We're all that stands between her and de Groot's vengeance. These guys would love to resume their little gnome works without our interference.

"There's no point assigning blame," Gamecock says. "Save that for later. How many Voors left your buses, your wagons?"

"Trekboers. Many," Rafe says.

De Groot clamps his jaw. "They go where home was."

Too many to fit in one wagon. Coyle asks, "Can they walk that far?"

"They die," de Groot says. "When hope it is gone, we go on

trek, like our ancestors. Dutch go hard on them, they walk from Cape Town to the Big Karoo and the Little Karoo. Our way."

"*King Solomon's Mines*," I say.

"That is right," Rafe says sadly. "Ophir. Right here we are. We are no danger. Set us free!"

Gamecock lowers his eyebrows a notch. Coyle shakes her head.

Vee-Def and Kazak have gone back to the northern garage at Gamecock's murmured instructions and now rejoin us. They confer with Coyle and Gamecock, away from Voor ears, and after a minute, Gamecock motions for me and Tak to come aside with them. Tak repeats his report. "We've got a good line of sight to the northwest. Lots of activity—there's a big cloud out there. Venn saw it earlier, just after we dropped. Well, now it's bigger and closer. There are tunnels and hidey-holes all through this place. We really need a map or a native guide."

I tell them about the southern watchtower and the control panel. Gamecock sends DJ to check it out.

"I'm not sure any of the Voors have been here in years," Gamecock says.

"Teal might know more, but she's terrified," I say.

"They keep calling this a 'pipe,'" Kazak says, drawing closer. "What the hell does that mean?"

"Volcanic pipe, like where diamonds are mined," Tak says.

"I saw something on a display up in the watchtower," I say. "A cavern or room, bright, shiny, crystals all over."

"Diamonds—here?" Gamecock asks, incredulous.

"Don't know that, sir, or where it is, even if it's in this formation."

"The big fellow did grab on to calling this place Solomon's mine," Coyle says. She points to me. "Master Sergeant Venn seems to have a relationship with the ranch wife. She showed you around, didn't she?"

"She's just scared," I say.

"Assume nothing," Coyle says.

Gamecock is studying me. I don't like that.

"I don't think she trusts any of us," I say.

"She's got to be lonely," Gamecock says. "She came here with nobody, to get away—but then she picks us up. None of the settlements like us..." Something continues not to convince or impress him. I have to agree—there are major gaps in every one of these stories.

Tak and I regard each other with owlish resignation. The dust and activity out there is almost certainly Antag, and they're either heading our direction deliberately, out to get us in particular, or we're on the path to wherever they are going. Given the nature of this place, if the Antags have tracked all these buggies from orbit, homing in on the Drifter like dung beetles to a pile, they're going to be curious.

Likely the Drifter has distinct gravimetry and until now the Antags have ignored it, as we have, because there's been too much else to do. But if they're in complete charge, laying down a heavy, long-term hand, they may feel the freedom to send out targeted recon.

"I want to know as much as we can know about this place, as soon as possible," he says. "There could be a hell of a lot more at stake than just us and them. Keep letting Teal think we're on her side. We may be on her side, of course. Captain Coyle, you go with them—chaperone. Take the big one, Rafe, just to let the Voors feel they're not being left out."

"What about the old guy?" Coyle asks. "He's the boss. And he's real trigger." She means a natural killer, remorseless and cold. "He might know more than the others. And the others won't do anything without his say."

"Isolate him," Tak suggests. "Defuse him."

"Take him away, the rest will get anxious," Gamecock says.

"I'll bet he's told his son most of what he knows. Rafe's the one you want to get separate." He presses his hands together, then splits them apart. "I'm pretty sure we're all going to be together in the shit soon enough. If we can keep them in line…Get them to fight *with* us…Maybe we'll die another day. But right now, we need to do our best to uplink and get instructions," the colonel concludes with a sour look.

DJ returns. "I've scoped out the watchtower rooms," he says. "Beetling brows over the ports." He salutes a caveman ridge above his nose. "No line of sight to zenith. Maybe to the horizon, but that's the long way."

"Even if we had working lasers," Gamecock says.

"We have helm lasers," Tak says. "On a clear night, we *could* get a horizontal link—for a few seconds at least."

"How? You couldn't hold steady enough."

"The sats could spot dust twinkle and do Fourier, then downlink."

"Why would they?" Gamecock asks doubtfully. "Antags can spot twinkle as well."

"If any sats survive," I add.

"Well, what if some do?" Tak says. "Sir, we can't *not* take chances. We need to compare our own tactical in real time, the updates between Captain Coyle's launch and drop and ours—not just chew over old news. Our angels are terrible at computing command decisions, especially when the shit sets up. But you *know* they will. And then, we have to do what they say." We have been instructed to follow angelic orders, even barring updates. That threat chills us all—all except Coyle, who stays cool, indifferent.

I note this with a slight itch in the back of my head.

"We're the deciders," I say.

Gamecock considers. "Captain Coyle—you, me, Tak, let's draw in the dust. Michelin, you and whomever the captain assigns work the layout with Rafe. Venn, take Teal back to that watchtower and look around. Keep her away from the Voors. And get back in your skintights, all of you. DJ…go outside through the southern garage. Shoot some beams. See if we can raise a sat."

DJ looks unhappy.

"Twenty minutes," Gamecock tells him. "Then get the fidge back in here."

"Just say 'fuck,' sir," DJ grumbles. "Bloody Gurus can't fucking hear us."

"Assume nothing," Gamecock says. "Go."

BACKGROUNDER, PART 3

I sit in the apartment's high morning light, flipping the inscribed platinum disk between my fingers, basking in a multicolored and subdivided square of reflected spring sun—with coffee. The lone box of breakfast cereal has long since become a village of weevils, a movable feast—if I regard them as food rather than company.

Doesn't matter. I'm not hungry. The dubious delights of being alone have worn off. I'm waiting for Joe to show up and tell me the outcome, as far as it goes, of his part of our long story.

I feel weirdly biblical this morning. Smiting and being smitten.

Lo and behold, heavenly visitors came to Earth, and at first it was good, though many were sore amazed, and some were affrighted and did rise up and protest.

That's all I got. Never did get into that shit much.

But about two-thirds of us decided it was okay, why be a wallflower at the orgy? The second year after the Gurus outed themselves, the major industrial nations recorded near-zero unemployment. All who could work, worked—there was that much to do to exploit what little they had begun to reveal.

But everything is context. Before the real kicker, the mother of other dropped shoes—the announcement that the Antags were in our backyard—the Gurus led with an opening poke, a diagnostic of our will, of our submission.

Maybe.

Gurus seemed reasonable, mostly. They took a larger view. No surprise, given their celestial origins. They didn't mind their benefits expanding to all nations, even those that refused to acknowledge they were real. They also didn't mind satires or outright blasphemies against their persons or activities—seemed at times to encourage them. Lets off steam. So be it. They are not *really* God or gods, after all. Like us, mere mortals.

And yet, like the God of Abraham, shrouded in His secure sanctuary, the Gurus do not show themselves to the greater world. In the early years, speculation ran rampant, but those in the know managed to keep quiet about what they saw and experienced, in the presence of our visitors.

And to them—to the Wait Staff, just before the truly shitty boot dropped—was passed the first edict of Guru kind. Call it a firm request.

The Gurus made it clear, however magnanimous they might seem, that they found offensive any and all sexual profanity. Words that showed disrespect to the sacred biological functions of reproduction. Blaspheme against the Lord or Allah or Krishna or Buddha or Brahma if you will, but the F-word and its irreverent equivalents were a foul stench unto core Guru beliefs.

No physical punishment would ensue should that word continue to occupy its favored place in literature, entertainment, and common discourse—that was not Guru style—but they would be highly displeased, and if sufficiently highly displeased, they could reduce their revelations, perhaps even pack up and depart.

Some found that amusing. Upon threat of suppression, the floodgates opened. For a few months, the channels of human discourse overflowed with sexual profanity of an amazing level of creativity and vigor.

And then, as promised, the Gurus clammed up. For three months, nothing new passed to the outer world from the Wait Staff. So began the worldwide clampdown on the F-word. After all, geese with sensitive ears who laid golden eggs now rocked our economy. No reason to be ungrateful. For the first time in human history, humans managed to mostly clean up their language.

Way back in the twentieth century, creative types conjured substitutes for F-words by the dozens, like ersatz coffee or fake cigarettes—or bootleg gin—to avoid purely human censors. That talent was now revived. A young blogger in Beijing, whose reports, in admirable English, were popular worldwide, made up the word *fidge* as the new expletive of choice. He carefully explained—for sensitive eyes and ears—that nowise and nohow did *fidge* have a sexual connotation.

Fidge it became: fidge this, fidge that.

Gamecock was always extra cautious.

And that's not all. Don't know if there's any relation, but respecting reproduction…

Maybe you know about the lists, the unsolved disappearances all around the world. They seem to have begun about three years after the Gurus arrived. A select group of men and even a few women are vanishing. Some have been connected with or accused of sexual crimes. Violent stuff. Like Corporal Grover Sudbury. Remember him?

The disappearances continue to this day. Certainly not mystery number one, but interesting.

WAKEFUL THOUGHTS FOR SLEEPLESS GRUNTS

I think more this morning of the Red. How, wearing a skintight and standing on a flat, lifeless prairie of old lava and blown dust and sand, sometimes, even before a battle, I could feel free, liberated, useful; whereas here, in the apartment, the walls are closing in worse than any faceplate; the ample air seems denser and more confining than the sour smell of packed filters.

There's an untouched bowl of cereal on the table. It's still moving. The weevils are active. I don't know whether to throw them out or sit down and talk to them. I've got it bad. I'm shaking, and it's not just the pure caffeine of freshly ground black coffee, a luxury hardly ever available on Mars. I'm shaking because my extended cat whiskers tell me a moment is arriving that will both explain and traumatize. I do not want to know. I've switched off my phone, cut the intercom and buzzer; nobody in, nobody out who doesn't already have a key. No news. No updates. Just the closing in and restlessness and shivering. No more, please. I'm a man without a center. I have no idea where the hell I am. Waiting for Joe. Waiting for anybody who can tell me what the hell happened and how long I have to lie low.

Christ, I am well and truly fucked.

I look at the door, above the rise and beyond the small flight of stairs, framed by the upstairs loft, clearly illuminated by rising glory reflected from a glass-walled skyscraper a few hundred meters across the downtown neighborhood—blue-green windows redirecting the eastern sunrise.

Someone's coming. It won't be Joe. That much my whiskers tell me. Someone new. I get up on autopilot, shivering uncontrollably, and move toward the door.

As my toe lands on the first step, the doorbell rings its Big Ben chimes. Very retro. It takes me a long while to answer, but whoever or whatever is there is patient. I finally unlatch the door and swing it open, half expecting I will take aggressive action— at the very least, jump out and scream "Boo!"

But I don't.

A small, zaftig woman with black eyes, a stub nose, and a close-cropped patch of red hair looks at me without expression— relaxed, composed. She's wearing a light gray overcoat and a red and purple scarf. She smells like roses, old-lady perfume, but she can't be much older than me.

"Yeah?" I say.

"Joseph sent me," she says with a knowing grin. "He told me you'd be here," she adds, looking past me into the apartment. "He's sorry he couldn't make it. But he said you'll understand."

I'm staring, goggle-eyed.

The woman who smells like roses explains, into my silence, "He gave me the code to the downstairs entry. And the elevator."

Still staring.

"Can I come in?" she asks. Straightforward. Steady. She's dealt with fidged Skyrines before.

"Joe's okay?" I ask.

"I haven't heard from him in a few days."

"Where is he?"

"I don't know."

"Is he in trouble?"

"He is *always* in trouble."

"You're his girlfriend?"

"Do I look that stupid?" But again she smiles. It's a lovely, gentle smile. "He *invited* me to come talk with you. Have you got the coin?"

"I've got some coins," I say.

"One important coin. Silver?"

"You tell me," I say.

"Platinum," she says.

"Yeah."

"What's on the coin?"

"Numbers," I say.

"Good on you."

I seem to pass, for now. The woman says, "In case you're wondering, Teal's alive, last I heard, but that was a while ago."

"How do you know about Teal?"

She cocks her head, holds out one hand, may she come in? I stand aside, let her in, and close the door. My shaking has stopped. It's better not to be alone. What I know, what I think I know, I really do not want to keep to myself. This might be progress.

"I smell coffee," she says.

"I can't smell coffee. Fidging Cosmoline. Miss that."

"Do you smell my roses?" she asks.

"Yeah."

"Good. Pretty soon, you'll smell the coffee, too."

"Okay. Thanks."

"Not a problem."

I go to the kitchen and get down a mug, pour her what's left in the carafe. She doesn't follow, doesn't move far from the entry, just stands back there, craning her neck and looking around the apartment.

"You guys do okay."

"Thanks. It's not my place," I say, and deliver the cup.

"You might put on some clothes," she tells me, eyes fixed on my chin.

I look down. I'm naked.

"Right," I say. "Sorry."

"Did Joe tell you I'm a nurse?"

"Joe didn't say a thing about you," I say over my shoulder as I go to collect a robe.

"That's surprising. Vac and mini-g medicine, combat metabolism, oxydep—Injuries from anoxia and hypoxia."

"MHAT?" I ask from the bedroom.

"No. Not that there's anything wrong with MHAT. Good for warriors in trouble. But my billets were orbital."

"Active duty?"

"Indefinite furlough," she says. "I'm facing courts-martial."

"That's good," I say.

"Hmm."

"What's your name?"

"Puddin' tame," she says.

"Great. Just a friend of Joe's, or a friend of Teal's?"

"A friend to Mars," she says. "I hope."

I've put on a robe and cinch the tie as I return.

"Can I see the coin?" she asks.

I've been clenching it against my palm like Gollum—*my Precious*—as I once observed myself doing on Mars, in the Drifter, but, now, shyly enough, I drop the end of the tie, open my fingers, and hold it out.

She reaches.

I pluck it back and close my hand.

"Name, rank, serial number," I say.

"First Lieutenant Alice Harper, U.S. Marine Medical Services, awaiting dishonorable discharge."

"Disability?"

"Multiple cancers, all cured—but leading to profound Cosmoline sickness," she says. "Can't take the vac anymore." Then she adds, when I look dubious, "That's my real name and rank, *fuckhead*."

Spoken like a true Skyrine.

Again, I hold out the coin. She picks it up between small, pretty fingers, nails cut close and clean and painted with clear polish, and turns it over, brings it to her eye, then hands it back.

"Looks good," she says.

"What does it mean? A second coin..."

"Tell me what happened," she says, and takes another step into the apartment. "May I sit?"

"Of course."

She sits on the couch.

And just as she does that, the awful reluctance returns. *I don't want to tell.* Telling is like making people die all over again. I stand in the living room, saying nothing, just looking out the window with a dumbass squint.

"I'm a good listener," she says. "Tell me what happened, and maybe I'll be able to tell you what the coin means."

I gather up my courage. I would like to know more. I already know some of it. Not a lot. Just enough. The Algerians and the Voors weren't the first to mine the Drifter. Not by three and a half billion years.

It's a big story getting bigger. Let's slip back into it slowly, like a scalding bath.

COMES THE HEAT

Teal and I return to the northern garage and put on our skin-tights. Scrubbed and recharged, my suit is almost comfortable. There's six hours of oxygen in the backpack, new filters—not pristine sweetness, but no longer pickle juice. Reassuring, if things get bad and we have to exit in a hurry.

"The Voors will kill you if t'ey can," Teal says under her breath. "T'ey hate brown people. And your fems are bossy, too."

"Brown people do better in the vac," I say.

"My fat'er t'ought so," she says. Teal's back is to me as we head toward the ladder leading to the cold high room, which I'm hoping is warming now that power is back on. She pauses at the bottom of the ladder. "Te Voors had all *t'is*," she says, shoulders tensed, back arched, everything in her posture asking me how stupid they must be. "Wealt' and food and metal and water power, as long as te hobo flowed. And 'tis still flowing, down t'ere, where 'tis safe and useful. But te Voors will never be happy. Na else wanted a work or trade wit' t'em, because of te wrong t'ey did te Algerians—and my fat'er."

I say nothing. My job is to look northwest. We climb the ladder in silence. The cold room is warming, just a little. The radiant heater mounted on one wall crackles as years of dust pop off.

Teal raises the shutter.

We both see at once. Where the steady brown blur had been, there's now a wide wall of dust, and it's no storm. Big movement all along the western horizon, an arc of at least thirty klicks, from one corner of the port to the other. Many things in motion.

What sort of things?

I close my helm's plate and dial down a pair of virtual binocs. The plate measures the angles of incident light from the front of the plate to the rear, does a transform algorithm, and voila— a lensless virtual magnification of the infrared projects into my eyes, along with my angel's analysis of what I might be seeing. More Guru tech.

Teal has pulled down the periscope, handling it gingerly. Not time enough to warm. Maybe it has its own magnification, but I doubt she's seeing all that I'm seeing. There's a phalanx of vehicles out there, deep in the dust cloud. The angel analyzes the most likely threat first, a large concentration of Antag vehicles. As well, aerostats are advancing slowly behind the dust, about fifty klicks from the Drifter: big suspended balloons, the smallest at least a hundred meters in diameter. But then the angel points up another, much smaller line of vehicles, moving at speed in front of the main mass, just before the leading edge of the dust. These outlines are more familiar, possibly not a threat—

The angel flashes purple, still collating—then chirps. Here's some good news. The advancing Antag front is driving a line of human transports. Not many, no more than twenty or thirty, but they're clipping along at a fair pace and will likely reach the arc that includes our position before the Antags.

"Not'ing but dust," Teal says, pushing back the scope. "What do you see?"

I've been quiet, except for clucking my tongue and tapping my gloved fingers, a habit when I see shit coming down. "Ants chasing rabbits," I say. "Cavalry, maybe." I don't say aloud, *but not enough, and followed right on their heels by a whole lot of Indians.* The biggest Antag push I've ever witnessed.

I try to raise Gamecock, but as before, RF is blocked by the density of metal and rock. I remember DJ is outside the southern gate trying to pick up a sat signal. He's on the wrong side of the Drifter and won't see what we see.

"Far Ot'ers? Do t'ey know we'or here?" Teal asks.

"No idea," I say, and lean in close to the plex, hoping my laser will carry that far. I murmur a message to the angel and it shoots a beam through the port, varying frequency to find a sweet spot. Not much chance it will get through, it tells me. Plex too thick. Too much dust between us and the advancing vehicles.

"No good?" Teal asks.

"Depends," I say. "We got to go. Shut the port. Don't want heat giving us away."

Teal closes the louvers. We descend and run back to the southern garage.

Gamecock and de Groot have agreed to a loose armistice, against the wishes of Captain Coyle, who does not enjoy being outranked. Gamecock has somehow convinced de Groot and the Voors to help us begin defensive prep. All the twisty-ties have been cut and discarded. Makes me nervous, but what the hell—it's our only option.

"I shot a helm burst east," I say.

"Might not have been a good idea, bringing them here," Coyle says.

"We need help," Gamecock says, frowning at her in puzzlement.

"Maybe." Coyle isn't happy about any of it. Again, her reaction seems wonky.

Kazak and Tak, with the help of Rafe and Andres, have sketched a crude map in the green dust of the key tunnels and external points of access, and when I pass along what I've seen, the Skyrines go into overdrive. Coyle orders three of her team lower into the Drifter to check out the supply situation, and asks Teal if she could act as a guide. Teal, with a glance at me, and to my nod, agrees. She trusts me. But fuck if I know what's going on.

They head out.

Rafe conferences with the Voors while de Groot talks over final things with Gamecock and Tak. If our forces received my burst and are speeding to join us, we'll open the northern gate and let them in—all the troops and as many of their vehicles and weapons as the garage can hold. Then we'll hunker down, hope the Antags pass us by—

But they won't. We sense that. They've laid down a heavy hand, they mean to stay, and that will take all the resources they can grab.

They still have eyes in the sky.

And they know we're here.

SHIT ALSO FLOATS, SOMETIMES

Before I exit, Teal returns with our three sisters. Her glum look leaves me with a strong impression that she suspects something is wrong, something that she does not feel at liberty to divulge. Does it involve our collaborating, even under necessity, with the Voors?

I wish I knew more about their history from an unprejudiced source, but on the other hand, Green Camp has been closer to the problem than anyone on Earth, and the tall dust widow is a serious, sober sort; she's suffered through her own kind of shit, her own kind of betrayal. Green Camp effectively forced her out on the Red. Then they alerted the Voors she was heading their way, all just to preserve a share of the Drifter, de Groot's pipe.

And now, she sees we're cozying up with her enemies.

Blows huge, all of it.

The generators are doing well, Coyle's team reports, and Teal agrees. Gamecock instructs Tak and me to post ourselves outside the northern gate, hiding behind the rock ridge, peeking over the top. We'll have a direct view of the approaching dust.

I check out the vehicle lock. It will only take three Skells or two Tonkas at a time, end to end. We won't be able to get all the vehicles inside, even those that will fit, before the Antags are upon us.

We pass through the personnel lock, which is big enough for maybe ten. Outside, it's coming up on mid-afternoon and very cold, but we aren't quite freezing; shivering knocks my teeth together, but that's okay, that's what we're used to. We can only hope the Antags and their sats don't spot our slim IR signatures and take potshots.

The wall of dust doesn't look any closer, but it does look higher. We can make out a few vehicles on the leading front with our naked eyes. Then the dust closes in. They must be fleeing in thick haze, and surely they know what's behind them. Makes me shiver.

Tak and I tap helms and talk to pass the time.

"How many days between space frames?" Tak asks. We both know the answer, but I say it anyway,

"Forty-three on average, depending on the season."

"How much equipment on the average sled?"

"Six hundred tons."

"How much of that is weaponry, how much transport and tents?"

We're not worried about fountains for the moment, because it's obvious we've found the mother lode of water and other resources.

"Forty percent transports, twenty weaponry," I say, rattling off the stats we're used to dealing with. Each delivery and drop can vary widely, and we won't know until we're updated; all this talk is snotsuck. But we're hoping our cavalry is traveling with platforms that can carry big hurt. Tons and tons of it, and lots of spent matter to mow down Antags.

"I could go for a steak," Tak says.

"Cue sad harmonica," I say, but grimace at the thought of sizzling meat.

"Play 'Danny Girl,' " he says. "The captain is hot."

"Captain Coyle is *not* hot. She's total big sister."

"Big Mama, you mean." Tak has *dignitas*, but he's no less male for all that. Irritating a watch partner is a true art form. Too little, and we might relax, become inattentive; too much, and we lose focus on the Red and start paying more attention to the argument.

"Guy can violate protocol on the Red anytime he wants," Tak says. "In his head."

"Hope angel doesn't note it."

"Duly observed. Angel, absolve me." Tak looks aside. "I heard Coyle went special ops."

"Something like that," I say. "And nothing about her after Hawthorne."

We think this over. Separate goals, separate orders. Special ops is like a hidden reef. Could protect, could sink.

Our angels are quiet. We never know what they record. So far, no Skyrine has ever had his loose talk or death video splattered over media; maybe we're too trusting. Or maybe we're too damned select and valuable to be messed with. Or—maybe we just can't afford to pay for the right video feed.

"How far?" Tak asks. We don't dare lase for range, a) because dust will absorb and scatter, and b) because the helm plates can guess almost as well with their incident angles and magnification transforms, like a camera finding focus. So Tak already knows.

But I say it anyway. "Five klicks for the lead group."

"Reinforcements. Transports and weapons."

Our angels now feed us rough approximations of what's stirring the closest dust. "Tonkas, four big ones," I say. "A bunch of Skells. A Chesty. And maybe a Trundle or two."

"Jeez. What's on the platforms? Stuff we trained with, or sci-fi crap we don't know how to use?"

Skyrines dream of that possibility. Major upgrades—MPHF, pronounced *mmph*, acronym for Mega Plus Hurt Factor—in our dreams these fabulous, decisive weapons are delivered by surprise, ready to link to our angels and upload instant training and serving suggestions. But training vids are the weakest link in Earth's military-industrial complex. Gurus leak us ideas for shit to use, but they don't tell us how best to use it.

Thinking there might be MPHF coming at us is too much to hope for. Hurts deep in my warrior soul. So we change the subject.

"That dust widow likes you, Venn," Tak says.

"She's in a tight angle." I tell him about her situation with the Voors.

"Shit," Tak says. "They want to paint her?"

"They would if they could."

"No wonder Coyle wanted them separated. I thought only enlightened nerds colonized Mars."

"Not hardly. Lots of folks wanted to get the hell off Earth. Rich and poor, nerds or just pissed-off."

"I do get the impression our guests don't much like brown people. Me, they don't know how to take."

"Nobody knows how to take you, Fujimori," I say. "Besides, why would any of them like Skyrines? Antags dropped shit on their settlement. It's our war, they claim, not theirs."

"Well, she likes *you*. What was it you found in those dungarees? What did Neemie say it was?"

"Platinum."

"Is there beaucoup platinum down there?"

"Maybe."

"Shit, let's do a *Dirty Dozen*!"

"You mean *Castle Keep*," I say. "Or maybe *Kelly's Heroes*."

Most Skyrines play Spex combat games or watch war movies when they're not crossing the vac or training or fighting. Some read. Tak does it all, but unlike Vee-Def, doesn't file away trivia.

Tak scoffs. "How far?"

"Three klicks and closing."

"See anything behind the Tonkas and the sleds?"

"Could be Millies. And high up, aerostats."

"Aerostats mean germ needles," Tak says.

"Wear a hat."

"Shit yes. Big steel sombrero." He holds his hands over his head, spreads them wide, pretends to hunker down more than we already are, squeezed into a narrow crevice in the rock.

Air support over Mars is difficult, because wings have to be so damned huge; anything like an airplane has to be big, clumsy, hard to maneuver—a perfect target. Antag aerostats are huge and even more clumsy, and in theory make good targets, but they seem to be cheap, easy to replace, and are surprisingly tough to shoot down. You pretty much have to slice away or burn out a few dozen meters of the aerostat's surface before it's fatally wounded and descends slowly to the dust, slumping like a big jellyfish on a terrestrial beach. We don't use them. I'm not sure why. We don't use germ needles, either. I'd say Antags know more about our biology than we do about theirs.

I rub the surface of the old basalt with my hand, feeling the age, trying to psych out some deeper truth.

Tak watches my hand. "Spirit of the Red? What you receiving?"

"Zip."

"Fucking superstition."

I'm not so sure. I keep seeing the coin, the platinum disk with its spiral of numbers, and it doesn't fit. It doesn't fit that some Voor miner would leave something so cool and valuable in his overalls—unless of course he died and nobody else knew. Still,

Teal seems to know. Possibly her father knew something and told her.

And maybe, just maybe, the previous owner of the dungarees was a caretaker, left behind...

And decided to go naked, without his dungarees?

Leaving his coin?

Maybe he's still down there, deep down, wallowing in green dust.

SNKRAZ.

"Three klicks," Tak says.

"Can't get a fix on how far behind the Antags are."

We're both thinking the same thing about the gates. Their outer doors will be like toilet tissue against Antag weapons.

"I say it's another five klicks. Gives us a minute or two to welcome reinforcements."

We enter the personnel lock and cycle through. We'll be back outside soon enough. The rocks look jagged enough to hide more than a few warriors. We're going to have to erect a slim sort of defense around both gates, set up a 360 atop the basalt hump-head, maybe find a kind of natural, high-point revetment for the lawnmower—the strong-field suppressor. It looks like a compact barbell with two handgrips and two nodes thrusting forward from the gray balls on each end. A triplex of spent matter cartridges hangs between the grips. Flip your guard and squeeze both grips and you spread tuned nasty over a wide arc.

We exit the inner lock hatch and stand before DJ, who is all alone and looks confused.

"Where is everybody?" he asks.

"Where's who?"

"*Everybody*. The Voor wagons are still over at the southern garage. The ranch wife's buggy..." He points. Teal's cylindrical vehicle is still parked beside the older hulks. "But all the people—gone."

"You passed through from there and didn't see anyone?"

"Just tunnels and dust."

"Where's the colonel and Captain Coyle?" Tak asks.

"Wherever they all went, I suppose," DJ says, exasperated and scared. "Nobody said a thing to me. How the hell should I know?"

I walk around the garage, examining the floor. There's a general trample of boot prints in the green dust, ours upon arrival, and then paths heading in several directions—nothing more.

"Goddamn Voors," DJ says.

"How the fuck could they overpower Skyrines when we have a lawnmower?" I ask. No answer. Tak is thoughtful.

Tak, DJ, and I are alone in the northern garage, with guests soon to arrive, and no plan how to greet them.

DRIFTERS AND HOBOS

Alice settles into our couch, draping her pleasingly plump arms along the back, feeling the leather with her well-manicured fingers.

"How did the Drifter get there?" I ask.

She looks at me. "Didn't Teal or Joe tell you?"

"I don't know what I don't know," I say.

"You're testing me."

"You test, I test. I'm asking meaningful questions. Doesn't that mean I'm on the mend, Doc?"

She lifts a corner of her lips, takes one last look at the platinum coin, and delicately deposits it on the glass table between us. I don't think she covets it. I think it scares her. "Nobody thought such a formation could exist," she says. "We've been telling ourselves an old, old story ... trying to get it to make sense, not quite succeeding."

"Who's we?"

"Experts and doubters," she says.

"You do geology?"

"I used to analyze orbital surveys. For a year, I even guided tactical mapping. First time I went out on a space frame, crossing the vac, to get up close and personal with the Red, we were caught in a massive solar storm—about halfway. Lasted six days. Fourteen space frames, everyone got full dose. Cosmoline couldn't absorb near enough. We arrived and parked in orbit. Fortunately there was an Ant lull at the time, perhaps because they were too smart to go out when it's that hot. Our frames got shipped back before we could drop anybody. Twelve frames returned, but two are still out there, endlessly orbiting—dead. I rode a hawk down to SBLM, ended up spending six months in Madigan rehab. Ended my career. Officers don't rise in ranks if they're stuck on Earth."

"And for that, they court-martial you?"

"That came later," she says.

"At least you're alive," I say.

She looks out the window, moves one arm on the back of the couch, lifts her hand. "I returned to civilian life, paid to get bored and blow my head off inside a year. That's the gamble, right?"

All too familiar among those mustered out of service for whatever reason.

"So I expanded my study program. Took all the available courses on settler history—what few courses remain. Universities have been dropping them right and left as funding dries up. Gurus don't like them, I guess. I took more science, then geology, focusing on Mars in deep time. Lots of civilian science about Mars, even now. Peaceniks, pure space types, libertarians. I fell right in with them, after a time, once they got over suspicions I was a spy. But nobody saw *this* coming."

"You split sociology, history—and geology?"

"Pretty much. After that, I interviewed with settler advocacy groups in Sacramento and Paris. Got picked up by a splinter of Mars Plus in New Mexico."

"Sandia Space Studies," I say. "Isn't that Air Force?"

"Yeah."

"Teal got a message through to them? Or Joe?"

"One or the other, I don't know," Alice says. "But Joe told us you might have something interesting to say. Describe this Drifter to me again."

I do. I'm full of metaphors. I tell her it's like a huge mandrake root almost submerged in a sea of cold basalt, descending many miles into the Martian crust. A lot of metals. Very heavy, no doubt. "Why didn't it sink?" I ask.

"Everyone wants to know that. I assume they're checking all over the Red now for others like it." She watches me too intently.

"Probably," I say. I feign ignorance—easy for me at the best of times.

"But maybe not," Alice says, drawing herself up. "Did you ever think the Gurus don't want us to know about this Drifter? Or any Drifters?"

"Why?" I ask.

"Not wanting to find them could explain why we've never paid attention to our own gravimetry. Which I had a hell of a time digging up."

Okay. But we're dodging the main issue. "So what is it?" I ask.

"Best guess, and not a bad one, is that it's a chunk of big old moon," Alice says. "One of many, maybe the biggest, that hit Mars a few billion years ago. Nine hundred miles or so in diameter, about the size of Rhea around Saturn. Metal and rocky core. Thick layer of ice and other volatiles. Probably got deflected by another passing object in the outer system, then fell downsun, approached Mars, and broke up as it passed through the Roche limit—the distance before tidal forces break a body into smaller pieces. The biggest chunks swung around Mars half a revolution or so—then fell right about where Hellas is now. The impacts melted through the mantle and wobbled the whole planet, rang it like a bell—also melted half the crust. Pretty much created the division between the southern highlands and northern lowlands.

"The impact in Hellas instantly converted most of the volatiles to superheated steam and blew them off into space. Some of the rest bubbled out through the molten impact basin for the next few hundred thousand years. Like a soda bottle." She grows flushed describing all this. To her, it's sexy. "The Martian crust and mantle congealed, solidified. But the big chunks of moon weren't completely absorbed. A couple of plumes of upwelling magma kept thrusting up the chunks—the last, unabsorbed remains—and floated them in place, like feathers on a jet of air."

"Jesus," I say.

Alice takes a deep breath. "Those days are long gone," she says. "The plumes are a lot colder. Most are solid. The Drifter has been sinking for a couple of billion years—but its head still pokes through, and there are lots of deep vent tubes carved by superheated lava, pushing tunnels right through to the deep roots, down to the main bulk of all those spectacular metals. Sound about right?"

It does. Perfect, in fact.

"All right, do I pass?"

"You pass."

"So do tell," she says, attentive without being needy.

GO DOWN IN HISTORY, DAMN YOU ALL

We've made our way to the southern garage and back, and now we stand beside Teal's buggy and the abandoned hulks. The tunnels between are deserted, as DJ described—as far as we could search. The weapons carried by Captain Coyle's squad are nowhere in sight, and so it seems likely that the tables have been turned and our Skyrines have been overpowered and taken away to be disposed of.

"The Voors must have had a weapons cache," Tak says, wandering around the walls. "They got the drop on the rest."

All we have are sidearms.

"No bodies, no blood," DJ observes.

No blood in the garage is a positive. Teal would likely be the first to get shot. After that, there are no positives. I'm not even sure we know how to open the gate and operate the locks fast enough to let in our reinforcements, if they arrive—if they *are* reinforcements and not prisoners driven ahead of the main column of Antags just to absorb our fire.

"We know the layout around here. I bet DJ can lead us through to the eastern gate," Tak says.

"Teal thought it was sealed," I say. "Like the western gate."

"Did you check?" Tak asks. "And what would it take to unseal it? The eastern garage makes the most sense."

"But the Voor wagons are still back at the southern gate!" DJ says.

"Maybe there was a wagon left outside," Tak says. "They could all fit into one now, right? Leave us behind, or kill us—get the hell out before the Ants arrive."

"I don't think they'd leave," I say. "It's too dangerous out there. If they get caught up in a battle, they're smoke and scrap, even if they have Coyle's weapons, which they can't use."

"Right," Tak says. "That could mean they have a dungeon down deep, hard to find—harder to get into. But how in hell did they overpower Coyle and Gamecock?"

I've considered all the possibilities, and one hypothesis remains unassailable, based on what little we know. I share it. There must have been one or more Voor wagons outside that Captain Coyle did not see and could not have commandeered. These latecomers could have arrived after the others, saw that something had gone wrong, and circled around to the eastern gate, then pushed stealthy raiders through the tunnels—where they got the drop on our comrades.

While those of us outside heard nothing.

I share this cheerful scenario. Tak considers with growing calm, not even frowning. The worse things seem, the calmer he looks.

"Shit, man," DJ says. "Why not leave somebody to take us out, too? We could *all* be stain by now."

"Because we don't matter," Tak says.

We quickly share the maps captured by our angels during explorations, with distances, elevations, quick video and photo notes on what was seen and where. Battlefield record keeping.

Nowhere near complete, but we come up with a good possibility for a passage to the eastern garage. And if the green dust in that tunnel is scuffed by lots of feet, we'll know we're on the right track.

Or we stay and let the reinforcements in. DJ says he might be able to operate the vehicle airlock from the control booth, but maybe not fast enough to get all the vehicles through...or any big weapons.

We're just churning.

I think I'm going to have to make the decision. I got my stripes before Tak. I get down on one knee. The others do the same, as if we're about to form a prayer triangle.

"Our buds out there don't even know we're here, unless they got my flash," I say. "We don't have time to get them all in, and besides, the doors won't hold long. Tak, you and DJ stay. I think I can operate Teal's bus. I'll go out and meet the approaching line, help them set up a defensive cordon around the northern gate, while DJ gets into the booth and you both try to cycle as many as you can. Maybe we can bring in enough to deal with the Voors."

Tak looks dubious but DJ looks energized. "Right!" he says. "They're looking for a place to turn and fight."

"What about the Antags?" Tak asks. "Won't they just cut through the small force, then blast the doors and swarm in?"

"Nothing better," I say. An old Skyrine nostrum. All that we deserve and nothing better. We glance at each other in the gloom. Tak and DJ tilt their heads, push out their lips, spit into the green dust.

Teal's buggy was not personally coded, as far as I could tell. Maybe she had an implant or a key fob, but I never saw her use it. The buggy was stolen anyway. We work our way to the buggy's hatch and push the big flat entrance button. The hatch opens. I climb into the lock. Then I look back at Tak and DJ. We nod. Last time into the breach.

As the big kahuna, our DI on Mauna Kea, told us on our graduation, *Last time no see anymore.*

Nothing better.

It's on.

ZULU TIME

can barely see DJ in the upper booth through the buggy's front windows. The bus's controls are not much different from a Skell or a big Tonka—a two-handled wheel on a stick and foot pedals. There's enough charge left in the batteries to get me out the gate and maybe ten or twelve klicks beyond—no time to wait for a full charge from the Drifter's generators.

Tak pulls the plug. DJ opens the inner doors. I rumble through, learning as I go—and manage to just scrape the edge of one door. Hope I haven't punched a hole, hope the door seals tight on the way back...

Hiss surrounds the buggy, the suck of retrieved air. Pressure drops in the lock. My ears pop. When the hiss is down to a light puff, DJ opens the outer doors and I shove the stick forward and to the left to go around the low end of the giant's arm. The only communication I'm going to have is radio. Can't rely on the helm laser this time—too much dust. So I start broadcasting across multiple shortwave digital bands. The dust looks thick and the vehicles are likely tossing up big grains—enough to interfere with microwave. But what the hell. If anybody human's listening, I can rev up the bus motors and wind them down in a kind of dogtrot EM pulse.

Soon, in just a couple of minutes, that arc of fleeing Skyrines and the Antags chasing them will arrive at the Drifter's northern gate. If the Skyrines know we're here, if they got my laser burst, they'll be heading for the gate. If not, they'll sweep around this bump in the Red like waves around a rock.

The air in the buggy smells like sweat and electricity. The batteries are old; the wiring may be shorting out as well. And all those pads from our skintights are doubtless festering in the rear hopper.

Outside, the air is an amazingly beautiful shade of lavender, shot through with high stripes of pink. The dust raised by the oncoming tide sweeps over the buggy, over everything.

Then it gets dark, very dark—black in just a few seconds. Martian night falls almost instantly and the only residual light has to come through the dust tops down to where I am—which it doesn't. Everyone out there in the dark and the dust is traveling blind, chasing blind, fleeing blind. And I'm moving out, broadcasting like a sonofabitch, pumping the engines up and down…

Then, to my left, a Skell-Jeep rolls up and throws a beam, almost blinds me, and passes so close it grazes a tire. The buggy shivers and complains. No doubt they know I'm here, but do they think I'm a Muskie? Or the idiot Skyrine who lased them?

Another vehicle passes me—this time a Tonka. My radar is shooting quick blips. I can make out hazy return in the general scatter and I'm still rolling forward, chuckling like an idiot child, when something or someone dogtrots a shortwave carrier. No voice—just up-and-down frequency variation. Answering my motor pulses.

"Someone wishes to speak to us," my helm says. "They want to know where we come from."

I then go all out on the shortwave and tell them we're friendly, give a call sign I hope is still good, ask to speak with the ranking CO. A rough, raspy voice gets back to me in seconds. "Who the fuck are you, and what are you doing way out here in the boonies?"

My face lights up in a big grin. Even with all the distortion and drop-out, I know this guy. It's Joe—First Sergeant Joe Sanchez.

"No time," I say. "We've found a rock up ahead with a door in it, leading to a bunch of caves—a pretty good refuge, but you'll have to buy time to get us all inside. Can you form a line on me?"

I am the only game in town, the only hope they have. My radar shows a fair number of our vehicles—at least ten, if I count through the ghosts and guesses—now forming a dirty curve about two hundred meters from end to end, like a mitt flexing to intercept a ball.

"If you'll just hold still a minute," Joe says, "you beautiful bastard."

"Gladly, First Sergeant." I pull back the buggy's wheel and pump the brakes, about a kilometer from the northern gate. This is where we're going to have to hold until or if the Antags decide to halt and reconnoiter. Not likely. But a battle in the dusty dark is nobody's ideal.

"Time to plow a hole with whatever you've got," I say. "You have to make the Antags hesitate. Then we'll withdraw in proper order to the rock."

I send the coordinates.

"Do you know how many Ants are on our tail?" the familiar voice asks, weaker and more raspy. "We haven't taken time to look over our shoulder."

Night is upon us. Nobody can see shit. Maybe the Antags are having the same difficulty.

"Rough guess," I say, "a hundred times your force, airborne and ground."

"Pick targets for maximum disruption," the raspy voice orders.

Another voice responds: "Sir, we'll provoke immediate fire. I don't know how we've—"

Another voice, female, shrill: "Die screaming, sweatrag!"

"Just fucking light 'em up!"

Then the dust glows in bright, quick flickers, like lightning seen through a filthy window. That makes me want to cry. We're in a real fight. We're all going to die, finally, and it's the best feeling in the world—kill and be killed! I wish someone was in the buggy to share it with me. I wish Teal could see me now. Or my dad. My uncle Karl.

Anyone.

The murk starts to really glow, almost steady, like a weird sunrise. Our buds are lighting up with all they've got, and judging by the purple tinge, they're using at least one big bolt cutter.

God, it's *awful* pretty.

Thumps rise through the bus's tires, shaking the frame. I hear ascendant whines cut through the thin air—through the muffling dust—and rise beyond human hearing. A Chesty's twin disruptors are hitting targets, slicing and dicing and electrifrying. Other sounds, other weapons. The Antags are firing back, I think, but it doesn't sound coordinated. It sounds confused. Of course, what do I know. I'm a blind duck in a truck.

Happier and happier.

I start singing.

Someone on the shortwave joins in. We're an insane duet for about ten seconds.

The murk fades, then the dust pulses again with pink and purple and finally green. Another big transport rolls up and around—a Deuce and a half, four sets of whanging tires, twice as big as a Tonka. I cheer out loud. The first part of our line is withdrawing to the Drifter.

At the same time, someone raps on the outer hull of the buggy, hard. I rise out of the driver's seat and go back to see who it is. At this stage, I'm loopy enough not to mind if it's one of the far-traveled enemy. Any change, please, to break the god-damn suspense, the awful grind of not knowing shit. Someone's cycling through. I'm tapping my feet and pushing off against the ceiling not to fly around in the cabin.

The hatch opens. A Skyrine pushes inside—and it *is* Joe, finally! Old friend. Old training buddy. Veteran of four previous mutual actions on the Red. Only he's got a lieutenant colonel's silver oak leaf pinned to his chest—rather, half of one, and there's blood all over his skintight, mostly dry, but some still foaming from the vac. Apparently not his own.

"Master Sergeant Michael Venn, my lucky day," Lieutenant Colonel Joseph Sanchez says, opening his helm.

I snap back and salute him.

"Screw that, it's brevet." Joe doesn't bother to brush down before he moves up front. I don't care. The cabin is already full of dust. He glares through the windshield, observing the with-drawal, then flops down on the step behind the controls. "Comm flashed they'd intercepted a hinky beam from somebody with your name—is that right?"

"Yes, sir!"

"So did the goddamn Antags, I bet. Where did you find this heap?"

I explain quickly about Gamecock and the Sky Defense brass in their sad, sagging tent. "Teal, the previous driver—a ranch wife—picked us up and took us to a lucky rock with a big door in it. After she unlocked the door and let us in, we accepted a visit from Captain Daniella Coyle and eleven sisters, who themselves hitched a ride with twelve hostile settlers—Voors. But they're gone now. Coyle and all her team, the Voors, the rest of my team—Kazak and Vee-Def and Michelin—seem to have disappeared deeper into the rock. We don't know where any of them are."

Joe stares at me through bloodshot, pale blue eyes, then shakes his head. "Outstanding! A dozen Voors. As in Voortrekkers?"

"Sort of. There could be more, if there's an unsecured gate... if they got reinforcements and overpowered Captain Coyle. They may have all the weapons, including a lawnmower. Which they can't use."

"Outstanding to above!" He's feverish from exhaustion.

"Sir, have you got recent tactical?" A silver oak leaf stomps any invitation to intimacy, especially when there's blood.

"Recent as of forty-eight hours, but they got most of our sats, and our new ones are being swatted down faster than we can find them." He grips my shoulder with one hand, and we exchange tactical. I close my faceplate to make sure I got it all. Little angel alarms and flashing pink dots in the upper corner.

I got it—but the angel is not happy. Position-wise, we are screwed—we should not be anywhere near where we are. I open my faceplate. "Angel's frantic," I say.

"Fuck it. Take the wheel and get in line."

I get behind the wheel and roll us into the retreating caravan. Another volley of purple pulses lights up the dust; the platform will withdraw last.

"Have you uplinked any of this with orbital?" Joe asks.

"Maybe DJ sent up something, but unlikely."

He rubs the bridge of his nose. "Vinnie, tell me how long before it gets so bad we shit our pants." We monkey-grimace and laugh. The thing about skintights is it's no fun pissing or shitting your pants because it doesn't matter—that's what you do all the time. So to signal that we live in fear, to express that we've lost all hope and fuck the big stuff—we don't relax our rectums. We just laugh. But not too long.

Time for Joe's story.

"Big Hammer two days back, we dropped right around a comet strike zone, lots of sparkly, lost maybe two-thirds of our frames, but three sleds came down intact, carrying six Trundles, five General Pullers, fifteen Skells, and six Deuces, all fully charged—but only ninety-two Skyrines. Most of command hit hard. And so…" He taps the bloody half leaf. "We salvaged what we could."

Another pulse and we can see the outline of the Drifter ahead.

"How many can you cycle through at once, and how fast?" he asks.

"Ten troops through the personnel lock, plus maybe three Skells or two Tonkas through the big gate. A Chesty won't fit, and I doubt the Trundles will, either. There's another gate on the opposite side, about a mile around the head—the hill. Might be big enough to take more Tonkas and maybe the Chesty. If there's time, maybe we can unload the platform."

Joe doesn't take long to think it through. "Cycle all the troops first. We'll divert big stuff around the head."

My angel gives him precise southern gate coordinates and he passes them along. I broadcast plain and loud to the Drifter and hope DJ and Tak are on the alert and haven't been swept by Voors.

Then I look left, south, on the driver's side vid. Three banged-up Deuces and the Chesty are pulling out of line to go left around the head. I can just hear them rolling behind us. Rear vid shows four Skells and a Tonka passing our buggy to cross right over the lava and old mud, preceding us toward the Drifter's arm. They're carrying troops and will go first.

"We're in sad shape, Vinnie," Joe says. "Save our sorry assets, and I'll hook you up with my seester."

"It would be my honor."

"She's ugly as sin."

"*Sin* rhymes with *Venn*, sir."

"Fuck you."

Outside, the dust is clearing, revealing night-dark sand and an amazing starry sky. We spin around and I scan the opposite line through my faceplate magnifier. The movement of Antags has stopped, but a few bolts are still being thrown out from the trundle to a largely quiet and unmoving line. They're just sitting and taking it, waiting, like a row of wolves curious as to why the rabbits have turned and bared their teeth.

Not scared. Just curious.

"It's a big drive," I say. "What are they hauling?"

"Major hurt, we assume. No time to stop and peek under their skirts."

The settling dust opens a space between us and the Antags. They have big black Millies, long and segmented like millipedes, little round wheels reaching out on a hundred legs. Haven't seen Millies that big before—at least fifty meters long and ten meters wide. Each looks like it can carry a couple of platoons, and there are *lots*. Plenty of parallel rollers as well, like big massage wheels on a rope—some supporting hooks to anchor the aeros, which float a couple of hundred meters above the hardpan like fat, shadowy jellyfish. Weapon mounts squat on flatbeds very like our Trundles, ready to deploy tuned relaxers, neural exciters—cause us fits. We call them shit-rays. Could be used to ease capture. But mostly they're prelude to unbridled bouts of execution—converting paralyzed, befouled humans to stain on the Red.

"We ain't paid enough," Joe concludes, a sentiment so universal it doesn't even register.

I see one of our bigger bolts has carved a Millie right down the middle, lengthwise. At that distance, I can more imagine than actually see movement of the injured, the dying. Hope and imagination combine forces. *Die, die. Breathe out and boil whatever you have for lungs.*

"Why aren't they shooting?" I ask. It's unnatural, not returning heat.

"Patience," Joe says, shaking his head. He does not know, does not believe our luck, if luck it is and not a pregnant pause. The Antags have us right where they want us. Why not just blast away?

Are they afraid of damaging the Drifter?

"Two more Tonkas around the left," Joe says after the first pair have vanished beyond the left shoulder. They are followed by the General Puller—the Chesty. The big Trundle has stopped firing and is soon kicking up a plume behind the Chesty. If I were Joe, I'd station the Trundle and a couple of Deuces just around the northern slope of the Drifter.

And so he does.

But there's still no Antag response.

"I know just what they're going to do," Joe says. "They're going to wait until we're all inside, then they're going to nuke us from orbit and boil us like lobsters."

"Don't think that will work, Joe, sir," I say.

"Why the hell not?"

"Because it's big and deep."

And because they want the Drifter as much as we do?

"But nukes would seal us in, wouldn't they?"

"Maybe."

I ask myself what it would be like to live like moles forever, breathing green dust, struggling to raise crops in the faded glimmer of hydroelectric power from a hobo that's mostly drained away. What'll that give us, a couple of months before we start dining on raw Voor and I fight for Teal's honor, or the Antags dig us out—

Joe sees my pensive gaze. "Stop thinking, shithead," he says. "Sorry to engage your fucking intellect."

"Yes, sir."

"Is there food in there?"

"Some."

There've been no shots since our last platform-mounted bolt cutters. But now an aerostat is on the move above the northwestern horizon, like a small black cloud covering the stars. It will be over us in a few minutes.

Joe looks at me. The vehicles have no doubt piled up behind the lava ridge, at the northern gate. I very much doubt they can all cycle through before the aerostat rains needles.

"Tell them to abandon the last vehicles," I say to Joe. "Tell them to run to the lock and pack in like Vienna sausages. And do the same at the southern gate."

"Right," Joe says.

If the Antags can hear and understand, this will be fun. For them, this will be a rollicking slaughter of frantic little rats. Needles will do the trick—no need to waste energy or big ordnance. Then they can perch on the Drifter and wait out the survivors.

"Our turn, Vinnie," Joe says. We quickly round the clenched fist of the lava arm and come up on the Skells and Tonkas. Skyrines are leaping out and jogging toward the rusty gate. A quick glance behind shows the aero looming, no more than a few hundred meters until it can loose the first curtain of needles.

We seal helms and exit the buggy's rear lock together. The run is a blur—feet barely touching sand and dust and rock, skipping, stumbling, rolling and jouncing on the upswing, zigging by abandoned Skells and a Tonka, almost catching up with our fellows, around the rough point of the ridge, into the rocky harbor of the northern gate.

Get in line, except there is no line. Skyrines are bunched up waiting to cycle through. DJ must be crazy, I think, not opening the vehicle lock, the big gate—but then I see it yawn wide, the first crowd has cycled through, and another group packs in—all but twenty making it before there's absolutely no way to add more without crushing bone or getting caught in the hatch.

The lock closes.

Joe and I stay back. Eighteen others pace, cringing, in the embrace of the ridge.

"Find cover in the rocks!" I call over suit-to-suit.

Seven guys try to fit into one cubby large enough for two. Joe and I have found low ridges we can hide under, if we dig out some sand. I can see him across the harbor, not far from the gate.

Ten left out in the open.

The aero is at zenith. Three or four minutes at minimum until DJ can cycle and open a lock again.

We've done our best.

Puffs in the sand. Dozens of little plumes shoot up and fall back quick. The ten out in the open are running around like rats in a dog pit. I can barely hear their screaming. Then I can hardly see for all the needles, a gray haze of falling death. Our stragglers cover their heads with arms and groping hands, but it doesn't matter—one needle and you go crazy and then, at leisure, twitching on the dust, puff up until your skintight splits its seams.

I can't bear to watch.

Four gang up to yank two Skyrines from cover, but get kicked off, then give up and just stand slouched under the deluge, heads bowed, hands stiff by their sides. Needles make them flinch.

They look like hedgehogs.

Then they begin that slow, awful dance.

Four more flail out from cover, plucking needles that have swooped in and found them.

Big gate still sealed.

I close my eyes and pray.

LAST EXIT TO HELL

The apartment is cool, almost cold, and sunset outside the window is a faint gray-yellow over the Olympics beyond the sound. I've changed out of my robe into civvies, Hawaiian shirt, and jeans. Alice Harper stands by the big window, arms crossed. "Wherever man goes," she says, and clenches herself tighter, "history sucks."

Can't disagree. The bad shit builds as I resurrect these awful memories. I say, "Do you think Green Camp actually wanted to flush Teal out on the Red?" I want, I *need*, to change the subject.

"Absolutely," she says. "Rationals believe in tight intellectual order, total logic, everything determined, DNA is fate, blue-blooded pedigree is your only hope—Asians beat whites beat blacks and Hispanics. Like a bloody-minded religion, only don't tell them that. Everything statistical, mathematically sound... Atheists by law, strict dogmatists, reductionists...Techno-racists. Libertarianism pushed to the ultimate extreme." She lowers her arms.

I watch her, fascinated by her calm, her weird *enthusiasm*. I wish I could be like that, feel as she feels right now. *Anything* not to be *me*. I say, "Just doesn't make sense."

"Use your head. Someone like Teal who apparently insists on one man at a time…no sharesies…She's baggage. The top bitch would shove her out soon as spit."

That would be Ally Pecqua, I'm guessing. "Pretty harsh."

Alice Harper shrugs. "It only got worse when Earth cut the data and stopped sending supplies. Mars not making anybody money, couldn't pay their bills. Time to slice the umbilical. Might drive anyone over the edge."

"What in hell are we fighting for, then? If we don't give a shit about the Red, why not just leave it to the Antags?"

"Because Gurus…" She gives me a stern look. "Rhetorical question, right?"

My turn to shrug. "I'm still out there. In my head. I have to sort it out or I'll never come home."

"So tell me more. Tell me what happened with you and Teal," Alice says.

That's not easy. I'm having a hard time moving on, still locked on the image of my fellow Skyrines dancing under that curtain of darts, until the aero passes over, circling at the end of its drag-line, and the rain stops.

It's coming back to me now in full force, that awfulness. I'm sweating heavy. I stink like a gymnasium full of wrestlers.

———

JOE BREAKS COVER and makes a run for the personnel lock gate. He starts pounding on it. Me and four guys join him, we're all pounding. I can't hear my fist hitting the hatch. I can't hear anything. I'm too busy looking down at my arms, my legs, too busy inspecting myself.

Then I stop. My heart stops.

There's a dart on my forearm.

Jesus.

Joe sees it, too. He doesn't pull it out, doesn't touch it, neither do I, because I'm not going crazy, it's only just pierced the skintight, might not have touched my skin, it was a ricochet, maybe, and hasn't yet pumped its poison.

Or it *has*, and adrenaline is just holding back the symptoms. Medics say that can happen.

My fingers reach down. Can't just leave it there.

Joe grabs my hand, then pushes his head in close to mine and looks through our faceplates straight into my eyes. "Don't," he says.

The smaller gate begins to grind open. We squeeze through the opening as it grows. The survivors are packed tight inside the lock by the time the aero is guided back over the shoulders of the Drifter. Everyone jostles, trying to get to the far side while the outer door closes. Joe makes a fence with his arms around me so nothing and nobody can jam the dart home.

My ears and throat feel pressure return.

The inner door opens and we spill out. Joe holds my clean arm, still gripping my hand, and we slowly spin like we're waltzing, because I'm trying to reach for the dart, and he's stopping me from doing that.

Pressure reaches Drifter max.

The other Skyrines see I'm darted. They stand clear of us, pushing at the inner door, which cracks open, slides slowly into the wall, and Skyrines exit, move through, but Joe still holds my hand, and I stop us spinning.

Hold out my darted arm.

"I'm not going to touch it," Joe says. "You know why."

"Up and down," I say, hardly able to draw breath. That's what the darts can do. Push up a *second* needle through the fletches and stick a would-be rescuer.

I'm on the couch with Alice.

I'm in the inner lock with Joe, my arm hurts, my muscles burn like fury.

I want to cry, *on the couch.*

I am crying, *in the lock, in my helm.* Sobbing like a baby.

We're through.

We're in the garage.

One of the Skyrines hands Joe a small needle-nose pliers. Good name. Part of someone's drop kit, maybe the gift of a relative before his transvac, use this, son, to pull out those sonofabitching things. Joe holds my arm steady, the tips of the pliers hover, he's shaking, I'm shaking, dear God don't push it down.

Jesus *don't even touch it.*

Then, he's got it. He lifts. He doesn't start shaking until the needle is out. He doesn't fling it aside. He doesn't drop it. Training kicks in after the near panic. Another Skyrine holds open a small silver bag. Joe deposits the dart into the bag and pats my shoulder. "We can't go back that way, not on foot," he says matter-of-factly.

The rocky harbor is littered with active darts.

———

ALICE LISTENS AND says nothing.

"I stink," I say.

"Please go on. Tell me what you can, what you feel like telling."

Christ, I *really* want Joe to walk through the apartment door. Jesus and God and Mary and Buddha and St. Emil Kapaun, I want that. If Joe doesn't come home, maybe I never will.

SKY BASIC

To go from an infant race of ground huggers to a force capable of fighting on other worlds, humans were handed a decent selection of Guru gifts, including of course spent matter technology, but also a thorough understanding of our own biology, chemistry, and psychology.

I suppose the Gurus knew us better than we knew ourselves. I've never met one—never met anyone who has—but I imagine them as wizened, wise, tall, and graceful, but tough sons of bitches to have survived their own long voyage across the awesome distances between the stars.

They knew our limits, political, biological, psychological. And so they helped us formulate Cosmoline, that greenish gel in which we are all packed and preserved like fruits in a can, not awake, not asleep, but not cold—not frozen—just quiet and contented while the space frames carry us to where we're going.

Some of us call it Warm Sleep. Old-timers will remember that Cosmoline was a patented petroleum-based product that helped keep rifles and guns and equipment from rusting. Not at all the same; a clever marketing wizard simply transferred the name and it stuck.

The chemistry behind our version of Cosmoline helped foster a thousand medical advances, of course. So it was one of those Guru swords that were already plowshares. In space, nobody had to rust or corrupt—not if they were wrapped in Cosmoline.

I've already described some of the side effects, but there are others, much worse. About one time in a hundred thousand, Cosmoline induces a complicated cascade of negative reactions. I've only seen it once. A space frame delivered a platoon of healthy Skyrines to orbit around the Red—along with one tube filled with corrupt Jell-O. Did the occupant die on impact? During the journey? Nobody explained, nobody asked questions. War is hell. We are all grateful not to remember the months we spend in the long rise to Mars.

Of far more concern to the usual breed of ecological worry-warts is spent matter tech. The Gurus knew how to suck all the life, if not quite all the energy, out of elements heavier than carbon and calcium. By reaching down to their inner electron shells and messing with a few quantum constants, atoms can be induced to give up a startling amount of nonnuclear energy. No neutrons, no deadly radiation, just remarkable amounts of pure power—but the resulting dead, *spent* mass is incredibly toxic. It's still matter, still behaves something like what it used to be, but that behavior is deceptive. Deadly. It's gone zombie. Spent matter waste has to be disposed of thoroughly and completely—in secure orbit. It should not be stockpiled on Earth or stored on Mars, and it should just not be shot willy-nilly into space.

Some have said that at the end of its energy draw, spent matter is toxic in terms of physics as well as chemistry. Dropped into the sun, into any star, spent matter might start a nasty chain reaction—literally slowing and then killing the sun's pulsing fusion heart. I don't know about that. But I do know that war is messy, and there are canisters of spent matter all over Mars, and probably in orbit as well, so the long-term consequences of Guru tech are still unknown. We should all hope the worrywarts are wrong and nothing will happen to the sun. But for the last couple of hundred years, some of those worrywarts have been spot-on.

Still, Gurus seemed delighted to help us recover from our own ignorance and greed...providing free visions of a boundless and bright future.

Until they told us about the Ants and recruited us to help fight their war. And their war became our war.

BACKING UP NOW

I thought I'd leap over to the good stuff, the easy stuff, all technical and shit, but that's not how it's going to be.

I just have to tough it out.

I cannot escape the burn from what happened in that embracing arm of sand-blasted lava, that little harbor of shelter outside the Drifter's western gate, filled with Joe's buddies. That may be the most horrible thing I've ever seen—Skyrines trying to pull each other out of cover to avoid the rippling curtains of plunging, swooping, *seeking* germ needles.

Fear is a drug you need to survive. Without fear, you die quicker; that's part of basic, that's what the old guys instill in us when we're fledglings waiting and eager to fly; fear is your friend, but only in controlled doses, never in such flooding waves that you panic. Panic kills you quicker than bullets. Panic turns you into doomed animals.

We panicked, all of us, in the embrace of that drowning giant's thick lava arm: those under cover, those out in the open, didn't matter. We would have killed each other rather than face the goddamned needles, and now that stokes my rage, the rage that eats me inside, that makes me less than a human being forever after, not just because I've seen my fellow Skyrines die horribly, but because I was forced to *want them to die* instead of me. I felt that little exultation that no needle was going to hit me, that I'd live to fuck again, maybe fuck their girlfriends, sympathy call, howdy, reporting to duty, sorry, ma'am, he's not coming back, but *I'm* here…

Fuck it! Fuck it all. I have so much rage at myself, at the Antags, at everything that made me grow up to be a Skyrine, a fighter across the stars, a heroic asshole coward who gave up being a sappy, naïve kid to fight in so many battles, only to finally panic on the Red, and then, like God is wagging His stony white finger at me, *shit*, that needle on my arm, just waiting to plunge in, you did not escape, you piss-scared little fuckwad, it's still *here*, and it's going to *get* you and eat you and you'll bloat up and burst, but only after you go crazy and somebody has to shoot you to keep you from hurting everyone.

Inside the dark, stone-walled garage…

Expletive expletive expletive. No words bad enough to convey that rage. No such language for what I am, what I feel. Just conjure up a deep, noisy silence, red with flashes of…why red? Not rage! Just deep, holy, animal disappointment, like what every gazelle must feel that falls to a lion, like any dinosaur that heard its sinews snapping and bones crunching under the razor teeth of a *T. rex*. First you panic, and then you die, one way or another.

I am no better than dead meat, broken, rotting, carrion, but I'm still here, still ambulatory. I just can't really tell the tale, not completely.

Not truthfully.

I died.

I did not die.

I keep trying to get back to the main current of our story, to the Drifter. But I'm going over history, technicalities, the kind of pop science deemed fit to stuff into a warrior's skull. Alice with her stiff, sad, not very sympathetic look confirms I'm just churning, I'm not getting my point across; she doesn't get it; she needs to change the subject.

"You were going to tell me about the caves," she says, looking out the big window. "I assume that means the crystals, the silicon plague. The Church," she adds.

She knows about the Church.

Okay. So that works. That knocks me loose. The beauty and strangeness and even those additional moments of horror, way down in the bowels of the Drifter. Sure. It's that easy, isn't it? Wonder trumps rage and panic.

Now my anger turns, quick as a bunny, into laughter. I laugh out loud, to her irritation, but it *is* funny. She wants the nougat center without the hard candy shell. Go straight to the point, skip all the spiky, nettle-wrapped stuff that makes us feel shitty and inadequate, that makes *me* feel and look and smell like a...

What? What am I now, other than a survivor, a lost Skyrine completely dead inside?

Something more.

Something *quite* different, thank you. Reliving the whole needle bit has reawakened snakes in my head. Snakes with broken glass for scales. But really, tell the truth, Vinnie old fellow— that isn't actually *it*, is it?

Strong tea. That's what DJ called it.

Green tea.

Ice moon tea.

Like Teal, only first gen, but nobody knows. There is redemption if I give in. But will it be *me* that survives?

My resolution sets up into concrete, but not the way either of us expected. "I'm done here," I tell her. "You aren't the one I need to talk to."

Alice turns her head, frowning. "I'm sorry," she says. "What can I do to—?"

"We're done. I won't explain."

"We need to know what you know," she says, angry roses on her cheeks.

"Get someone who's been there," I say. "Someone who doesn't think I'm crazy or about to be. I'll tell it to them, maybe."

"I don't think that," Alice says. "Honestly, I don't."

"Why did they send just you? Why not the whole committee?"

"There's a committee?" she asks.

"Yeah, there's a committee, all ready to overturn the system, set it right, just get them the information, listen to me confess to what I saw out there. Sure, they'll use us to overthrow the system—then shoot us in the back of the head and toss us aside. Like the Kronstadt sailors." Fidge me, how did *that* get in there?

"I don't understand," Alice says slowly. "You know that Joe wanted me to come here and talk to you."

"What's his moniker? His tag?"

"Sanka," Alice says. "Teal would say that was his nick."

I very slowly deflate. Letting out the snakes, maybe. Sucking down to what's actually going to happen, nothing I can do about it. I don't know what to think or feel.

"You know where he is," I say, but without conviction.

"I wish I did," Alice says. "There was just a delayed message. And there is no committee, not yet anyway…Just a beginning, a suspicion, that maybe there's something I can do, we can do."

"No committee?"

"None. We're too ignorant and stupid to be organized," she says, and I see she means it, and her tell is the cold disappointment that she's ineffective, that she's as ignorant as she says.

"Sorry," I say. But I still won't look at her. I wish she would go away and leave me to the Eames chair and the night and the endless lines of ferries and freighters. What we fight for.

"I wish Joe were here," Alice says softly. "Or another Sky-rine, like you say, someone who can understand what you've been through, because I *can't*. I won't say I can. I never will. *I don't want to feel what you're feeling, ever.* All right?"

That's honest. Still deflating. The snakes haven't left, but they've settled down a little.

The *other*, though...

My new memories, the oldest memories of all. Maybe I like it. Maybe this great, expanding volume of memories makes me more than what I am, provides a bigger refuge for my broken soul.

Alice's eyes are targeting *me*, holding me there in the chair, and suddenly, I like it, I like being targeted and pinned by this zaftig female in our clean steel and blue apartment, earned by all that money, all that comp. She's got some strength and she's not as arrogant as I thought.

Best of all, she doesn't want to understand.

Good. Fine.

But still silent. Frozen.

"I can leave you here and come back later," she says after a minute, "maybe when Joe gets here. Or I can just leave for good. Let you be."

I have no idea what expression suddenly comes to my face, but it makes her jump, startled. I lean forward, my voice a lit-tle high. "There's something very strange happening to us, to Earth, isn't there?" I ask. "With the Gurus and the Antags and going out to the Red."

"Hell, yes," she says, eyes flashing. "You're just starting to realize that?"

"Some things are coming together, maybe. I'm almost there now."

Another pause. We're watching each other, hawk and mouse, mouse and hawk.

"Then take me along, please, if you can, take me there with you," Alice says. "Maybe then we can start unwinding all the threads and figure out what we've got ourselves into. Maybe *then* there can be a committee, and you'll be on it."

I grit my teeth and shake my head. "No committees. We got a get out a here. I need a walk somewheres."

She narrows one eye at the accent. "Okay." She gets up, ready to go, but I'm still sitting.

"Yesterday, a grandma in a blue electric car gave me a ride and told me her son became a hero on Titan," I say. "Know anything about that?"

Alice shakes her head. But the merest shift in her frown says, maybe that wasn't good, maybe that shouldn't have happened.

"Why would she know that, why would anybody tell her?" I ask. Then my thoughts focus. "She said she was a colonel's secretary. At SBLM. Maybe that's how she knew. The brass told her. A security slip, too much sympathy, but they tell her."

Alice lifts her hand a few inches, noncommittal.

"Titan!" I say. "That's out around Saturn. That's out by the rings and shit, one and a half billion klicks across the vac. That's out where a *lot* of the moons are covered with ice, isn't it? Deep ice, with liquid oceans underneath—some of them?"

Alice takes a deep breath. "We both need a break," she says, standing. "I'll buy groceries, if you'll let me fix something to eat."

"There's not much here that isn't spoiled," I admit. The room feels lighter. The air is sweeter. Maybe I'm okay.

Maybe we're just putting off the rough shit for another couple of hours. But that's good, isn't it?

"Can I buy the groceries, Master Sergeant Venn?" she asks very softly.

"Yeah. I'll stay here."

She's firm. She insists. "I'd like you to accompany me to the market. I'd like you to go shopping with me, Vinnie."

I pretend to think that over. I'm acting like a child. To tell this story, to live as a whole man after this moment, I have to go back to being a child. Feels funny and right at the same time. All us Skyrines are children, before, during, and even *inside* the end. So the experienced ones tell us. The DIs and veterans.

"I went to the market soon as I got back," I say.

"What did you buy?"

"Celery."

"And obviously, nothing else. So...shall we go?"

I do like it at the market. There're other children, and the old bronze pig, and toys. Doughnuts. Pastries. Jerky. Fruit and candy. I need to stand up and walk around and maybe eat more celery.

Why celery? I think I know. Ritual. As a kid, I loved celery. My mother would hand me a stalk filled with bright orange Cheez Whiz, whenever she made a salad. She'd smile at me, perfect love, tree to apple, simple, no judgment. I was just a kid and she was my mom.

Welcome home.

I don't want to cry now or get lost in myself.

I get up. Alice takes gentle hold of my elbow.

"Let's go to the market," she says. "Let's walk there and then walk back. It's only a couple of miles. If you have the legs for it."

MOVING FORWARD AGAIN

have the legs.

I enjoy the air, the streets, the hill down to the market, the climb back, though it makes my knees wobble. I enjoy walking beside Alice Harper, who takes it all without breaking a sweat or one little huff, Earth girl that she is; she looks zaftig, but it's muscle and no small determination all bundled up and concentrated.

I enjoy walking. I enjoy walking with her.

Nobody pays us much attention.

I'm starting to smell like a human being again.

At the old fish stall, where the guys and the ladies still flash naked biceps and fling salmon to each other, Alice buys whole cooked crab and clams and cod and snapper, and after, we walk down a hallway to a smaller indoor shop lined with dark wooden shelves, where she picks out herbs and spices and the clerk scoops them out of glass jars into little plastic bags; Alice is sure we don't have such back at the apartment—we don't—and she says she's going to make a good fish stew, *cioppino*, if that's okay, if I like fish stew. I probably do, I don't know. It's been so long since I've been served a home-cooked meal.

The walk back is easier. I carry the groceries.

This is nice.

But I still refuse to trust her. I just can't. It's far too dangerous, with what I have bottled up inside me.

———

I SIT ON a bar stool at the kitchen counter while Alice works. "This is a great kitchen," she says. "You guys should use it to do more than microwave pizza."

"We never spend a lot of time here," I say. "After a few days, after we stop stinking and get our land legs back, we go out."

"Hunting?" she asks with a wry face.

"Yeah," I say. "Or just looking. Cosmoline—takes the edge off for a while, you know. One of the downsides of transvac. Or the benefits, if you're a monk."

"Pushes you back from the responsibility of acting human?" she asks, with a quiet tone I can't read, and a side look as she chops the celery and tomatoes and begins to simmer a fish stock of scraps she bought at the market. I can smell again, it's mostly back. Being able to smell is half the job of coming home. I can smell Alice beneath the rose perfume. It's not like she smells sexy, not yet, but smelling her is a treat, a revelation.

"It's okay," I say. "We're not very good company for a few days. You'll vouch for that."

"I will," she says, terse but not judgmental. She puts a lid on the simmering pot, after adding more onions and celery. She snaps off a stalk and passes it across the counter to me. I hold it, look it over. Nothing like it on the Red. Nothing so crisp and fresh, nothing this crisp and alive, even after it's been pulled from the bunch and trimmed. Likely Teal has never bitten into a stalk of celery. Nothing like this for decades to come, probably.

If ever. How brave was that, for the Muskies to fly out to the Red, knowing what they'd leave behind, just to see something new, something few humans had ever seen?

"When company was coming," Alice says, apropos of nothing, "my mother used to lay out a tray of celery stuffed with Cheez Whiz."

That makes nice sparks burst in my head, lovely bits of glow, soft and gentle, like a thousand little night-lights following me around in the dark. "Really?"

"True salt of the Earth. Emphasis on the salt." Alice smiles and keeps adding to the pot. Onions, olive oil, garlic, saffron, so many fresh herbs I can't count, black pepper, white pepper... bewildering.

She turns down the heat, watching me with a light, open-lipped grin.

I lift the celery, fence the air.

"Yeah," she says, and taps the pot with a wooden spoon, also purchased at the market, and fences back. Celery crosses spoon. Spoon wins. I finish off my losing weapon.

"This will take a while," she says, putting down the spoon, "but I guarantee, it'll be the best you ever tasted." She reaches into the last canvas bag and lifts out a bottle of white wine, natural grapes, no GM stuff—not cheap. She pours a good splash into the pot.

Then, she asks, lifting the bottle, "Ready?"

My body does not cringe.

"We have juice glasses," I say.

"Poor boys."

It's getting dark outside. Another sol is passing—I mean, another day. So *unreal*. The apartment smells wonderful. I'm not sweating, I'm not shaking, my legs are almost back to normal, memories a little less jagged.

Not that the worst part is over. I was hoping *that* was the worst part, but I know it isn't. In jerks and starts, I try to continue. My voice is steady—for a while.

She pours a couple of juice glasses. We hoist, toast Earth, the Red, all of it: the dead, the living, the irrational and unfinished. Silent but comprehensive. The wine tastes good. Crisp, green, like rain over spring hills. Alice pours the fish stock through a spaghetti basket, puts aside the bones and shriveled fish heads—stuff that brings back bad memories. Could be like what fills the skintight of a Skyrine stuck with a germ needle…

Then she whisks the scraps aside and returns the stock to the pot, adds more vegetables, sluices in a little more wine.

"Never enough wine," she murmurs. "Fish and crabs come next, in a few minutes. Clams at the very last. They're still alive…"

She pulls back, regretting that bit of information, but it's not life and death per se, or going into the pot, that gets to me.

"Tender morsels," I say.

We return to couch and chair.

"How are the legs?" she asks. "Sore?"

"Steady."

Alice crosses her legs, holds up the last of her wine in the twilight, suspended in her fingers, city lights twinkling in the juice glass. I manage to say some things. Then more things. It doesn't hurt as much.

She gets up to add the fish and crab. In a few minutes, she adds the clams, and a few minutes later, serves it up. Oh my God. It is good. I eat four bowls. Airplanes pass in the night sky. A double-egg and hawksbill crosses the Sound, heading for SBLM. More Skyrines returning from the vac. I put down my bowl and stifle a tremendous belch. First time I've done that in modern memory.

"I'm ready," I say.

And she listens.

WHAT THE BIG BOYS WANT YOU TO KNOW

There are thirty-two of us in the garage, including DJ, still up in the high booth, and Tak, who's standing clear of the new arrivals, the survivors, and standing clear of me; we might have more darts. Before they had to close up for good, before the shower of germ needles, they managed to bring in twenty-three of Joe's troops, three Skell-Jeeps, and two medium-sized Tonkas. Teal's buggy and a few of the smaller vehicles are still outside, some in the shelter of the giant's arm, but they all might as well be gone.

We don't know if any of the other vehicles and big weapons made it around to the southern gate.

Joe tells Tak to check us over and don't touch anyone.

One of the new Skyrines, the one with the needle pouch, fishes a handful of fresh pouches out of his leggings and gets ready to receive more. Tak does a thorough job of checking us over, telling us to spin, lift our arms and then our legs, show the soles of our boots. All our skintights are clean, no rips, no poke marks.

DJ descends from the booth.

"Got water? New filters?" Joe asks.

"I'll look," DJ says. He sounds sad, guilty to walk among the strung-out newbies, who are still shivering and wild-eyed. He climbs up into a Skell-Jeep and rummages through the bins, manages to retrieve a clutch of filter pads, then climbs onto a Tonka, accesses the heating system, drains clean water into a can, and passes it around.

One of the newbies—Corporal Vita Beringer, young, baby-faced, and almost completely zoned, is slowly, methodically trying to peel out of her skintight. Joe slaps her hand down, reseals a loose seam, tells her she's better off for now keeping it on. We don't know whether the Voors can selectively flush air in the Drifter—suffocate us. I know he's thinking that, but he doesn't say it out loud. He just knows when's the right time to be blunt, and when it's better to be quiet and soft. Gently persistent. Joe is good that way.

DJ tells me, in an aside, that he doubts the outer gate can withstand much of an assault. No news there. "They're pretty rusty," he says. "I wonder the Antags aren't already knocking."

"They're patient," I say. "No need to rush in."

Or is it some other reason? They can skip around the Drifter, leave it alone, leave us here, if they want. Island hopping. I suppose the Drifter is the closest thing to an island there is on the Red.

Joe approaches us, waves Tak over, tells us to gather behind a Tonka, away from the others. He and Tak served together three or four times, shared a few weeks of OCS prep at McGill. We huddle behind the Tonka like boys getting ready to play marbles and brief Joe on what little we know about the Drifter, transfer what little knowledge we have managed to collect.

"Thanks for the reception," he says. "Our drop was a shitty

blender. Sisters and brothers, different frames, broken platoons. All mixed up."

"De nada, sir," Tak says. "Par for this course."

Joe points down. "How deep is this thing?"

"More than a mile, maybe a lot more," I say. "Deep mining interrupted by a hobo—a wandering subsurface river. It's been flooded up to here for at least twenty years, Earth years—but now the water has subsided, opening up the workings. We haven't been down very far." I lift my hands. "It's mostly guesswork."

"How far has anyone gone?" Joe asks.

"DJ's been back and forth a couple of times to the southern gate," I say. "Teal took me through a few side tunnels. There are a couple of watchtowers, lookouts, up in the head—the mound. The western gate is welded shut. The eastern gate was supposed to be closed up and welded as well, but that could be where a second pack of Voors entered."

"We don't know that for sure," Tak says. "But it makes sense."

"Settler equipment and supplies?"

"A depositor mothballed in a side chamber. Looks to be in decent shape."

"Barrels of slurry?"

"Some. Maybe a lot."

"We have to check that out," Joe says. "We have to secure whatever resources we can find. So...DJ knows his way around."

"And can operate the southern gate," I say.

We'll end up repeating what Gamecock tried to do, but we have no choice. And maybe the newbies will do it better.

"First order of business—let's send a welcoming party to the southern garage. Then let's get the fuck away from here before Ants come knocking."

Tak calls over three of the survivors, a tall major named Jack Ackerly, an equally string-bean warrant officer named George

Brom, as well as a shorter corporal, a sister, Shelby Simca. As the trio stands at attention, Joe reaches to open his faceplate, as if to rub his eye or his nose, but Simca stops him with a cautionary hand.

"Dust, sir," she says. "We haven't had time to brush down."

"Right," Joe says. "Thanks. You two go with Corporal Johnson, DJ—accompany him to the southern gate and let in as many of our team and big vehicles as you can, post guard, then reconnoiter. Leave bread crumbs. One of you will return and report. We'll rendezvous halfway."

"Yes, sir," Simca says, and the trio runs off to gather up DJ. I'm sure he'll be delighted to have company.

Joe lays down more orders to the rest to form up, prep weapons, charge bolts, finish stripping the Skell-Jeeps and Tonkas of supplies—make ready to move out.

"Let's not join our friends right away," Joe says to the assembled troops. The specters of dead, bloated Skyrines on the other side of that lock are enough to motivate everybody. After what they've just been through, the newbies move fast.

Joe rejoins us behind the Tonka. "What the hell happened?" he asks. "Vinnie shot some of it at me on the Red, but we were distracted. Give it to me again, slower."

Tak takes a stab at summing up. "A month ago, Sky Defense must have dropped a battalion of Eurasians on the Red, to prep and defend fountains, cache weapons, get ready for later drops."

"You found them?" Joe asks.

"Some," Tak says. "All dead, at first. We found a few tents, one darted but two functional, enough to keep us alive. No working fountains. Then Lieutenant Colonel Roost found us, he was driving a Skell, alongside a Korean general. They took us over to where more survivors, mostly Eurasian brass, had holed up around an old, broken fountain. They had a command tent but not much in the way of resources, not for so many. Mostly injured, some severely. The fountain was beyond repair, at least with what we had. By the time a Muskie buggy arrived—"

"Driven by Vinnie's girlfriend," Joe says.

"She's from a settlement called Green Camp," I pick up, ignoring the gibe. "A refugee—an outcast. Her name is Teal. She saved us just as we were about to crap out on the Red. The only survivor from the command tent was the Korean major general, named Kwak. Kwak and Gamecock, Tak, Kazak, DJ, Neemie, Vee-Def, Michelin—she picked us up, shared air and water and filters, and transported us here. She called it the eastern Drifter.

"Shortly after, Captain Coyle and her troops arrived at the southern gate. Another scattered drop, I guess. They forcibly hitched a ride with less savory settlers, the Voors. The Voors were also coming to the Drifter, maybe to intercept Teal."

"Voors—Voortrekkers?" Joe asks again, and there's a glint in his eye, the same glint I saw the first time he asked—as if this was not unexpected.

"Yeah. Then, while Tak and I were outside—something happened inside. All but DJ vanished. He didn't see or hear a thing. We'd asked him to go outside the southern gate and try to establish a satlink."

"Vinnie thinks another wagon full of Voors showed up, maybe at the eastern gate, and took our people by surprise," Tak says. "But that gate was supposed to be welded shut. We just don't know what the hell happened."

Joe looks down at the green dust, scrapes it with his glove tip. Rubs the dust between his fingers. Most of it sifts to the floor. "How come we didn't detect the Ant forces in solar orbit? Flying downsun to intercept Mars?"

"How come we didn't detect comets?" I add.

"Fucking shambles," Joe says tightly. "Lousy coordination,

crappy intelligence. If we get back, I am definitely going to write a letter."

We update Joe on the character of the Voors, who could become a second front in our little set-to.

"They hate us, I get that," Joe says, "but enough to destroy all chances of survival?"

"Maybe," I say. "The patriarch, de Groot, is a real strutter. His son, Rafe, may be more sensible. The others...pretty strung out—and in mourning. They lost their settlement to the comets. They may be the last of their kind."

Joe's eyes get bigger. "Are the Voors expecting to team up with the Ants?" He looks us over with his wild, pale stare, and I hope I'm not seeing the last hope drain out of him, because frankly, we're all going to need a little of that, just a sip, from his cup.

"I doubt it," I say. "They won't be beholden to anything or anybody."

"Just like my pappy," Joe says, slipping into drawl. "Biggest sonofabitch in Memphis, ran a plumbing outfit, cheated on his customers and his women, never paid his taxes, but at least he wasn't a fucking joiner."

Tak and I reward him with weak grins. Joe's pappy is famous—and various. Joe never knew his father.

"Who's on top of our pyramid?" he asks with a sniff, and covers the silver leaf with his hand.

"Gamecock."

"Never here when you need them. Let's grab our shit and move."

Just then, to emphasize our situation, the outer lock doors resound like they've been hit with a fistful of boulders. It doesn't take us long to gather what supplies we can carry and abandon the northern garage.

TWO BALLS, ONE HEAD—YOU'RE GOOD TO GO

The reconnaissance group sends Ackerly back. We meet him a third of the way through the tunnel going south, just where a side jog took Teal and me to the first lookout. All clear to the southern gate, Ackerly says. DJ worked the locks and brought in the survivors who made it around the Drifter's shoulders.

"Needles fell in a second wave from the aero. They were caught outside, trying to get from the Tonkas and the Trundle. We lost all but two of the Tonkas and couldn't fit the Trundle. The Chesty is inside, but it's badly damaged."

"How many got in?" Joe asks.

Ackerly lowers his eyes. "Thirteen," he says.

Joe's lips work. He turns to Tak and me. "We have to assess, find out how many can fight, get our teams back in order," he says. "Then we have to locate Captain Coyle and the Voors."

Ackerly leads us to the southern gate. The thirteen new arrivals are of all persuasions, all walks of life, all colors, tired and stretched to breaking, but all are beautiful. Six corporals, three sergeants, a warrant officer—CW5, black eagle eyes surrounded by wrinkles; could be outstanding, another major, a tough-looking first sergeant, and another captain who's too zoned and beat up to do anybody any good.

In addition, we now have two lawnmowers, six heavy bolt rifles, eight boxes of spent matter cartridges, and kinetic projectiles of all sorts. Plus the Chesty—the General Puller, a long, narrow tan and red carriage sitting on eight tall wheels, supporting four side-mounted Aegis 7 kinetic cannons and the big draw: a triple-rail, chained-bolt ballista—but only ten percent charge remaining.

Joe asks how many of the new group have more than a few minutes' reserves in their suits. Two hold up their hands. We start distributing the filters and tanks taken from all the vehicles, including the Voor wagons. The survivors are quiet, trying to deal with their emotions, their short-term shock response to what they've been through. The usual acid mind-burn that comes after an engagement, when there is still no relief, no chance to really think, just adrenaline and bad shit dogging us while we run and pretend that we're still iron-ass Skyrines and not damaged goods.

It's going to take some real leadership to bring us back up to snuff. Joe picks the warrant officer, Wilhelmina Brodsky, a tough old bird with a face carved from teak. Brodsky is given the task of organizing new fire teams. Tak helps with the distribution of hand weapons. Not all of the weapons will be carried by rated Skyrines, but we'll make do.

"We're going to defend this gate with all we have," Joe says. "Most will stay here for now, rest up, scrub suits." He turns to Tak. "I want to station three sentinels just before the northern gate. Comm doesn't seem to work very well down here, so make sure they can all run fast. Vinnie, pick three. Then, I need to know about that eastern gate, and wherever the hell everyone else might have gone."

DJ says he understands the tunnels pretty well around here, and even down a few levels. I ask how he knows that.

"I seduced the panel in the southern watchtower," he says. The same place that Teal took me when we saw the Voors arriving. "Time on my hands while you were out on the playground. All dead-dude crypto. I got me some pretty pictures."

"Upload?"

"Eyeballs only. No way to link, like I said."

"But your angel recorded, right?"

"Some of it. Then the console crapped out—all the displays went blank. But it's still up here." He taps his head—not the angel, the skull beneath his helm. I remember Teal saying that the digs continued even while the Drifter was deserted, even while it was flooded. I say nothing about that. No sense confusing people with things I haven't seen and don't yet understand.

"Eastern gate open and receiving visitors?" I ask DJ.

"If the Voors or the Algerians welded it shut, they didn't inform the console," DJ says. "But the map says it's definitely there. Entrance lies about five hundred meters that way," he points to our right, then down, "and fifteen meters below… Comes in at a heavy mining level, meant to receive big equipment, maybe send out shipments of ore."

"Any visitors logging in or out?"

"I asked the booth AI about that multiple ways, but no joy, no grief, nothing one way or the other."

"Can we get there from here? No flooding, no other obstructions?"

"I think so," DJ says, thoughtful.

"Can the booth AI here tell us if someone breaks through the northern gate?"

DJ shrugs. "It really doesn't seem to care. It's pretty old and worn-out."

"Sentinels," I say to Joe. Brodsky continues putting together teams. She enlists Tak to help refresh two teams on the rifles.

"Yeah," Joe says. "DJ, stay here and tell them how not to get lost." DJ does his best.

Joe sends Beringer, Stanwick, and the burned-out Captain Victor Gallegos north, then leans against a wall and makes motions like he wants to smoke a cigarette. A couple of minutes of this odd charade and he's up straight, brushing the imaginary cigarette against the wall. I've never known him to smoke.

"Now, Vinnie...can we go take a look around?"

I lead Joe back to the southern watchtower. The console is indeed dead, so we pull down the periscope and do a 360. Soon enough, we understand our situation. The Drifter is surrounded by a solid circle of Antags standing back at about a klick, black Millies lined up with the big shiny heads forward, like a string of beads draped over the hardpan—platforms just behind them, dark gray with faint gleams of light as they are charged and tended by their gun crews. A full division, if we can effectively judge Antag order of battle—at least five infantry brigades carried and supported by over a hundred Millies, six mobile weapons battalions, other groups we can't make out to the rear of the forward forces.

They've completed the perimeter—and haven't just bunched up before the gates. Holding all fire. Waiting. A hell of a lot more than enough to obliterate us. If we decide to break out.

Not cautious. Confident.

Fucking arrogant.

Joe pushes up and stows the periscope with a grim look. "They could take this place in an hour," he murmurs. "What the fuck are they waiting for?"

"Orders?" I suggest. "Maybe they're as screwed up with tactical as we are."

"They're just playing with us, I think. Cat-and-mouse." His hands keep clenching. He hasn't slept since maybe before their drop. He whispers, "Take DJ and Brom and Ackerly and reconnoiter the eastern gate. Check integrity, evidence of another Voor team—wagons, supplies, whatever. Explore at will, grab what you can, expand on DJ's map—and get back as soon as you can."

"What do we do if we encounter the Voors?" I ask.

"Avoid getting killed," Joe says, eyelids heavy. "Tell them the truth—if we don't pull together, we're all going to die in here."

Back to the southern gate. Tak sees Joe's situation and takes him away from me, arm over his shoulder, with a backward glance.

"Take a break, sir. Five minutes," Tak says to him.

Rugged.

"Ackerly, Brom, DJ—on me," I say.

ANT FARM

When I was a kid, I used to love ant farm tales—the kind of stories where a clutch of ordinary folk are cooped up on an island or isolated in something strange, like a giant overturned ocean liner or a lost starship, whatever—didn't matter. Cooped up, the people all started to act like ants in an ant farm, digging out trails through the sand between the mysterious plastic walls, acting out little dramas, retracing familiar old trails, bumping into each other—like that. And what I loved was, all the inhabitants of the ant farm seemed oblivious to any larger drama, careless of what the farm might actually be—a child's toy, for example. Most of the characters hardly gave a damn about the big idea of their situation, paid the large questions almost no attention, because, I guess, it was insoluble at their level of information and smarts and faced with that, we all revert to what we do best—socialize, mate, preen, strut, fight, talk a lot, wonder a lot. Ant farm stories are just like life. We have no idea why we're here, what we're doing alive, or even where we are, but *here* we are, doing our best to make do.

And that's another reason I prefer not to think of the Antags as Ants. Because if I do, then it means they've somehow managed to escape *their* glass walls, their farm, and cross the stars. Ants are peering in at our solar system. Peering in at *us*, on Mars, stuck in the Drifter.

Wonder what they think of us? Do they pity us, so backward and *stuck*?

SNKRAZ.

Note to self: Stop thinking. Follow orders. Rely on training. Those are a Skyrine's protective glass walls.

DJ takes the lead again, right up to a tunnel that veers abruptly to our right. "This way," he says. Brom and Ackerly exchange glances with me as they pass. Our guide whistles. The sound echoes eerily ahead. All Tom Sawyer stuff to DJ. Gotta love him. Drives me nuts.

A few minutes, and we arrive at a wide spot in the tunnel, with a railing surrounding a shaft about seven meters wide. The walls of the shaft have been carved to shape a steep flight of steps, a spiral staircase, like something Basil Rathbone and Errol Flynn would have a sword fight on, running up and down—the first of a number of such shafts and far from the worst.

The deeper we descend, many meters, maybe a hundred or more, the shinier and more purely metallic the walls become, reflecting our flaring helm lights—big metal crystals, what are they called? Formed in deep space over ages of slow cooling...

NEWS OF JOE

Widmanstätten patterns," Alice Harper says. "Nickel iron crystals. How big?"

I spread my hands apart. Fifty centimeters, maybe. Chunky as hell, but smoothly polished, like an art project.

"My Lord," she says. "You were descending through the core of the old moon. Right there on Mars!"

"Right there," I say. My head aches like fury. My neck is stiff with talking, remembering, and I want to delay like anything what's coming up. "I got to take a couple of pills."

"Go take," Alice says. She looks at her phone, as if expecting a call.

Vac supplements are recommended while coming off Cosmoline. I've been avoiding them the last few hours because sometimes they flush the system. Part of the glamour of being a spaceman. I'm in the bathroom, staring into the large mirror, disembodied head swimming in my filmy gaze—seeing nothing I like or respect.

I rest my hands on the sink. A phone wheedles in the living room, not mine. Alice answers, her voice low. I've left the bathroom door open for the moment and clasp the vitamins in my hand, deciding whether I want to become human again—find firmer ground through more food, good company—or give in to the vac in my head.

Alice is speaking on her cell. Something's up. She sounds energized, but I can't quite hear what she's saying. I swallow the vitamins and scoop water from the tap to chase them. Then I emerge. The food in my belly is behaving. My legs are behaving. My vision is clear. I feel stronger.

Alice stands on the step up to the hallway, smiling a very odd smile. "That was Joe," she says. "He wants you out of here."

"And go where?"

"He didn't say, and I don't think we want to know—not yet. Get your stuff together."

"Moving out? Where?"

"I do not know. Honest."

"Do I have a choice?"

Alice—the same Alice who walked me around the market and made cioppino, who's listened to everything with sympathy and firm understanding—glares at me, brooking no dissent.

"It's *Joe*," she says.

"Why doesn't he come here?"

"I didn't ask! Let's move."

She helps me put together a packet with pills and fills a bottle of water from the tap in the kitchen. Somehow, I have run out of questions.

But she tells me, "Keep talking," as we take the elevator. "Keep your mind on what happened. Don't lose any details."

DEEP PRIDE

At the bottom of the spiral stairs, three tunnels run straight outward like spokes for as far as we can see; DJ has led us to a circular chamber at the center of a perfect shooting gallery. No star lights in sight. I signal for us to take positions away from the tunnels, close to the chamber wall.

But there's only darkness and silence.

Out on the Red, there's always the faintest hiss of ghostly breeze, almost inaudible except during a sandstorm, but down here, there's only a muffled hint of withheld human breath, the superlight scuff and rubbery tap of boots, and beyond that— beyond these very thin noises—

Nothing.

We switch on our helm lights. We can all see that the main trail of prints and streaks in the dust leads down one tunnel. The dust in the other tunnels is almost undisturbed—except for some tiny pocks and thin lines, which I ignore, because I can't explain them and my head is already overloaded.

DJ bends to draw a map in the dust. He lifts his forefinger to his lips as if to taste the dust on the tip, then catches me watching and drops his hand. "There are sixteen main levels connected by twenty-one shafts—right down to the torso. Most of the levels were closed due to flooding before the Voors packed up, I think—but they've drained now. All but the deep hydro."

"We should go back," Ackerly says, kneeling by the human tracks. "They're ahead waiting to ambush whoever follows."

DJ has an odd look. "Okay. *This* tunnel goes to the eastern gate—but *that* one does not." He points to the well-traveled tunnel and taps the middle of his map, then draws a staggered cascade of lines down through the Drifter's long axis. "It drops at a shallow angle and then intersects one side of a ring. Go halfway around the ring, and you'll meet the first of a series of shafts descending to a tall cavern—a big void. Right now, we're only in the neck—"

"What?" Brom asks.

"This whole Drifter thing is like a big swimming guy, trying to stay afloat, isn't it, Master Sergeant?" DJ says. I nod. "We've only gone down as far as one side of the neck."

"I do not get that swimmer shit," Ackerly interrupts.

"Try to imagine something for once," Brom tells him.

Ackerly frowns. "Backstroke or crawl?"

"Just the upper head and forearms and part of the neck reach above the sand," DJ says. "It's kind of like a giant doing a backstroke, I suppose. Head and shoulder, the harbor of one arm, thrust out in front—the northern gate. Another out behind, the southern gate. Yeah, backstroke."

Brom laughs. "Fuck," he says. "I can *see* the arm now. Big elbow. Hand below the sand. So what's down *there*—way down in the belly?"

"The big cavern. A void. The console labeled it the Church."

"Why the fuck is there a church down here?" Ackerly asks.

"It's what the Voors called it. Down in the gut."

"If *this* tunnel goes to the eastern gate," I point, "nobody's used it. These thin tracks could be pebbles falling from the roof or something, but there are no boot prints around here."

DJ absorbs this but looks stubborn. "Well, I'm fucking solid this goes to the eastern gate."

"Up in the booth—were some of the digs marked in blue and red?" I ask.

"Yeah. Way below, lots of red—mostly around the Church."

"The gut," Brom says.

"Bowels of Mars," Ackerly says. "Love it. Love it. We are heading into the shit for sure!"

"When Teal saw the red and blue traces on the larger diagram, she seemed to think the digs continued after the Drifter was abandoned," I say.

"Who's Teal?" Brom asks.

"The ranch wife who saved our bacon," DJ explains. Then he catches on and squinches one eye. "Still mining—even in deep water? Who would do that? *What* would do that?"

Brom and Ackerly look between us, blank-faced. We're talking way above what they've managed to understand.

"Let's get to the eastern gate," I say. "First order of business is figuring out where the Voors might have come in, and how vulnerable the upper works are to Antags."

DJ shrugs and heads down the tunnel he thinks—or remembers—leads to the eastern gate. "These are *old* digs," he says. We can hear him clearly enough, even above the scuff of boots, because his voice is naturally high-pitched, penetrating.

"How can you tell?" Brom asks.

"The grooves. Dig marks. When I went back and forth between the gates, I could see some were a lot older than the Voors."

"Really? How old?"

DJ flashes us a weirdly chipper look. "Millions of years, maybe. The marks here," he brushes one with his glove, "these are softer—they've been *eroded* by lots of flowing water, you know, the hobo, the underground river. And that must have taken millions of years, because, right? It doesn't flow all the time, it just *hobos* around under the surface, coming back every few million years, flooding, withdrawing…"

He keeps walking, throws out his right arm, and we all turn right. "This is newer, less erosion," he observes in the next tunnel.

I honestly don't know what to think. The tunnel excavation marks back there *do* look worn compared to these. But that could be a difference in machines, mining tools, techniques…

"Head and neck and shoulder," Brom murmurs. "Belly below. What's below that? How far down does this fucker go?"

"Maybe two or three dozen klicks," DJ says. "Based on the pictures I saw."

He has also neglected to reveal that, until now.

"What in hell *is* this place?" Ackerly asks.

"God's candy bar," I say. "Dropped it on His way to Earth. Creamy nougat center, I hear."

Ackerly thinks that over. "Really?" he asks with a boyish innocence you got to love.

The tunnel curves and then rises, and in a few minutes we're at the eastern gate—another hangar-sized cavern, completely dark—no star lights, nothing but our helm lanterns flaring through the cold, clear air. We're the first to disturb the green dust on the floor.

We wander around the cavern. No buggies, no wagons, no vehicles whatsoever—and no equipment. I approach the inner lock hatch, shining my light from top to bottom—pretty big, at least as big as the southern gate lock. The lock has been welded shut, then completely blocked by cross-welded beams and a big pile of basalt boulders—mine tailings, probably. Closed long ago, undisturbed since.

Nobody has been here for a very long time.

Ackerly sneezes and picks at his nose. His finger comes away green. "This ain't Mars dust," he observes, then wipes his finger on his forearm. "It's the green shit that's all over. We're sucking it in. What is it?"

"Algae, maybe," DJ says.

"What if I'm allergic?" Ackerly says.

"Not even a control booth," DJ says, standing beside an old, rusted frame that might have once supported such a structure. "I'll bet when they sealed it off, they covered the outside with rocks, too. So's nobody would even know it was here. Paranoid bastards, but smart, right?"

"No Voors came in through here," Brom observes, turning, his light sweeping around the walls of the garage. "How'd they overpower Skyrines without help?"

Then my own beam returns as a glint—back in the tunnel that led us here. A little speck of reflection that almost instantly seems to be obscured, as if by a shutter, a *blink*, then jerks aside— and vanishes.

"Did you see that?" I ask, retreating to the center of the hangar.

"See what?" DJ says.

"An eye," Brom says, throat tight. "I saw it, too—a blinking eye. Just one."

Ackerly bumps up against us and we're a tight square, facing outward, sidearms at the ready. "I didn't see anything," he insists. "Are we going back that way?"

"Only way out," DJ says.

It takes a few minutes to get these exhausted and thoroughly unhappy men to see clear reason. We cannot finish our mission without retracing our steps—following our boot marks. I look down at the green dust and our own tracks with obsessive interest, trying to make any sense of where we are, what's happening. What we're seeing or not seeing.

DJ takes the lead again. I take the rear. We're all in stealth mode, moving with as little sound as possible, trying not even to breathe loud.

Then Brom gives a little grunt. "Look at this," he says, bending, moving his light along our tracks. There's a very clear boot print, fresh, in the dust. One of ours, doesn't matter whose. Pointing to the garage.

Someone or something has planted an even fresher pockmark, and pushed aside a little line of green dust, right across that print. A few minutes before.

Without leaving any other sign.

"Ants!" Brom says, his voice rising. "They're already inside. We are truly fucked!"

"I don't think so," I say, mind working so fast my thoughts feel like sparks. No panic. Draw them back from panic. "We've all seen Antag tracks on the Red. Individuals leave bigger marks—double circles, side bars. Bigger boots than ours."

"Not Ants, then," DJ agrees.

"Calm down," I say. "Mission first. We have to get back and report."

We return to the radiance of tunnels at the bottom of the first spiral staircase. Alone, unmolested.

"Something with one shiny eye," Brom says thoughtfully. "If not Ants, then what?"

"Let's finish this level and see if there's something we need to know," I say.

We've gone on for a few hundred meters and it's becoming obvious that DJ no longer knows where we are.

"We've walked too fucking far," he says. "I'm turned around."

"Lost?" Ackerly asks.

"No, man, just turned around. Put me right and I'll find the way. We can follow our tracks."

We've made a wrong turn, it's dark—no star lights hang on these walls, and the grooves seem fresh. DJ is silent for a while until we stop again and he turns and looks back at us. "These digs weren't on the map," he says. "I think we're nowhere near where we're supposed to be."

"Then we just go back, right?" Ackerly asks.

"Green dust will show us the way," Brom says.

"If you'll notice," I say, pointing to our feet, "no green dust."

"Shit," Brom says. "It's supposed to be everywhere, it clogs my nose like snuff—why not *here*? Why not when we need it?"

"Because it's not *funny*," DJ says. "There's only green dust when it's funny."

But we're not going to let him off easy. We group around him, tight, as if we can squeeze out a better answer. Not threatening, mind you—we'd never threaten a fellow Skyrine. More like we're really strung-out chain-smokers and we know he has a pack of cigarettes on him somewhere.

"Give me room to think, goddamn it," he says, head low, eyes shifting in our beams. Which are, of course, slowly dimming. At least the air is fresh—fresher than ever, I think, like a slow, continuous mountain breeze way down here. "There was a side tunnel back about a hundred meters," he finally says, and pushes through our pack. "We'll try that one."

"I did not see it," Ackerly says. "Did you?" he asks Brom.

None of us saw it except DJ, and he's murmuring, "I didn't think it was the one, not right. Didn't feel right."

I have nothing against Corporal Dan Johnson—really. Decent tech, dedicated Skyrine, sometimes tries to be funny. But the thought that our lives depend on DJ's self-described perfect memory brings no joy. Ackerly and Brom are stoic. I think they made their peace out on the Red, running before the Antag wall of dust, and the rest has just been prelude to a foregone conclusion.

I'm trying to figure the lack of dust and the walls' fresh grooves. Recent digs?

Even after the water receded?

Slowly it's beginning to dawn on me that we might be dealing with another kind of participant in our weird game—a third party or group of parties, origin unknown, nature unknown.

But carrying a camera.

"What the fuck are you laughing at?" DJ asks me. "It's not funny, man."

"Find that side tunnel," I tell him.

"Yes, sir. What if it's not there anymore?"

"Find it."

Ten more steps and DJ spins around, shining his beam right at us. He points to his right, our left, face bright but damp. "There, just like I saw."

It's a smaller, narrower tunnel, barely high enough to stoop into. DJ bends over and heads in anyway, and then pops out like a cork, arms flailing. He's caught in a weird kind of web, pieces of thin translucent stuff, like flexible glass or cellophane noodles, that have stuck to his helm and shoulders. Grunting like a desperate pig, he plucks off the glassy fibers and flings them to the floor while Brom and Ackerly and I stand back, afraid to touch him, not at all sure what he's blundered into. But finally he's mostly cleaned himself off, all but for little fragments, and I tell him to stop, stop wasting energy, let me look you over.

He freezes like a statue, chin high, arms out. "Are they needles?" he asks, high and squeaky.

"Don't think so. Hold still."

I carefully pluck away one fiber, hold it out and up in our beams. It's about five centimeters long, twenty millimeters across, very much like a cellophane noodle in a bowl of Asian soup, but stiffly bendy. I pinch it lengthwise, not too hard, between my fingers. It flexes, then seems to grow rigid—to actually straighten and harden. Weird material.

Pieces of the shattered web lie on the tunnel floor all around DJ. But nothing seems to have pierced his skintight.

"Fucking spiderweb," Brom says.

"No!" DJ husks. "Fucking heavy-duty *no* to that shit!"

"Fine," Brom says. "No spiders."

"I'm cool with no spiders, too," Ackerly says.

My turn. I bend over and shine my light directly into the cavity that was supposed to be our turning point, our salvation, if ever I trusted DJ. "Something's jammed in here," I say.

"Trapdoor!" Brom says.

Now Ackerly takes umbrage and cuffs him on the side of the head.

My curiosity is piqued. Really. I am not in the least afraid—not now, just feeling a weird kind of wonder. Sad wonder. I feel as if I know what I'm going to find. Or at least *part of me knows*. Part of me feels a separate truth, not...

Human?

"It's not moving, whatever it is," I call back. I've pushed through the rubbery, brittle fibers and found the thing that might have made them, and it, too, looks like it might have come out of some crazy glass-blowing shop at a county fair. There's the eye, like a lens all right, on a tubular kind of head, transparent and blue-green, now slumped on a short neck. Behind the head and the eye is a jumble of glassy limbs about as thick as my wrist, which might have once been flexible and tough but are now shot through with cracks, dry, brittle. Looks like I could crunch them to dust with a poke of my finger.

"I doubt it's Antag," I say over my shoulder. "It's not moving. Old. Ready to fall apart. Decaying—"

Something that crawled in and died in this little hidey hole. Or just stopped working. What is it I'm recognizing, acknowledging, in this sad clump of fibers?

Brom sticks his head in behind me and shines another light down the narrow tunnel. "Looks like a dead end. What is that thing, a fossil?"

"Don't know. But…I think it didn't come from outside. I think it belongs down here."

"Get out and let's go," DJ says, voice still shaky.

I'm becoming more and more interested. I get down on my knees, very cautious, in case any of the fragments are still sharp, and examine its shoes, pads, feet—if it's one thing, one creature, or a creature at all!—about two or three dozen of them, at the ends of a maze of triple-and-quadruple jointed legs. I grip a pad and lift it—it's not all that light—and then, the leg above breaks and white dust rises and okay, it's time to back out, time to find another way, this is almost certainly not where we should be going—the hidey hole is feeling pretty tight.

I exit and hold the pad under the dimming beams proffered by Brom and Ackerly. DJ moves in to inspect with us. The pad masses about half a kilo and the bottom is hard, finely grooved in a cross-hatch pattern, but not your ordinary nail-file sort of grooves—more like the rotating cutter on a big digging machine back on Earth.

"It's a rock grinder!" DJ says, curiosity getting the better of fear. Then our eyes meet—and I recognize something in DJ's look. Knowing, acknowledging. I turn away before he can give me a little nod, before we join a really weird club.

"Maybe it dug these new tunnels," Brom says. "That thing's a fucking *kobold.*"

"You just make that up?" DJ asks.

"No, man—kobold. Mining spirit. Like gremlins, only down in the ground."

"Let's go," I say. I'm holding tight to the pad, the cutting foot. Joe has to see this. Our whole situation is out of control in more dimensions than I can track.

Because what Brom and I saw in the useless and welded-tight hangar of the eastern gate was *not* a long-dead fossil stuck in a hole. What I saw had the same single, shiny camera eye—but it had *moved*.

These tunnels are new.

Kobolds may still be hard at work.

———

DJ IS LOSING focus, distracted—frazzled. He's murmuring to himself and leading us back to the eastern gate, hoping, I presume, for another branching tunnel, another shaft, something we missed. Brom is telling us all about kobolds, which he knows from a game he played as a kid on Earth. Ghostly diggers, spirits of dead miners; in the game they were horrible, flesh-eating wraiths that pickaxed you in the top of the head, caught the spurting blood in pelican-like beaks, then tore into the rest of you, bones and all, leaving nothing behind.

He's no better than listening to DJ, and finally, Ackerly tells him to just shut it.

"Right," Brom says. "Sorry."

This time, I'm the one who shines his helm light to the left at just the right moment, and instead of seeing metal crystals or black basalt, I see—a wide opening. A branch to the left, pretty straight, sloping down about ten degrees.

DJ inspects this with a puzzled look. "Don't remember any passage at this kind of angle," he says.

"You don't remember *shit*," Ackerly reminds him.

"This one's new, too," Brom says, pointing to the grooves.

We begin the slight descent. The tunnel grows wider, which I appreciate. DJ insists on taking the lead, and I don't deny him that much; he may still have a clue. The rest of us do not. He's stopped mumbling. Ackerly and Brom are silent as well. As the saying goes, it's quiet, too quiet.

"Will you please just *whistle*, DJ?" Brom asks after maybe ten minutes.

"No spit," DJ says. "Running dry."

All our suits could use a good, long recharge. We've been away from resources for hours; suits can typically run for two or three days, but ours have not been fully charged since prep before our drop. They can take all kinds of abuse and keep us alive, but staying comfortable is once again not an option.

"Where are we, anatomically?" Ackerly asks.

"Below the neck, in the chest, I think," DJ replies.

"Anywhere near the bowels?"

"We might be below the eastern garage, down around the heart," DJ says. Then he pulls up short, hunching his shoulders and letting out a moan. We've come to a round chamber, older, with rust on the walls and a damp floor. His helm light flashes up, around, and he backs off to show us what he's found. A body.

Human.

I walk around him, and then we gather and focus our lights, which are now almost orange. The sight is ghastly. A man has been cut in half and the walls have been scored in a weird, elongated spiral, all the way down another passage to the right… into darkness.

"Lawnmower," Brom says.

"It's a Voor, isn't it?" DJ asks, staring at me as I turn my light up to his face.

"Yeah," I say. "The one they called Hendrik."

"Here's another," Brom says. He's gone about six meters down another passage, also sloping, but this time up. "What the hell?"

"Must have been a firefight," DJ says.

Just two bodies. Both Voors, both cut to pieces while running away—by a lawnmower shot indiscriminately into the passage. Way overkill.

The evidence chills me.

"We need to get back *now*," I say.

Our discoveries are not over. DJ leads us past the second body, up the ascending tunnel, and a few dozen meters beyond, in another circular chamber with four more branching tunnels, we find three more Voors—lined up against a wall and shot with bullets: back-of-the-head-shots, execution-style. No recognizing any of them. Hendrik and the other may have lit out in desperation to escape this organized carnage.

"This is bullshit!" DJ shouts.

"But was it *authorized* bullshit?" Brom asks. "Who the fuck's in charge?"

Not Gamecock, I'm pretty sure of that. I'm having to revise everything I've thought about our situation. No additional party of Voors from the eastern gate, no reinforcements, no Antags breaking in yet—we'd probably be dead by now or see a lot more destruction if that last were the case.

Looks as if Coyle and our sisters might have scratched an evil little itch, all on their own. But why leave the southern gate? Why abandon *both* gates? We'd support them no matter what they did because that's what Skyrines do.

What are Captain Coyle's orders? What does she know that we don't?

Does Joe know what she knows?

DJ has fled up the widest tunnel. We're losing cohesion. Then he starts shouting, not more than twenty meters ahead. "It's a fucking boneyard! They're all over in here!"

Very reluctantly we join him in the biggest chamber we've

found yet, about sixty meters across, a great, dark stone hollow surrounded by a head-high shelf of foggy-silver metal. I'm expecting to see dead Voors and Skyrines smeared all over—a hecatomb of combat mayhem.

Nothing of the kind.

"More kobolds!" Brom says, voice down to a hard whisper.

Hundreds, maybe thousands of them, massed around the walls like a river-piled deadfall, their jointed tubes and pads jumbled in with long heads and camera eyes—still pale, still supple, but motionless, silent, and in such confusion I can't begin to figure out what the mass would have looked like alive and working.

Maybe the kobolds had come together like Tinkertoys to become a single machine, to more efficiently carve out the lava and metal with hundreds of grinding, cutting pads, still busy, still digging—

DJ splashes through an ankle-deep pool. The chamber appears to have been expanded within the past few days or weeks. Water could have been kept longer in the lower tunnels, allowing the kobolds more time to keep digging—until they connected with a dry passage and everything drained. But draining water wasn't what killed them. They can move around for some time even after the water is gone—I saw one do just that. Maybe they can even keep working.

A gigantic mining machine, a big operation—

Until somebody—possibly Captain Coyle herself, or Gunny de Guzman, whom I first saw with the lawnmower—ran rampant and sprayed beams all through the hollow. Spiraling scorch marks rise across and around the walls, cleaving the thick masses of kobolds, up to the rugged ceiling. By definition, a lawnmower is excessive—so what's an excess of excess? Mad, thorough destruction.

Our sisters might have figured they were about to be attacked. Maybe they *were* attacked. But we see no blood, no human bodies—except for Voors.

Ackerly and Brom and DJ stand at the center of the hollow, stunned. "This is *our* shit!" Ackerly says, his voice very low now, trying to reason through the threat, the cause. "What if these fucking kobolds are Ant scouts—little buggy drones or shit? They're inside, checking things out, making their moves, so our sisters righteously carved them into lunch meat!"

"These aren't Ant drones," Brom says quietly.

I agree. They don't fit any known pattern, don't carry weapons, and haven't hurt us or even threatened us.

"Maybe it doesn't matter if you're a kobold whether you're alive or dead," Ackerly says. "Maybe they can revive and spring up and grab you...like zombies! Soda straw zombies."

"Shut *up*," DJ says in fierce disgust.

They're all looking right at me. It's never good when Skyrines start plumbing the depths of their intellect.

"We have to get back to Sanka," I say. It's all I can think to do: finish our mission, pass the buck—inform our commander the eastern gate is locked, we haven't seen any Antags in the Drifter...

Only kobolds, whatever the fuck they are.

DJ walks ahead and we follow, muttering in the shadows and damp as he flings his arm right, then left, guiding us. We're moving fast. Our heads hurt from all the pressure changes.

He halts at a wide spot in the tunnel and slams his hand against a hatch set into the wall, covering an opening in the floor about two meters wide, not an airlock but maybe watertight. "Okay," he says. "I know this one. This covers a shaft that takes you down maybe fifty meters, to where nobody's been except maybe the Voors. If we can get it open."

"And you know that *because*...?" I ask.

"I told you!" he shouts. "The booth. It's…up here, you know?" He taps his head again and I feel a sudden anger, an outrageous urge to just start kicking him and the walls, because it's all so nuts. Would a little certainty and sanity hurt whoever's in charge, please, just this once?

Instead, I ask, "Will it take us any closer to the southern gate?"

DJ thinks this over. "No," he says. "Deeper, down to a big void, no idea what's inside." He kneels and manages to pry up one side. "Look, it's not locked."

The door is light, not steel—probably some polymer printed out by the depositor.

"Is there space down there for a good-sized group to hide?"

"Definitely," DJ says. "Really big."

"Fucking hold fire!" someone shouts from down the tunnel— a woman. "Seventh Marines, Akbar!"

I recognize the voice. It's Captain Coyle.

"Fuck," Brom says under his breath.

First down the tunnel walks Vee-Def, pushed out front by Sergeant Mustafa, and he doesn't look happy. He gives me a warning glance as helm lights flash. Theirs is not a cordial relationship.

"Fuck this shit," he says wearily, and Mustafa taps him on the back of his neck with the butt of her sidearm. He reels forward and falls to his knees.

Ackerly, Brom, and DJ form a tight square around me, and we all palm sidearms.

Mustafa glares. "He's being an asshole," she says, then reaches to help Vee-Def back to his feet.

Coyle and four of our sisters come out of the shadows and join us in the wide spot, where they surround us like it's old home week, checking us over, casually checking status of our sidearms, monkeys picking nits, social as shit in a chute—but my head is buzzing, my adrenaline is way up.

Shrugging off Mustafa's help, Vee-Def stands. His eyes are heavy, and not just with pain. Betrayal. Rage.

"What the hell happened to you?" I ask Coyle.

Without meeting my eyes, she softly, gently tells us about the unexpected arrival of twelve more Voors, coming in through the eastern gate, fully armed with pistols and assault weapons. Her voice is flat, deadly calm, like she's on some sort of drug.

"The Voors drew down," she says, pacing around the hatch. DJ bends and swings the hatch up. At Mustafa's scowl, DJ backs off. "There was a brief struggle, nearly everyone returned fire. Two Voors were killed by bolts, two of ours were killed by projectiles, and we overwhelmed the rest. Some broke loose and ran down here. When we got here, they ambushed us, attacked us again."

"What about Lieutenant Colonel Roost?"

"Killed in the first attack." Coyle suddenly looks right at me, face like an angry little girl's, defying me or anyone to say she's a liar, but that's exactly what she is, a liar—and we all know it.

The ladies have sidearms out and charged. De Guzman levels that goddamned lawnmower, expression total trigger. I idly observe that if she fires she'll take out not just us but half her team.

"Ladies, ladies," Ackerly says, holding up his hands.

DJ's sweating, losing focus.

"Where's Teal?" I ask.

"I don't know," Coyle says. "Doesn't matter."

The sisters loosen their ring but not their vigilance.

"Listen up," Coyle says, her voice ringing against the walls as if she's addressing a platoon. "We have orders. New orders. The Antags are going to overwhelm this place, and command doesn't want it to fall to them. So we're taking all our spent matter and mining explosives and shit…rigging it to release all at once. We're going to collapse the upper works."

Brom and Ackerly shake their heads and look dubious. DJ stands aside, back hunched, like he's going to be sick. He keeps looking at the hatch.

"Sir, why not mount a defense until they reinforce?" Brom asks pertly, as if rational questions are still in order. Ackerly pokes Brom in the ribs but it doesn't seem to register. "We have the weapons, you say we have enough charges—"

Coyle ignores him and turns to me. "Where have you been?" she asks.

"The eastern gate," I say.

"Find the Voors?" she asks, bold as whiskey.

"We're on board, Captain," I say. "Carry out your orders. We'll move back to the southern gate and wait for all of you before we abandon the Drifter."

"I need your assurance that you understand my orders supersede any others," Coyle says. There are dark moments coming, that's what I get from her weird, *don't hit me*, little girl look. Orders are orders whether you like them or not. Captain Coyle does not like her orders. Not one bit. But she's an excellent Skyrine.

SNKRAZ.

"I don't know why you didn't confide in us in the first place, Captain," DJ says dreamily, rubbing his neck. There are streaks on his cheeks, I notice for the first time, like he's been rubbing them with green dust.

"What's with him?" de Guzman asks.

"He's tired," I say. "Like all of us."

"Execute in sequence," Coyle says. "Need to know. Anyway, it's all out now. We came back because our detonators aren't up to the task. We're taking another pair down to the Church, and then we'll climb up and join you at the southern gate. Apologies, Master Sergeant. We'll leave Lance Corporal Medvedev with you."

So she, too, knows about the Church.

The ladies slip down the hole beneath the hatch, covering us as they depart. De Guzman goes last. And just as suddenly as it began it's over, like a wicked, ugly dream.

"Don't listen to them," Vee-Def says. "They want us dead. All of us. It's a suicide mission."

DJ says, "Strong tea, ain't it?"

COLD COMFORT

Alice Harper has called a minivan to the curved drive outside our building. In the rearmost seat, far away from the driver—who sits behind a plastic shield anyway, and probably isn't listening—I continue my story, speaking low, eyes darting at the bright, cloudy day, wondering where she's taking me but not really caring.

I feel very funny indeed. This isn't Cosmoline, nor is it getting used again to Earth air and gravity. My mind is filling again with ghostly thoughts, visuals, details, all fragmented and swirly. Not direct experience, not sensual input or something I read or saw, more like a direct feed into my cortex. Maybe it's another kind of angel taking form in my skull, trying to awaken. It hurts, sort of—but this is an interesting sort of pain, like freshly exercised muscles.

Then my mood flips. All things unexpected turn out badly; that's the truth of battle. Most of the things we *do* expect turn out badly, as well. I'm not a happy camper, in any case, and my innards are knotting—both stomach *and* brain.

"I'm going to be sick," I say.

"No, you aren't," Alice says.

"I *am* sick, inside," I say.

"Not really," she says. She sounds like she knows something but she doesn't want to tell me, not here, not yet. And suddenly that's okay. I'm compliant again, complaisant. I do feel strange, but I trust her. That makes no sense, even if she is pretty and a good cook and knows how to take charge.

She fed me cioppino. Fish and clams and crab and vegetables. Delicious.

"Did you drug me?" I ask.

"No," she says firmly, and pats my knee before unhitching and moving up front to talk to the driver. When she returns, she tells me, "You didn't come back as Master Sergeant Venn, did you?"

"No," I say.

"Joe sent you back with another ID, and in the crowding and confusion, out on the dust and on the orbital—nobody checked, right?"

"Or didn't care. Focus on getting us all home."

"Joe figured the brass would take a couple of days to start putting together all your stories. A couple of days before they decided to round you all up and isolate you. That's why he told you to stay away from MHAT."

"Right," I say.

"He didn't think it would be a good idea for him to join you right away. Too many eggs in one basket. So he sent me. And no, I did not drug you. But you are now full of essential supplements and vitamins."

"Are those making me sick?"

"You're *not* sick," she emphasizes, a little ticked. Her patience is wearing thin. I am trying her patience. I am trying her patience on for size and finding it's just too sheer. I can see through it. I can be either patient or impatient.

Shit, I am drugged—looping out and in, flying free…

And then, *not*.

My head is clear as a ringing bell.

"What the fuck happened up there?" I ask her.

"You tell me," she says. "But not here. We'll be where we're going soon, in an hour."

"And where is that?"

"Safe, quiet, remote. Joe says he'll try to be there when we arrive."

"We both made it, you know. We both got off Mars."

"I know."

"They wanted to kill us. All of us."

"So I heard."

"But you want me to wait before I learn the truth, don't you? Before I figure it all out, or somebody tells me."

She nods. "Patience. Won't be long, Vinnie."

On the return trip, before we slipped into the Cosmoline, the orbital crew promised us all campaign medals stamped with our company blaze. But what's inside my head, what's happening to me, and maybe to others besides me—to DJ, for example—

Will shove all that aside.

I'm being hustled away by a zaftig, pretty female who's a great cook, knows how to sling and deliver the right supplements, claims she knows Joe—and also knows what's good for me.

"One last thing," I say.

"One last thing," she agrees, leaning in on the bench seat, watching me closely.

Very softly, so the driver can't hear, "I'm valuable, ain't I?"

"You're fucking irreplaceable, Vinnie."

TEAL'S WAY

We make steps, one after the next, getting farther and farther away from the chamber of kobold slaughter, from the hatch, from Captain Coyle, just picking a way out, a way up. God help me, my brain is still on overdrive. I need distraction from thoughts about Coyle, about our sisters, about orbital command.

And so I think about kobolds. What are they hoping to achieve? Are they like automated termites, just digging for the hell of it—turning the entire Drifter into a rotting log of rock and metal? Maybe that's it.

We've been moving this way and that, ever upward, for about an hour, when we see a light fly back across the shining metal ceiling over our heads, and DJ shouts, "It's Michelin! And Neemie!"

This passage is not very wide but we all pack together, shining our beams in each other's faces. Neemie and Michelin look like they've been through a grinder. Their skintights are badly lacerated, helms broken and faceplates torn away, and Michelin is clutching his arm to his chest. It looks broken.

Ackerly tries to help Michelin but he jerks aside, eyes show-ing whites all around like a terrified horse.

"Where are the others?" I ask.

Michelin points up, down, then around with his good arm, face ghostly white. He says, "Shit's falling from so high we can't even smell it."

Neemie grimaces. "Don't mess with him," he says. "Talk to me. While I still have a clue."

Michelin starts to sing, *"If I only had a clue…"* Neemie gen-tly puts his hand over his mouth. Michelin folds down against a wall and slumps his head.

"Tell us about Coyle," I say.

"She got final instructions from that Korean general, Kwak, before he died. That's why they're all here, I think."

"Fucking command," Michelin mutters.

"What instructions?"

"They came with beaucoup spent matter charges. In their back-packs. Somebody back home wants this place blown to gravel, that's what I gathered, that's what Gamecock—I mean, Lieutenant Colonel Roost—figured when Coyle and the sisters took us over, us and the Voors. Poor Muskie bastards didn't stand a chance."

"Coyle killed them all?"

"De Guzman tried. Too tight for that. Some got away, don't know how many."

"What about Teal? The ranch wife?"

Neemie shakes his head. "Michelin and I got away, and I think maybe Gamecock. But you know what's really scary? There's something else down here! Like bundles of thick straw, only moving and fast."

"We've seen them," Brom says. "Kobolds."

"They filled the tunnel and flooded in on Coyle and her team just as they were zeroing the Voors—executing them, man! Coyle was a fucking fiend—"

"Had her orders, she said," Michelin adds. "Weird fucking face on her."

"—and de Guzman with that fucking lawnmower…" Neemie swallows but it won't go down and he strokes his throat as if to help it. I'm amazed he can still talk. "But then we were backed into a big space and it filled with those straw bundles, straw creatures, coming in from all sides, and I swear, I swear this is true—"

"It *is* true," Michelin says, looking up.

"Coyle's team pulled us out of there, laid down more lawnmower, pulled us into another tunnel where there were these crystals, big, clear crystals. And when they started laying charges, pulling them out of their packs like Girl Scout cookies—the crystals turned black! The walls turned to, like, black *glass* and got spiky, and the spikes snagged Magsaysay and then Ceniza, ripped her suit—and, *man*…"

"Help me up," Michelin says.

"They both turned all black, shiny," Neemie says. "Like statues."

DJ throws me a look as we help lift Michelin back to his feet.

"Medusa," I say and instantly regret it. Ackerly and Brom are ready to book to the top and run straight out onto the Red. It's just a matter of seconds before everything closes in on all of us.

"We didn't see the finish," Neemie continues, "but they were pinned on the spikes and their legs and skintights and everything—"

"Solid, shiny, filled with fireflies," Michelin says. "Some fucking defense!"

"Whose defense?" Brom asks. "Who's defending who?"

Time to get back to essentials.

"Where are they now?" I ask.

"Coyle was going deep before everything mixed," Neemie says. "Down to a place the old Voor called the Church. They strung him up and he tried not to tell them, but Rafe…"

Michelin's eyes go horse-wild again. He throws out one arm, bangs the walls, as if he'd break that one, too.

"Hold him, Brom," I say.

"He's *hurt*, man," Brom says. "We have to get him to the top and out of here." Brom's eyes beseech.

"Don't forget what's waiting outside," Ackerly says, voice cool. "Are they still holding good Skyrines?"

"I don't know who's good or bad," Neemie says. "We got away in the freak. Kazak and Vee-Def were helping Gamecock. Coyle beat the colonel down bad when he questioned Kwak's orders. And then Kwak dies—he just *expires*. Still spouting crap about old moons and dust and shit, and that snaps everybody. Believe it. *Nobody* goes home."

"Who's in charge?" Michelin asks. "I'll follow orders if I just know who's wacko and who's not."

"DJ," I say, and he perks up instantly, "guide us back to Sanka. Now."

"Right," he says, and turns to the others. "Southern gate, fellows. On me. We're packing up to go home."

I don't contradict him. It's a good story. Maybe we are, maybe we aren't.

DJ leads us with firmer conviction and a lot more motivation. He's still intent on running his gloved fingertips along the grooves, as if he's reading the walls. There's green dust again—these tunnels are older, the grooves more worn, and somehow that's reassuring. We follow them back along a scuffed trail of many footprints.

DJ looks back at me and whispers, "This dust, it's fucking strong tea. I'm seeing shit. What about you?"

I don't want to hazard an opinion. We're stretched way too thin. I'd rather die on the Red than face rogue Skyrines or black spikes. For the moment, thinking things through is more than I'm good for—but even so, there's a peculiar *newness* in my head.

Something fresh and unexpected.

And then—scaring the hell out of me—

Takahashi Fujimori.

His face rises like a dull orange ghost in our beams. Behind him are Brodsky and Beringer. Believe me, Skyrines can shriek like little girls.

Then we get real quiet. That kind of shock is not good. We could have killed each other. Jangles subside and we catch our breath.

"Where you guys been?" Tak asks.

"We're retreating in good order to the southern gate," Ackerly says, strolling past. "Permission to abandon this shithole, Master Sergeant."

"Follow us. Sanka's up ahead." Tak asks me, "Any sign of Captain Coyle and her squad?"

"Could be way down deep," I say. "They're going to demo this place. Blow it the fuck up. We don't know anything about anything, Tak."

"Yeah. We were sent to find you. We make one last attempt to locate Captain Coyle and her team, see what the fuck they're up to—issue a final notice that we're all gathering at the southern gate, organize vehicles and weapons," he shoves out his hands, "and push through the Antag line. There's a dust storm outside, a real good one."

"Saw it from a watchtower," Beringer says. "Great screen. Might give us cover."

"Outstanding," Neemie says, fingering the rips on his skintight. "Blind and out on the Red in our pajamas."

"We're hoping the bright boys in orbit have decided to regroup and open up a distraction," Tak says.

"*Hoping?*" Brom asks.

"In here, it's fucking bughouse," Beringer says.

"You're telling us?" Michelin asks.

Ten minutes later, we've come to the roundabout just before the southern garage, where Joe is squatting beside a Voor—de Groot's son, Rafe. Rafe is in decent shape considering but minus his skintight, face bruised, sullen.

Joe, with a sour look but no words, takes us all back to the southern gate. There de Groot and two of the Voors are lifting Gamecock on a stretcher, up into the cabin of the Chesty.

"He's not going to make it," Joe says, out of our CO's earshot. "They have some story to tell. You?"

I try to pass along what I might or might not know. As I finish Kazak comes around from the vehicle's lock hatch.

Tak and Kazak and I slap backs, but it's a brief moment. Kazak is in surprisingly good shape after what he's been through.

Rafe stands beside his father after they finish loading our CO. Both regard us with weary disgust. De Groot looks to have been chewed all over by rats and his face is swollen almost beyond recognition, but he's still upright, proud, defiant.

Joe sums it up. "Coyle and her squad are working from a different set of orders. The Voors are coming with us."

"Who's been lying the hardest?" I ask.

Joe ignores the question. "Any sign of the rest of our team?"

"None we've seen."

"The ranch wife?" Joe asks.

"Nothing," I say.

"She's gone over to the Drifter," Rafe says, but before he can explain what that means the floor shakes under us. The walls shiver and dust sifts from the ceiling.

"From below?" Kazak asks.

"From above," Tak says. "Bombardment."

"Antags getting ready to move in."

"I strongly doubt it," de Groot says. "You do not see at all, do you? What is happening, who is working behind you?"

Joe assigns Kazak to watch over the garage and prepare for

our exit. Then he picks four of us and signals for us to move out. "DJ, you've still got some sort of map in your head, right?"

"I think so," DJ says.

"Find that hatch again. We're going to locate Captain Coyle and see what her disposition really is. Try and get her team to come back with us."

Joe says, in a low voice, so that Rafe and de Groot can't hear, "I don't get these fucking kobolds. What are the chances the Voors invited the Ants in? And the Ants killed some of them for their trouble?"

"Not likely," I say.

Joe absorbs this. "Then it's true. Coyle and her orders, Major General Kwak, what the Voors have been saying…"

I'm about to ask what the hell else could possibly be true when DJ comes trotting back. "Found the hatch," he says. "There's a shaft, something like steps but cramped as hell, not designed for people. I don't know how our sisters made it down."

Rafe comes forward. "It is old and for the Church," he says. "Not for us."

Joe acknowledges this contribution with a nod, then points for us to move out. DJ leads the six of us to the shaft opening and lifts away the hatch. Christ it *is* small—just two meters wide, steps tiny and tall; we'll be crawling down more like worms or snakes than men.

DJ says, "If you're down here digging long enough, maybe you get all big-eyed and greasy like, you know, Gollum."

I'm actually fingering the platinum coin in my pouch, but when he says that, I stop.

Joe has had enough of DJ's nervous chatter. "Cram that shit back in," he says. "We go down, find Coyle and our survivors, find Teal and what's left of the Voors. That's that."

We begin one by one to drop through the hatch. I volunteer to take point.

"Dick down the hole," DJ says.

I hear murmuring up above, establishing order as the defensive lines break and join us, until there are just two covering our rear, awaiting a signal we've come out in a better place.

Beams bounce and flare.

One sidelights Tak grinning through his faceplate like a lacquer mask.

HOW LOW CAN YOU GO BEFORE IT'S UP AGAIN

Just a few meters down. On top of everything else, like a final fillip of perversity, the skinny shaft is really getting to me.

We did mine training at Hawthorne Tactical in Nevada, suspecting there were going to be circumstances where we might have to worm around under the Red, and there was a particularly awe-inspiring old turquoise and silver mine shaft that we, a squad of ten, plumbed for almost a quarter of a mile, taking instruction from a fifty-something DI named Marquez about how to stay calm under an overwhelming burden of rock. "There's a whole goddamned *mountain* over your head right now," he kindly informed us. "Look at those braces, look at those *beams*—think there's *termites* in that old wood? Are there termites in Nevada? You know there are. Wood-chewing, white ants. I think there's termites in *all* this old wood…Plus, fidging overburden shifts all the time, seismically active, *wow*, did you just feel *that*?"

As we stooped and crawled, he lectured on how to conduct live fire in a confined space, he'd learned it from a guy who learned it from a guy who once went after Viet Cong in their spider holes, and *he* learned it from a guy who did the same in Korea, and *he* learned it from a guy who sent in Dobermans to clean out tunnels in Okinawa and then took in gunny sacks after—

Jesus, *I hate this fucking place.*

I do not want to think about other places that were worse because my skintight is already filter-clogged and I'm sweating like a bastard, dripping from the lip of my faceplate, and Joe's boot takes me across the back of the neck when he slips, and I start thinking about my integrity; maybe he's ripped the fabric and if I fucking get out of this I'll just hiss out on the Red.

Why is the air still good down here? Who set up diffusers to spread clean, breathable air throughout the Drifter? The Voors? Kobolds are more likely. Better engineers. Hell, the old silver mine at Hawthorne, the deepest shafts, was reputed to be filled with sulfurous fumes from deep under the mountain—so that syphilitic cunt of a sadistic motherfucking DI told us—but nobody had ever been that deep, it was off-limits, he said, maybe we're already over the boundary, and then he taunted, "Smell anything, Skyrines? Whiff that stink? Other than your own butt-gas?"

He was just trying to flunk us out but no way, that pay hike shined over our heads every day we trained at Hawthorne bigger than claustrophobia, stronger than deep-Earth butt-gas.

Joe and I and the eight others had already been through seven circles of Skyrine hell. Only two would not finish. But they gave that DI immense satisfaction, those two. They flunked out in the drowning pool, floundering in skintights in zero-g prep. The DI had issued suits with leaks. Pointless, we thought, so much water—that much water on Mars! Seemed ridiculous, unfair, but I survived the mine shaft and kept my calm in the drowning pool, I made it, Joe made it, the other six made it, who were they? Fuck I'm forgetting so much, is the oxygen really all that good down here?

"Off-limits," Joe mutters above me. I'm still mad because he hasn't apologized for the boot in my neck, but my own boots are slipping on these inhuman steps.

"Fucking off-limits," I affirm, banging my knee, and again integrity will be an issue. I'll have to check myself all over and hope somebody brought the right patches.

"Don't remind me of that fucking old mine," Joe says. We're in memory sync. "I hated that place," he says. "Didn't you?"

I'm trying to hold on to the edge of a long, long step. "Loved it like my mother," I say. "A total stone vagina squeezing out born-again Skyrines. Just like here."

Joe snorts. I'm paying him back for his boot in my neck. Orderly descent. All an Antag has to do is lay down a couple of bolts from below and we'll cook, we'll fry in this shaft like—

My foot hits something that gives. That clacking sound again, only like rocks or plastic striking, not metal. I know that sound. I can imagine what's making it. I shine my helm light straight down between my legs and something shines back up at me just for a moment, like the lens of a camera, not an eye, not wet or alive—but shiny and round.

I suck in my breath.

They're keeping track of us.

And then it's gone. The spiraling shaft below is empty, as far as I can see—a couple of meters—but for a moment, I've come to an abrupt, stunned halt and Joe is right above me, knees doubled just behind my head, cursing.

"What?" he shouts.

"Tell DJ I just stepped on Gollum," I say, still processing the visual, hoping my angel caught it and we can all replay and judge when we're at the bottom. Then I see a black void and my boot kicks out from a step into empty air.

"Bottom, I think," I say.

"Shove through, goddamn it," Joe says.

I do that and then I stand up in a bigger darkness, a blessed black openness, and start shining my helm light around.

"Go ahead," Joe says.

I move on, relieved to be out of the shaft, but there's also that newness in my head. Feels right, feels *good*. Seems to help me find my way around. Problem is, I'm less and less sure I know who I am or who I'm with. I focus and try to hear those behind me. But I've lost them. Maybe I've turned left when they turned right.

I don't mind.

Strong tea.

I'm surrounded by complete darkness but I switch off my fading helm light, touch fingers lightly to the grooves in the wall, feel the grooves rise and drop in an interesting rhythm.

I keep walking. It's possible I'm just losing my grip, possible that the green dust is infiltrating my brain and I'm descending in a spiral to a place where no one will ever find me. There's a certain comfort in that. I like it down here. Maybe I won't have to deal with whatever's happening with Captain Coyle and our sisters. I can leave that to Joe. But then, I won't see Joe or Tak or Kazak or any of the others again, and I won't even be able to compare notes with DJ, possibly the only other Skyrine feeling the tea as strongly as me.

I haven't a fucking idea what's happening, really.

But fairly contented.

———

I'M SOMEWHERE BELOW the neck of the homunculus that is the Drifter, winding down. After a couple of hours, I realize this is *way* down. It's getting warmer. The air in the darkness is rich and moist. Electric. I'm smelling that living planet again. The walls are damp. Then I'm on my knees, crawling, occasionally touching the grooves to coordinate the noise in my head with where I am, possibly *who* I am, which is not at all clear.

I hear somebody or something up ahead. Down this far, deep into the chest of the Drifter, more than likely I'm about to meet up with one or more kobolds. That doesn't concern me, though it should.

I like kobolds.

Then human instinct kicks back in and tells me to get my shit together, think of something to counter the strong tea.

I remember reading an article about cat ladies.

Brain really digresses here: there is such a huge difference between a cat lady and Catwoman. Funny how that works. *Not funny at all, asshole. Get it together!*

Cat ladies—not the slinky gal wearing a mask with perky little ears, rather the kind that just loves kitties and can't stop filling houses with them: this article I read back on Earth said that cat ladies were more than likely infected by a parasite found in cat shit, *toxi something something*, that is *supposed* to end up in rats, where it takes over their rat brains and makes them unafraid and bold, but also makes the rats *love* the smell of feline urine; well, cat ladies are probably infected with this parasite and it's in their brains and so they never clean the litter boxes, just keep piling on the kitties and rising to heaven on the smell of cat pee...

SNKRAZ!

I'm thinking the green powder makes DJ and me love darkness and depth. Makes us seek something, I don't know what. I sure as fuck hope I don't acquire the urge to dig. To keep myself as human as possible, I begin to hum pop tunes but somehow end up with Grieg, "In the Hall of the Mountain King." "Dump dump dump dump *dump* da da, *dump* da-da, *dump* da-da..." Finally, the tune runs out of my head. Legs getting tired. Nose clogging; I sneeze a lot.

There's a kind of dream I'm having as I walk, not at all unpleasant, but in other circumstances it would be an honest-to-God nightmare. Funny stuff. Weirder and weirder.

Very strong tea.

I'm swimming across a muddy plain beneath upside-down hills of ice, blue-green and white, festooned with hanging meadows of luminous flowers, and the hills are dripping shiny twisters, downward-flowing rivulets of supercooled brine, and I don't know *what* I look like but I'm sure I'm more like a crab or a trilobite or a spiky worm than a human because, of course, humans could not survive here.

I avoid the brine—tastes bad, too many minerals—but those glowing flowers are food as well as light, and when I meet up with dozens of others like myself, in a low ocean valley, we're all very interesting and good-looking (*ugly—the ugliest fucking shelly things I've ever seen, multiple joints and grooves, waving arms and shit I can't begin to describe, and they all seem to be ridden by,* I'm *being ridden by, a skinny, spidery parasite with a set of odd, multi-faceted eyes—I love this parasite, it's my best friend, it keeps me safe and warns me of bad stuff*)—

We're each of us big, maybe four or five meters long—and as we gather, we look up in admiration and pride at something we've all made, something immense and beautiful: a great pillar rising thousands of meters from the middle of the valley, all the way to a high, dark, inverted dome of ice.

Below us is the rocky, metal-rich core, the solid heart of our world, heated by internal radiation, heated also by tidal friction from outside, while above, the ice forms a protective barrier between us and the greater universe, allowing us to grow for a billion years—grow and develop in peace.

My God, how *thick* is that ice?

One hundred kilometers.

And only in the last thousand years have we managed to dig out and look around, like breaking out of an immense, frozen egg—

The cause of our long, gestating ignorance, and soon, of our destruction. Because we can infer what's coming—

Moonfall.

We know it's going to happen, we feel the changing tides, we're no longer where we *were*, wherever that was, around a great, steady source of gravity and the constant rhythmic, reliable tides...

We've been knocked away from all that. Our world has been growing colder for a long time and we've been slowly dying off, but meanwhile building, encapsulating, encoding, and preserving.

Getting ready.

The walls of the pillar are made of tiny crystals from which slough great cascades of what can only be called slime, luminous, thickly elegant slime filled with writhing, transparent tubes that join and come apart within the cascades.

The pillar is *working*.

The pillar is *ready*.

Really bad things are about to happen, but we're as prepared as we're ever going to be.

I'm so distracted by this second life, this tea dream, that I barely notice I've bumped up against somebody in the darkness. Fumbling, I switch on my helm light, which is so dim and orange it barely illuminates anything. But it shows me whom I've bumped into.

Not a crab, no outer shell at all—very tall, very slender—female. Slowly I recall my humanity and this female's name: this is Teal—nick for Tealullah.

She regards me with wide, calm eyes; no surprise that I'm here. Like DJ, she's rubbed her pale face with green powder. Maybe I should do the same. Can't get any weirder.

Then she looks beyond me.

I turn slowly and see Joe and DJ and Tak and Beringer and Brodsky. They were with me all along. I must have thought they were giant crabs.

Saying I've been confused does not begin to cut it.

"Didn't want to interrupt you, Vinnie," Joe says as if speaking to a child. "You followed the grooves. You found it."

"Yeah," DJ says in admiration.

Teal blinks at them, then focuses on me. "Come wit' me," she says. "Afore 'tis gone, you have a see it."

"How'd you get away from the Voors?" I ask.

She shakes her head.

"Some are dead," I say.

"I know. One would ha been a new husband. But he didna feel it. The ot'er life did not take. And I didna want t'at, with him na brushing old trut'..."

Even befuddled, I realize this is a new version of her story. Which do I believe?

"Other life?" I ask.

She takes my hand.

Jesus! Her touch fills my head with sparks. She whispers in my ear. "You are *t'ere*, you feel it, doan you?"

"Yeah. Maybe." I can sort of see Joe in my peripheral vision. The others: not at all.

"Go ahead," Joe says distantly. "We're with you."

Maybe they are, maybe they aren't.

Teal walks beside me into the largest chamber in the Drifter: the Church, the void. Scattered strings of star lights glow along the outer wall, profiling one side of what might be a shaft hundreds of meters high—a great cylinder. Someone has raised nine or ten of the miners' wide work light panels on tall tripods and connected them to the Drifter's hydro power through thick cables. Teal walks from one panel to the next and switches the lights on, and now I see the galleries hewn high in the metal walls, all the way to the top.

The void, the Church, is like an inverted Tower of Babel.

The last thing that catches my eye, oddly, is the most

startling and prominent, as if I've seen it so often before it can be ignored—but of course I haven't and it can't.

A pillar of glittering crystals rises through the center of the Church, big, though not nearly as large as the one in my waking dream—my green tea dream—and broken, cracked all over. The pillar is held by embracing spars of rock left in place, but also by hanging nets of interlinked tubules like those making up the kobolds, only thicker. Basic units of construction. Tinkertoys.

The void is the center, the focus of the greatest mining operation in the Drifter: a carved-out and liberated pillar of something like living diamond—a diamond skyscraper, struggling to restore and remake itself after billions of years of being trapped, encased in stone and lava and metal.

And now I can see the connection. The big story.

This pillar, like the one in my vision, oozes a glistening gelatin that slides down around the supports and braces, cascades slowly from level to level, pooling near the base—where unfinished kobolds stir sluggishly, trying out new connections, apparently without direction. Some, however, have begun a laborious journey back up the braces, climbing with agonizing slowness to become part of the thing that will eventually surround the pillar and reinforce the mined-out galleries, filling the deep heart—or mind—of the Drifter. Recreating the immense crystal pillar in those ancient, ice-roofed seas.

The green powder lies thick all over. It forms a thin scum on the churning slime. Maybe the powder *comes* from the slime.

For a crazy moment, a panicked resistance sets in; all my training and paranoia and battle fatigue and all the bad shit a Skyrine falls heir to rises up like a twister filled with knives and all I can think is that somehow the Antags have drugged me, drugged us all, or maybe command drugged the Cosmoline, and some unknown new enemy (maybe we're our own enemy) has infiltrated the Drifter to create a literal fifth column, something big and awful and nasty-subversive...Something that if it is allowed to complete its work will spell the end of all that we fight for.

But none of that makes sense.

I'm caught between competing indoctrinations, competing information, and I drop to my knees in the glare of a work light panel, shade my eyes, and look high into the void to try to find that other life again.

The life that had purpose and majesty, yet is now gone.

"Very, very old," Teal says, getting down on her knees beside me. "Te moon fell on Mars in pieces, long ago. T'is wor one of te pieces. Te Algerians and t'en te Voors part mined it out but at first knew not'ing...T'en te Voors found te Church, but broke a dike and let flow wild te hobo, and when t'ey fled, te old crystals had years and enow water a shape old servants...First of the awakening."

"Kobolds," I say.

"After te Voors abandoned te Drifter, te servants dug and searched."

"The red and blue parts in the map," I say.

"All yes. In te beginning, Fat'er lived an breat'ed te green powder all t'rough te old spaces, blown up from te deep hydraulics. He had time enow a feel te ot'er life, time enow a guess what t'wor."

"He told you?"

"No need. He wor first gen. He inhaled green powder like all te rest...Gave him weak sight a life a te old moon. T'en, te Voors sent his first wife out a te dust. 'Tis why he went a Green Camp. Better t'em t'an Voors. And he fat'ered me. What he only slightly felt and dreamed slid deep inna my genes...and grew.

"But word got out. T'wor traitors in all camps. T'at's why te Voors came a Green Camp a trade for me. By t'en, te doctors told, te child a te exposed man and woman will be te one—'tis *t'ird* gen will grow and finish te big story.

"De Groot had only sons—said he'd atone for what t'ey did and trade for me. Wanted a see te Drifter clear, work it, use it… T'ought it would give t'em power over te Earth and over te Far Ot'ers, too. And maybe 'twill. But look…Drifter can defend*T* itself…"

We follow more cables, thinner—leads from Skyrine demolition packages. Explosives have been rigged around the bottom of the void, around the pillar, and even more hang higher up from the growing tubules and braces—dozens of spent matter charges rigged to expend their energy all at once, a rather impressive show of force—what our sisters carried in those heavy packs when they arrived, hitching a ride with the very folks who could take them where they wanted to go.

All planned.

"Captain Coyle?" I ask. Joe and then DJ are right behind me, listening. My focus is on Teal, but they're here, too.

"The Voors tried a stop t'em. Your women shot t'em," Teal says. "I saw some die."

Coyle and the ladies were assigned a special ops mission, a mission we were not privy to. None of us are expected to survive.

Teal walks ahead, crossing rock bridges carved from the mass of old stone, a kind of elevated maze over a slow lake of glass-clear, shining ooze, filled with half-made kobolds, rippling over a thick bed of glowing red and blue flowers, the foodstuffs and guides of my deep ice vision.

The old moon trying to come back to life…

Trying to *remember.*

Captain Coyle's wires extend across the lava bridges, to the other side of the pillar, where more charges hang prepped and ready to blow. Collapsing the entire void, possibly pulling the head and shoulders of the Drifter down beneath the surface of the Red, ending all the labor that the Algerians and the Voors had put into this amazing formation.

Putting an end to all the possibilities, all the raw materials, and why?

"Why kill such knowledge?" Joe asks. And now I see it, too. Knowledge more dangerous than opportunity and resource. "Crazier still, why kill *us*?"

DJ comes into my filmy sidelong view. "Strong tea. We've got it, and *they* don't want us to have it."

"Abody dinna want knowledge," Teal says.

"Which abody, I wonder?" Joe asks.

DJ's moved ahead of us, over a high bridge, but Teal calls for him to stop, holds up a finger, points out an extrusion from the base of the pillar: a dark, hard, shiny material we have not seen before but which has been described to us. Not rock, not metal. Throwing up a dark meadow of sharp spines, thick as grass, silvery black, translucent, at once beautiful and frightening.

The spines are *growing*.

"Te an*T*ent knows how a fight," Teal says. But the look on her face tells me she *dinna* know what this is, what it means, only that we should not come near, should not touch. She keeps us back, but DJ is already in the forefront and he stoops to look at the growing spines, then turns, rises again.

"Fuck!" he cries. "You gotta *see* this. This is important."

Cautiously, Joe and I push around Teal's blocking arms. We cross the bridge, extra cautious around the spines, around the dark, spiky growth, clinking and spreading through the clear, gelatinous lake. Where the spikes intrude the lake itself and the kobolds within are also turning dark, hardening.

"It's like silicon," Joe says, wondering despite the danger, the strangeness. Maybe the dust is slipping deep into his thoughts. Maybe we're all touched by the strong tea.

We're all turning first gen.

And then comes a soft, girlish voice, half hidden behind the extrusion, calling to us.

Asking for help.

Another few steps.

It's Captain Daniella Coyle. She must have hauled fresh detonators and another satchel of charges to this side of the pillar. She must have slipped and brushed up against the spines, or maybe they reached out...

She lies across one side of a wide arch of ancient stone, partly covering the satchel, hand grasping the straps to keep charges from falling into the squirming ooze. Her lower body, clothing, flesh, bone, even her sidearm, has gone dark. Shiny. She's turning into whatever this hard, shiny shit is. The silicon darkness is moving rapidly up her torso, freezing her one remaining arm, stilling her grasping fingers around the straps of the satchel, holding them in mid-twitch. Only her chest and head are left and she's having difficulty catching a breath. Her eyes are filled with fear but she doesn't seem to be in pain. Even so, she can barely speak.

Coyle murmurs, "Get me out. Help me up. Get me out."

The satchel and the charges have themselves become dark. God knows what happens to high explosives when touched this way.

DJ kneels close. He tries to take hold of her shoulder, but the spikes crawl up the fabric of her skintight, bristling toward him, aiming for his reaching hand, or warning him away—and he shakes his head violently. He's crying, by God.

"No can do, Captain," he says, but then his voice falls into soft reverence, and his next few words shape a kind of prayer. A soldier's prayer for a fatally wounded comrade. I would never have expected this of DJ but here he is, ministering, caring, coaching Coyle across the unknown border in a way that Joe and I could never manage: instinctive, inappropriate in any sort of polite company—divinely foolish.

"It's out of our hands," DJ says, eyes fixed on hers, and now she's watching him intently, like a newborn watching a mysterious father; his is the last human face she will see and know. "You're a very brave sister, Captain Coyle. Sorry I can't join you, not yet anyway. Soon though. We all know we're short. Just ease into it, Captain. Don't fight it, go with it. There. There it is. Tell all of them hello for us."

Then, gentlest of all, "*Semper fi.*"

Where Coyle has been touched and turned, little reddish lights move in the depths of the dark material, terrifyingly pretty, growing into beauty, like thousands of fireflies in an endless night.

Captain Coyle's last words rise through the Church, high, soft, even girlish, "*Momma! Momma! I'm not ready, Momma, hold me, please wait... Momma!*"

All Skyrines are children, before, during, and even *inside* the end.

Her lips freeze in polished translucency. The fireflies move up inside her neck, gather behind her eyes. Her eyes become greenish torches in the perfect sculpture of her face. Then the lights spread out, flow from her transformed body, back into the greater mass, the extrusion.

Coyle's eyes go dark.

There's quiet between us for the longest time, silence but for the gentle, slippery noise of wavelets within the clear, thick lake, and the light, wind-chime tinkle of the dark spikes as they strike and grow.

DJ rises and lets out a shuddering breath, then brushes past us, wiping his face, leaving green streaks across his cheeks, and stands with the others back beyond the maze of bridges.

Stands and waits, arms at his side like a chastened little kid in this old, old Church.

Far above, a hideous, shuddering slam drops onto our world like the stomp of a giant boot. The high pillar vibrates, making the supports flex and squeak; bits of crystal shatter away and strike the upper galleries, plash into the lake, scatter in bright pieces across the maze of stone bridges.

"Right," Joe says. "We're done here."

And that's it, we're off.

LARGER ISSUES

Out on the Red, surrounded by Antags, in a dust storm and in your pajamas," Alice says. "And yet...here you are. Un-fucking-believable."

"Yeah," I say, still not back from the last of Captain Coyle.

We're driving north on 5, ten lanes, crossing wide new bridges, between wide farm fields and lumber yards and casinos and outlet malls, stuff that's been here for decades, not looking very futuristic, looking damned old and traditional in fact.

Alice adds, "I believe almost anything nowadays. Like, I can almost believe you and Teal will get together and she'll pup out a litter of lobsters."

"That's disgusting," I say.

"Really?" She watches me.

"Not the way it works."

"How do you know?"

"They're gone. They're dead...billions of years gone. They aren't coming back, not like that."

"What do you feel now?" Alice asks. "Still having visions?"

I wonder whether all this talk has done either of us any good.

And why she's indulged me. I could not possibly explain most of it to her.

"No," I say. "Not strong ones, anyway. It just messes with me in general. I don't know where I am, so I don't know *who* I am."

"What was their plan, then? For third gen?"

"Knowledge. Wisdom. I don't know."

"What if somebody *does* know but doesn't want it to happen? Doesn't want us to know the bigger picture—to get smart that way?"

I watch her closely. "We're not going to meet Joe, are we?"

"We are," she insists.

"But we're going to *Canada*. Why not just stop this thing and let me off," I say. Cold, calm. I've known, I've felt, I've *suspected*, but I'm still not decided, I'm still stuck between more than two worlds.

"He's *in* Canada," Alice says.

"Canada isn't signatory."

"True enough."

The driver, up front behind his plastic partition, looks back, checking up on us, making sure we're still okay. That I'm still keeping my shit together.

I am. God knows how.

"What's Joe doing in Canada?"

"Getting away from the bullshit," she says. "Must have been interesting coming back in Cosmoline. Sleeping one place... then another. I can't imagine what that was like. Thinking you were an ugly, shelly thing, out under the ice of an old moon. Wow. What happens when you get away from the green dust? Does it all fade?"

I'm feeling less and less at liberty to go on. I'm thinking of Captain Coyle and our sisters, those who were part of her special ops team, and how only two of them returned with us, with me, but not on the same space frames.

Joe and DJ and Tak and Kazak and Vee-Def, also on another frame.

Michelin and Brom and Ackerly and so many of the others...

"We've got half an hour before we reach Blaine," Alice says. "Canadian authorities will meet us there. If they haven't figured out it was you on that returning hawk. If someone hasn't alerted border security on this side. And if you want to follow through. Do you want me to explain what happens after that?"

"I'm no longer in the Skyrines?"

"In any case, you won't return to your previous life. But you knew that. You're smart."

"Captain Coyle...different orders. She was willing to kill us all. And die herself. Why?"

"I went through special ops training before I switched to medical," Alice says. "I remember Captain Coyle. A great lady, maybe the finest I ever knew in the Corps. There was a time when I would have done the same thing she did, followed the same orders. But then...I met Joe. He took the scales from off my eyes, so to speak. Not to cast any aspersion on scales, shells, crab eyes, whatever. Whatever you feel you are now."

Is this odd and variable and now crude and insulting woman playing with me? Testing me? Making sure I know my own mind?

Or have a mind, *any* mind, to know?

"*One question you should ask,*" Teal said in the southern garage; her face was suddenly thoughtful, sympathetic and distant at once. "*How t'is strong tea, as you call it, knows to fit humans? A just snap inna our tissues, our genes?*"

"You tell me," I murmur.

"First, finish your story," Alice Harper says. "Make it clear, cement it down. Then I'll try to tell you the rest. All that Joe has told me. All that I've learned. I need perspective, and I'm sure you can provide some of that."

MEETINGS, PARTINGS, SWEET SORROW

In the southern garage, Michelin and Kazak have run the troops through final prep for our sortie, our breakout maneuver. Mustafa and Suleiman, from Coyle's team, have wandered back, in shock—and been accepted, because I suppose nobody knows the whole story, or their story, and we're all Skyrines.

Or maybe it was because after they managed to recover some of their wits, they volunteered to go out through the gate, scope out the rocky harbor, and assess the fitness of the vehicles that didn't make it inside the garage. They rigged a kind of broom of old wire and used it to brush off the germ needles scattered out there, brush a clear trail; they did this by themselves, Brodsky and Neemie say.

After the special ops sisters returned, Neemie and Beringer stepped through the lock next and tried to establish a satlink. Nothing going. We're still on our own.

And so now we know. The northern gate is blocked by rubble. There's been substantial bombardment. Outside the southern gate all of the deuces have been destroyed. The Trundle was hit but there's a possibility one of the disruptors is still functional. Another Skell-Jeep seems to have survived and might still run, and two more Tonkas appear intact and not booby-trapped. The vehicles outside the harbor can't be seen through the blowing dust, which is still heavy enough it darkens the dawn skies.

Inside the garage there's the Tonka, with two fixed disruptors and a rear-firing multigauge cannon, the Chesty with its four Aegis 7 cannons and chain-bolt ballista, and two lightly armed Skell-Jeeps—kinetic rifles only.

Joe and Gamecock confer, tapping the lieutenant colonel's remaining energy to figure out how to move the platform's disruptor and its power supply onto the General Puller. The Chesty was designed to fight but also to tow and haul and do light repair. It has a folding crane behind the cabin and its own weapons that might transfer a disruptor.

Simca and Vee-Def think they can take the guts out of a Deuce's triple-rail bolt gun and mount it to the carriage of a...

I'm losing all that. Everybody's yakking. I listen, but I'm not getting it. Tak and Kazak are working hard and I'm doing hardly *nothing*.

Then Joe walks by and says, "We're all going to die out there. I'll make sure you mount some heavy shit before you expire."

"Outstanding," I say.

Teal watches this interchange with that same strange, beautiful calm. Second gen and now more days breathing the strong tea. Ice moon tea. Where does she live from now on? I mean, in her head, but maybe I also mean, on Mars as well.

Where does she go if she lives?

———

OUR WOUNDED—VOOR AND Skyrine—have been loaded in the Chesty's enclosed cabin, including Gamecock. Joe and Vee-Def and Rafe have made one last survey from the western watchtower and report the sky is still thick with dust and winds are up to two hundred knots.

Tak has taken a third turn around the rocky harbor outside the garage.

The Voors are quiet.

Teal: utterly still as she stands in the middle of the garage along with DJ and me. I hear the reports with half my head, half my self. I realize I'm standing beside Teal, not being helpful, and DJ is sticking close, like we're all separated out, quarantined; we are still smeared with green dust and after the reports of what happened to some of Coyle's team, nobody's at ease being around us. They think we've gone over, whatever that could mean.

"I miss my weird-looking parasite," DJ whispers, and looks at me with a smirk. "The one that sat up here." He touches the back of his neck. "Don't you?"

Maybe we do.

De Groot and Rafe tend to Gamecock but he's fading, getting worse, and his eyes show he knows it. Typically a mortally wounded Skyrine will not be allowed to fill a slot in a jump-up. Not be allowed to take up space in a returning frame, if there is one up there waiting for us. Cosmoline doesn't work on major injuries and there are no hospitals in orbit.

One major difference between Skyrines and ground pounders. Helps define us. Not that any of us likes it.

We have four who may not make it, including Gamecock, but we'll take them with us as far as we can. We owe them that much.

The Voors, of course, will not find a slot in any of our jump-ups. Even if we offered—and we won't—they wouldn't take them. Joe says they're getting their wagons back, those that still work; enough to carry their survivors to wherever they can go. Another camp, another settlement, if any will have them. De Groot works like a sonofabitch along with Rafe and two others, hauling and tending.

SNKRAZ.

Our plan is simple enough. We don't know what will happen when we break through the Antag lines, but attempt to break through we will—and dispose of as many of the enemy as we can. The Voors will follow.

Joe approaches Teal and then me and then DJ.

"I'm handing Teal over to de Groot," he says. "She can't come to Earth; they'd never accept her. The Voors will take her with them to a settlement. Rafe seems to think there's a chance Amazonia will take them all, if it's still there. If they can make it that far."

Teal doesn't react to this news. When Joe walks away to help patch skintights using Voor repair kits, she turns to me and says, "Come back if you can."

"What about me?" DJ asks hopefully.

"All of you...if you brush te ot'er life."

I can't stand that anymore, just so fucking *weird* and confusing, and so I walk away to join the others while Teal stands there watching us, beautiful, calm, scary as hell. De Groot can have her, I think, but I don't mean it. I just can't stand the thought of never feeling that touch again—that beautiful connection to something utterly beautiful and strange.

Teal.

Ice moon tea.

"We're not going to make it anyway, Master Sergeant," DJ says, noting my gloom as he walks beside me across the garage to our Skell-Jeep. "Question I have is, which heaven will we go to? Crab heaven or pearly gates?"

Our teams have assembled. We mount our vehicles.

The little side lock opens, Neemie enters and nobody bothers to brush him down because we're going to immediately shove out anyway.

But then he shouts, "I got satlink! There's lots of fresh orbital. Our orbital. Don't know disposition or tactics, but it's up there! Want to see what I got?"

We share, those of us who can. Some of our angels are still working but for most of us, the skintight charges are too far down, the suits too damaged, some of us now wear Voor helms, and so...

"Push out!" Joe calls. Vee-Def will operate the locks and run to join us when we've all exited.

Teal climbs up behind Rafe into a Voor wagon.

That's the last I see of her.

I'm on my Tonka and true to his word, Joe has assigned me to a multigauge cannon. DJ is on the second cannon. Michelin pilots. We have eight passengers, including Beringer, Brodsky, Mustafa, and Suleiman.

Vee-Def in the garage booth fuses a safety circuit and the main lock gates slide open together—inside and out. Air rushes by with a lion's roar. We're blown around for a few seconds, my skintight fabric ripples—our vehicles rev and lurch and roll. The engines all around grow quieter in the thinning air, but the Tonka's rumble still comes up through our asses.

And then we're outside, blind—flooded with the barely tactile whisper of a Martian dust storm. Mustafa grabs my arm, I reach over to Michelin, he slows the Tonka for just a moment—and Vee-Def runs out of the obscurity, leaps up onto the vehicle, and squeezes between Mustafa and Beringer.

The Chesty immediately starts laying down barrages right and left. Nobody pauses at the platform to transfer shit; we're already taking incoming fire, bolts, shells, and then a lancing disruptor beam plows the stone beside us, rises like an electric cobra, and shaves a curved blade from our right rear tire, which immediately digs into the dirt and starts to heave us around.

Michelin ejects the bad tire and it flies off into the swirling murk. Five tires is still enough. Four is enough, though the tail will drag. Three and we're stalled.

Once again, the dust goes purple all around with ghostly lightning, heavy, dull thumps vibrate us in our seats—something bright green and throwing out curling threads of plasma screams overhead like a ghastly firework, then abruptly descends. It misses us but the Skell-Jeep to our right takes the direct bolt hit and leaps in flaming pieces, bodies and blood soaring into the storm—

We're keeping to our course, DJ and I are laying down blind cannon bursts—taking opposite arcs right and left—the Martian wind is rising, buffeting like an angry, dusty ghost...

I'm definitely focused. On the Red now and nowhere else, in combat mode, stuck in this all-too-mortal and coldly frightened body, hanging on to the multigauge and my seat, knocked around by rough terrain, wind, concussions. Michelin's head jerks from side to side in the pilot's seat. He looks up over his shoulder in disbelief.

Still here!

We've managed to push about a kilometer from the Drifter. We can barely make out the Voor wagon ahead of us, can't see a thing in front, and then—

Air, dust, rock—all lift up behind and cast shadows as it flies over. There are four more bursts just like that in rapid succession. Rocks fall around—meters wide, bouncing and rolling, throwing up great gouts of shattered basalt and sand—and a Millie plummets out of nowhere directly in front of our Tonka, outlined in molten glow, tumbling end over end, cracking open, spilling dozens of weird dolls in jumbles of arms and legs all in the wrong places, all twisting wrong—Antags!

Michelin's arms wheel as he almost casually steers our Tonka around the wreckage and broken bodies.

Joe takes the comm: "Ants at nine o'clock! Prep sidearms—they're on foot, fast and close!"

Now we're going to have our chance to engage the enemy at close quarters. Pity it won't get reported, pity it won't get out, what we'll see.

What we've already seen.

BIRDS

"What *do* they look like?" Alice asks.

We're about fifteen miles from the border. Traffic is backed up; lots of folks heading north for vacation. Cheerful crowding. Canada's not signatory, but still prosperous, nobody's retaliating, Gurus don't want discord. Gurus want political stability while they dole out their technological gifts, so that we can head out to the Red and fight.

"Like birds," I tell her. "They were pretty thickly suited up. Long in the neck, wide helms, with a long nose—thick bodies, really long, strong arms, a kind of hanging sack below the arms."

"Like where wing feathers would hang," Alice says.

"Yeah. Maybe. But the eyes…"

I hear something above the light electric hum of the traffic. All these electric cars and it's so soft, so quiet, you might think you were out on a meadow with the wind blowing through the grass, that's what it sounds like on the road to the border, to Blaine.

But I'm hearing something more powerful, louder. Higher.

Alice hears it next, and the driver notices as well. He turns around, and we can't understand what he's saying through the plastic barrier until he switches on an intercom.

"What should I do?" he asks Alice. "We can get off at the next exit, we could go inland, there's a—"

"Quiet," she says. She puts her palm to her chin and taps her nose with a manicured finger.

I'm looking up through the side window, straining on my seat belt, and I see them first. Four hover-squares, quadcopters in civvy parlance. Coming low over the countryside, the fields, the freeway, slowly swaying side to side, searching for something.

"Are they looking for us?" the driver asks.

Alice shoots me a querulous look. "Who knows you made it back?" she asks.

"Nobody, I think."

"The apartment's clear. Joe made sure of that," she says, more to herself, then back to me. "Did you walk from the mob center?"

"I walked. Hitchhiked, actually. A lady in—"

"Crap," Alice says.

"Nobody told me to walk all the way to Seattle," I say.

"No, that would be silly," she says in an equally low tone. "The one who picked you up—somebody from the base?"

"She said she was a colonel's secretary. Older gal."

Alice looks right at me; she hadn't heard that part. "Anyone else?"

"A short cab ride."

"How'd you pay?"

I hold up my finger.

The hover-squares have leveled off about a hundred meters on each side of the freeway and are running north in parallel to the stuck traffic, no doubt scanning everybody through the windows.

I lean back in the seat and close my eyes.

OFF THE RED

Vee-Def shouts through the roar and the dust, "That's our incoming! From orbit—they're carpeting the Drifter!"

Which is how we got through the lines. What started out sporadic has now become constant. Maybe it's for us, to allow our escape, maybe not. But for the moment, while we're on the run, the Antags are in total disarray.

We've gone four klicks. A long chain of explosions ahead of us has halted for the moment and seems to have temporarily put the Antag infantry on pause. Our tires may actually be rolling over some of them in their trenches. I think I see a kind of fountain in a gully, figures scrambling through the morning shadows and the gray and purple-lit dust. More boulders arc out and fall around us from the barrage over the Drifter—bouncing. I can see the Voor wagon off to our right, plunging in and out of drifts of dust and coiling, wind-whipped smoke, and I think I see Antags popping up like arcade cutouts between us, but it's hard to make out anything real, we're shivered by one concussion after another. Michelin is driving like a madman, veering right and left, and I barely hear him shouting in his helm, or singing, can't tell which.

Mustafa and Suleiman cling to each other. Vee-Def is huddled beside them, head down. Michelin and I have temporarily ceased firing the multigauges because we could hit our own vehicles, flying across the rock and dust, escaping from the Drifter.

Five klicks!

By God, we're going to make it!

And then there's this black thing right in front of us, so fucking big it blocks the Voor wagon, the Chesty, the Tonka. Like an entire ridge of rock just flew up out of Mars, only it didn't fly up, it came *down*. The impact throws us all up off the Red a couple of meters, and now we're landing hard, bouncing, and Mustafa and Suleiman have been knocked off the Tonka and I've been snapped out of my harness. I'm clinging to the barrel of the cannon, which is still hot, and my gloved fingers are starting to burn so I let go, drop slowly off to the side, land on my feet, just stand there, fighting spasmodic chest muscles to get my breath back.

A hundred meters of Drifter, a shard from the half-buried swimmer, the deep homunculus, has been lofted by the concussions and dropped almost upon us, and something in me feels utterly lost, such a turnaround from the exaltation of believing we might have actually made it—

All finished, ended, done with—after billions of years!

I don't know how long it's been, I'm rattled, but Vee-Def is beside me and amazingly he has his shit together.

"Sidearms, ladies!" he shouts.

And then the Antag infantry is up and coming at us.

I see two Skyrines running from the Chesty, which has landed on its side, and just behind them, a smoky wave of Antags, recovered enough to search around this side of the fallen ridge, and the dust storm has been completely interrupted by the rockfall, and I'm on one knee, aiming at Antags, hoping I'm seeing them clearly, not aiming at Skyrines in dust-covered skintights.

They're returning fire, moving in to clean us out. It's going to be close.

We're suddenly silent in our helms. No more words. Coordinated fire. I look left, cringing, just as Vee-Def's head flies off, right beside me, and the bolt that took it whangs and fries and sizzles against the side of the Tonka. All those bad jokes, those movies, now hot pink mist. At leisure, his body begins to slump.

My pistol is getting off bolt after bolt, and then, just as an Antag weaves to within a few meters, it runs out of charge—of course—

And I'm down to bullets, and then *they're* gone, and I'm down to waiting for one of the Antags to build up the courage to come in and grapple. Why not just shoot me?

Because the Antag has dropped its weapon or I can't see a weapon. Maybe they long for hand-to-hand or claw-to-hand or whatever, for honor, for glory. And then it's on me. God, it is strong! Those long, flapping arms and three-fingered gloves wrap around my chest, lift me up, and I see another Antag stand atop the Tonka, firing blindly down at Michelin, but Michelin is firing back, and that one topples, and I've got my own gloves straight on the Antag's helm, and I'm digging in my fingers, trying to grab and grip and rip, and I can see its face through the wide, narrow plate, above the long jutting of the helm, the nose, the beak, but mostly just its eyes, looking up at me, as it lifts me, my ribs starting to give.

I look *right into its eyes.* It has four of them, a smaller central pair, red and shiny, between two large outboard eyes, staring expressionless, but I've brought my pistol up and am using the butt like a hammer repeatedly on the plate, and then it lets go, but too late, I've cracked the plate—it has other issues to deal with.

And then I see two Skyrines come around the sides of the Tonka. One is Tak; the other is Joe. Tak is hefting a power supply that must mass two hundred kilos, and Joe's got the rail gun, wrenched from the Chesty, and they're laying down fire, clearing the area around the fallen ridge, the rock, which must have landed on a whole battalion of Antags, clearing a way, because they toss the heavy shit aside, grab me, grab Mustafa, who's still alive—Suleiman nowhere in sight—and we join Michelin and run, leap, around the right of the sizzling ridge of rock—crackling and splitting and powdering from all the energy unleashed by the blast that tossed it here—around to open dust and lava, familiar Red stretching out before us, air clear like there was never a storm.

We keep running. Running forever. I think Kazak may have joined us, can't be sure, because there's six of us running in a line.

And then we stop. We all fall over.

Into a gully just deep enough to cover us.

Instinctively, I roll and start to check integrity, first on my suit, then on the skintight of the Skyrine next to me, Kazak, and then I'm up over to Joe, who pulls me and shouts, "Keep fucking *down*," but I check him anyway, picking nits, social as shit in a chute, my eyes sliding into narrowing tunnels.

Joe grabs my shoulders.

"Hang on, Vinnie," he says.

"Sure!" I cry out. "Love this shit! Love it!"

We're all crying in our helms.

"The wagon," I say.

"It was up ahead," Joe says. "I think the rock missed it."

"Chesty got wiped," Kazak says.

"Sure as shit that rock took out the Antag line!" Tak says. We eyeball each other for a long moment, too tired to say anything. Then we flop back in the gully, studying the bands of dust that flow overhead like pink and gray rivers, and we jerk in unison as a stray bolt draws a sparking trail to the north, perk up as our angels try to come back online—flickering displays and crackling comm, voices out there, so few, far away—maybe from where we all go when our heads get vaporized.

We're back where we started. Before Lieutenant Colonel Roost, before the ranch wife in her buggy, before so many saviors—and who can expect another such round of saviors?

We've worked through our supply.

Power low. Maybe ten minutes of air.

If I slow my lungs down. Stop gasping.

Stop crying.

INVALUABLE

Alice and the driver have stepped outside. I'm still strapped into the bench seat, best place to be, because it's quiet in the van.

Seven men and women from the hover-squares approach us, weaving through the other stalled vehicles: cars, trucks. They aren't cops, they aren't MPs—the hover-squares are unmarked.

And now the seven are interested in the van.

COMING HOME AGAIN

Joe pulls off my blaze, grabs my helm, smashes the angel with a rock. He reaches into his pack and hands me the helm from a dead Voor, tells me to switch it out, put it on in the pop-up, discard mine—then get back to Earth as best I can.

"For God's sake, after all that's happened, stay away from MHAT," he says.

"Pop-up being delivered right now," Kazak says.

Joe gives me Gamecock's blaze and pins me with his own broken silver leaf.

"Aren't you coming with me?" I ask him.

"Right behind you. Second pop-up. I'm going with DJ."

"He made it?"

"As much as DJ will ever make it," Joe says.

So I'll come back with no ID or the wrong ID, which is not a problem, because the pop-up crew will pack us in and hoist us all to orbit, to the return frames, and the orbital crew will soak us in Cosmoline and send us back to Earth; that's what we can count on.

I'm going in and out when I feel a breath of fresh oxygen. My eyes stay open. I can hardly credit what I've seen, what Joe has done, but new Skyrines in beautiful fresh skintights are tending to all of us, to Tak and Kazak and DJ.

One sister leans over me—a lieutenant named Shirmerhorn. "Where the hell have you been, Lieutenant Colonel Roost?" she asks me.

"Mismatch on the DNA," says a tech with a very young voice. He lifts a bio-wand and shakes it by his ear, as if it might rattle.

"Screw the bookkeeping," Shirmerhorn says. "They won't notice. Rack 'em and pop 'em."

And so they do.

I've come through all this shit relatively unscathed. Broken ribs, a greenstick fracture of my tibia, a concussion, oxydep-burned lungs. A long session in Cosmoline is called for. Most of it will knit just fine on the way home.

I see Kazak and Tak and Joe and DJ lying beside me in their plastic tents, peeled out of their skintights.

Joe lolls his head. "You'll touch Earth at SBLM," he says. "Seattle was Gamecock's town." He tells me to go to the Seattle apartment, reminds me of the address—makes me repeat it. "Stay out of trouble. I'll join you as soon as I can. Lots to tell."

"What?"

"What it all means, asshole."

Tak's listening, lying almost on his side.

Kazak rises up behind him. "What the fuck are you two whispering about?" he says.

Joe smiles. "We're going home."

"If they don't pump bolts into our frames," Kazak says, falling back, ever the optimist.

"Vee-Def got it," I say, that image still searing. "He got it quick but bad."

"Listen close, Vinnie," Joe says. "This is important. It's why Coyle was out there, and why all the brass was out there, and I was out there, and why the Antags were out there, chasing us all. There's a bigger picture, and now you're part of it, get me? Lie low and just relax for a while, until we can all sit down, private-like, and talk about it. Lots more to come. I'll be back when I can."

"Back to the world where we can't say 'fuck,'" Tak says.

Joe has a funny story about that, and so, while we're waiting to be delivered to the pop-ups, he tells us. Maybe someday I'll tell it to somebody else. If there's time.

If I'm in the mood.

My moods are getting stranger and stranger lately.

OOPS

Alice and the driver are in custody by the side of the road, and the civvies in the other cars are watching, critical, irritated, thinking we must be smugglers.

"Did you bring anything back with you, soldier?" one of the plainclothes guys asks as he helps me down, very carefully, from the back of the van. "Any crystals—black crystals, white crystals—diamonds or whatever?"

"No, sir. No crystals."

They have a kind of plastic bag they want me to wear, so I oblige them and put it on. Upper baglike torso encloses my arms, no sleeves, but the lower half fits around my legs so I can walk. Even has a separate breathing apparatus. They load me carefully onto the back of a hover-square. The pilot looks back from the cockpit as I'm loaded and secured, then looks forward, touches his mike, and reports, "Fugitive retrieved. ETA twenty-seven minutes. Prepare Madigan."

Fucking Madigan. I don't care *who* hears me. I do not want to be laid up with doctors and needles and idiots who think I'm carrying something contagious.

Even if I am.

Joe had arranged that I come home as a different man. Relying on typical Corps inefficiency. Thinking I might have some time before the docs found out somebody came back who shouldn't have, who wasn't on the list. Who should have died up there, if Captain Coyle and her team had done their job.

No matter.

It was always a long shot.

I had a weird time in Cosmoline on the way back. Unlike most trips, I didn't just sleep it through. I did some heavy-duty thinking, and not always with my own, difficult brain.

With a new, strange, and friendlier brain.

———

THE FOUR WIDE blades on the corners whir their dusty lift, and we're abruptly up and out, flying over the farmland, away from the border.

My plastic bag-suit crackles as I move.

"Welcome home, Skyrine," says the guy sitting next to me, in his forties, graying, hard-muscled but bulky, eyes darting, fatalistic. Could have been a Skyrine himself once.

Inside the plastic sack, I reach into my pocket. Finger the coin, my Precious. They haven't frisked me yet. Teal also had a coin, given to her by her father—a kind of key to the Drifter. And now here's another key. Maybe that means there's more than one Drifter. Makes sense.

Lots of chunks of old moon fell on Mars way back when.

———

I HATE TRANSITIONS. Borders in time, in space, the thin lines between one state and another are the most dangerous. We cross two big borders in life, both equally difficult—being born and dying.

Darkness on either side.

I'm afraid, always afraid, of such thoughts, because I do not slide well between states—war and peace, happiness and grief, friends alive, friends dead. I watched a cat die once. It had been hit by a truck backing out of a driveway. It zipped one way, scared by the motor noise, then suddenly, panicking, turned around—dashed right under a tire. I kneeled beside it after the truck had gone. Last few seconds of life, it looked up at me in greater pain than I wanted to imagine, and then it just shivered and closed its eyes. That cat made the grade. It knew all about borders and transitions.

It crossed over without a sound.

I can only hope I will do the same.

For the time being I'm in Madigan, in a secure facility, with no prospect of going anywhere. But at least I'm getting three squares of hospital food, which is better than I expected, and there's lots of air and lots of water and no smell of pickle, and I don't have to wear a skintight, so that's good.

I don't know what happened to Alice. Maybe she's here, too, somewhere—in quarantine because she spent so much time with me. I still hope Joe will come for me, but that's crazy thinking.

Been doing a lot of crazy thinking since I was put into orbit and fell home. But Earth isn't really my only home now. I dream and think a lot of crazy things.

CAESURA

Okay, I'm ready to spill some conclusions.

Listen close. Tell this to Joe. He probably knows already, but maybe not.

DJ's strong tea, the green powder, isn't spores, isn't an infection of any sort we understand—it's memory. It's what the intelligences from the old ice moon designed their crystals to leave behind when the water runs out, so that kobolds can pick up the work later, when water returns.

But the memory dust affects humans, too. It slips into our cells, into our heads. We begin to remember things we never lived. And there's only one explanation for that.

When the old moon collided with Mars, eons ago, it must have dropped trillions of tons of ice and rock—its icy shell, inner oceans, and deep, rocky core—onto a previously lifeless Mars. The old moon seeded Mars. Rain and snow fell all over the Red until oceans covered the young beds of lava, and Mars came alive for a few tens of millions of years.

But some of that debris blasted back from the impact, far out into space, and drifted downsun.

To Earth. On rebound from Mars, the living things within the ice moon also seeded Earth. In part at least, we're their descendants...Open to the history carried in the green dust, heirs to all that ancient knowledge, if we know how to decode and restore what the kobolds have been trying to preserve for so many millions of years. The secrets of another kind of history. Knowledge, perception, judgment—primordial wisdom.

And the Gurus know it. They must have ordered command to send in Coyle and her sappers. That means they'll do everything they can to stop us. But *why*? Aren't they here to help? Maybe not; they're not from around here, this is all separate from them, counter to whatever they've planned.

What is it they don't want us to learn?

And I'm thinking, if the Antags came here strapped to an old chunk of Oort ice—what the hell does *that* mean in our big picture?

The massive Antag buildup, decimating the Koreans and the Euros and the Russians, then fidging our drop, tracking and chasing Joe's platoon—and meanwhile, slinging comets—maybe hoping to take out anyone who's been subjected to ice moon tea?

Settlers and warriors.

Is it possible *everybody* wanted to erase the Drifter and all it contained?

IN STIR

Got most of it down, including the stuff I told Alice. Packing it all away, sending it out. Along with the platinum coin. Madigan was reluctant to do a cavity search on a contaminated man, and when they got around to it...too late. Won't tell you how or where. But suffice it to say, somebody here at Madigan knows someone who knows Joe, and Joe is still out there.

Joe is legendary here.

A trio of doctors came to visit last Monday—Moon Day— and talked to me through my room's big, thick window. They told me I'm going to spend a few more weeks in quarantine, and when that's finished, they'll hand me over to the capable hands of the Wait Staff.

That could mean I'll be dead soon. Or I'll get to meet Gurus. If I live, I hope they don't mess with my memories of either world. But if they do, or I'm gone, and this is all I leave behind, think on this:

Titan. Out around Saturn, more than one and a half billion kilometers from Earth. Some of us have already become heroes out there. What kind of suits do we wear? Nitrogen and methane

atmosphere, mostly, with traces of acetylene and propane helping shape a billowing, yellow-orange haze over a plasticky, oily
geology rich with long-chain hydrocarbons—sitting on deep ice
and an ocean way beneath *that*, flowing over a weirdly uneven,
stony core.

Undisturbed…until now.

Old and cold.